NESTON

#1 in
The Neston Novels
Series

TESS ADONE

ALSO BY TESS ADONE

#2 in The Neston Novels Series:
The Dragon of Neston

Respect and Respectability:
Susan Price at Mansfield Park

NESTON

ISBN 978-1-7323955-3-4 Paperback
ISBN 978-1-7323955-4-1 E-book
ISBN 978-1-7323955-5-8 Large Print Hardcover
ISBN 978-1-7323955-6-5 Hardcover

Published by Tess Adone
Essex, Vermont
www.tessadone.com

For Arabella Grace Stout

Now people were bringing the little children
to Jesus for Him to place His hands on them,
and the disciples rebuked those who brought them.
But when Jesus saw this,
He was indignant and told them,
"Let the little children come to Me,
and do not hinder them!
For the kingdom of God belongs to such as these.
Truly I tell you, anyone who does not receive
the kingdom of God like a little child
will never enter it."
And He took the children in His arms,
placed His hands on them, and blessed them.

Mark 10:13-16

Chapter 1

I COULD JUST PICTURE Dad's surprise when he looked up from pumping air in the tube and realized Marcia and Donna had left Gabe and me behind in the car. He and Mom had lugged the heavy ice cooler and big plaid Thermos bottle to our favorite picnic spot, but instead of staying to look after us, my sisters had dawdled behind them with an aluminum chaise under each arm.

Gabe had managed to remain sound asleep through the ruckus of unloading. The frame of his baby car seat was hooked over the middle of the front seat. It had a steering wheel with a horn that squeaked, and after he tired himself out make-believe driving, he often fell asleep behind the wheel.

I looked around while he slumbered. School was over for the year, and the public beach at Île de L'eau was crowded. We were joining Carl and Frieda, and their car was parked a few spaces away, so I knew they had arrived early to stake out tables at the remote end of the picnic area. The station wagon that my best friend's parents drove was in the lot, too. I'd catch up with Debbie later. So far, so good.

But I was also on the lookout for those I dreaded seeing. It would be a real spoiler if I bumped into Tina Henry or Janice Armstrong. One day at school, all of a sudden, they wouldn't play with me, and they started making fun of me. Well, my name anyway.

Due to a mix-up of labels in the infant viewing room at the hospital, I was given a boy's name. The mistake was caught, but not before the birth certificate was signed with my name as Etienne. Mom and Dad were so grateful that I went home with the right Durand family that they never held it against anyone. They nicknamed me Ette. That declared me female, and since I was premature, also happened to describe me as being small. I still am.

I thought Etienne was a nice name, but once Tina lopped off the end and started calling me Eddie, Janice joined her. They taunted me with it when no playground monitors were close enough to hear, so I was back at square one, only worse, a reject. I wished the mistake could have been with a name like Kim.

Both boys and girls were named Kim, but Kimmie was distinctly feminine. Everyone simply loved to say the nickname Kimmie and couldn't say Kimmie often enough. The mere name created popularity, which wasn't fair because Kimmies already tended to be smart, attractive, and above average athletically. I knew two of them, one older and one younger.

Since Janice and Tina lashed out with Eddie when I tried to talk to them to find out what was wrong, I backed off. They were a year ahead of me, so I was able to avoid them as much as possible. I wanted to keep it that way.

Eddie was a different kind of wrong label. They say words can't hurt you, but name calling is never just about words. I figured it was part of an ugly stage that some people went through. All I could do was wait it out.

I pushed the hair off Gabe's moist forehead. He opened his eyes and mashed a hand against my cheek. I nibbled his fingers, smacking my lips.

"Mmm, yum, Gabe tastes so good!" He gurgled.

"Got your keys?"

I rattled his big play keys, and he grasped the ring. I slung his diaper bag across my back and lifted him. He pushed up.

"Atta boy, Gabe."

He clasped me around the neck, gripping his bottle with the tiny teeth poking through his gums.

"I missed you all day when I was in school, but not any more. Now we're going to have the whole summer together."

"Ahh," he said. As soon as he opened his mouth, the bottle fell. We looked down at it rolling away in the pine needles.

"It's okay, Gabe. Plastic, eighth wonder of the world."

I couldn't hold him and the diaper bag and pick up the bottle at the same time, and that was when a knight in Bermuda shorts arrived on foot.

"Hi, I'm Frieda's nephew," he said, and I believed him. I immediately saw the resemblance to Frieda in his blond hair, blue eyes, and features.

"Hi," I said.

"This is the only wood-paneled wagon, so you must be Etienne and Gabriel." He saw the bottle and picked it up.

"Yeah, this is Gabe, I'm Etienne."

"Great name," he said.

That was a first.

"Most people call me Ette," I said.

"Ette," he said. "I'm Dietrich. Most people call me Dieter."

"Ahh," said Gabe.

"Hi, Gabe," said Dieter. "What can I carry?"

"There's just the diaper bag."

He took Gabe so I could remove the bag, and in the transfer, I accidentally swished across his chest. I felt like the fire drill bell at school had gone off.

And that was exactly when the crowd that hung out at the Beach Bun concession stand saw us. As Frieda liked to say, it triggered more buzz than a Geiger counter at a Nevada test site.

I saw Debbie. She waved. I waved back. One of her brothers pointed. Her whole family, who always sat as close as possible to the concession stand, turned and stared.

That couldn't have been another first. Dieter must have been by there already. He was what's called a looker.

We never bought anything from the concession stand, but unless you peed in the water or went in the woods, it was just a matter of time before you'd end up on your flank of the stand, where his-and-her plywood entries led to clammy bathrooms.

Farther on, Tedeschi's Bait & Tackle rented rowboats, and according to its sign, sold *Everything Under the Sun*, so people would know it was more than a specialty store. The rowboats were docked on one side of Tedeschi's pier, and people fished from the other side.

Even if none of your friends was at the beach that day, there was always some reason to head to one place or the other.

Dieter veered away from the shoreline route and took the wooded path instead. "Do your parents have a habit of leaving you like that?"

"No." I thought for a second. "But these things happen. Last year when we went to the fair, Dad took a picture of a big sign that said *Parents find your lost children here*, except find was spelled *f-i-n-e-d*."

Dieter laughed.

"Dad has a whole bunch of pictures like that."

"They'll be fun to see," he said.

"Yeah," I said. I guess Frieda's nephew would be coming over.

The path narrowed and he took the lead.

"Root," he warned a couple of times.

"Check," I responded. I knew where all of the gnarly roots were exposed, but I couldn't be too safe holding Gabe.

Carl spied us first. "Here they are," he announced.

"There, everything's fine," Dad reassured Mom.

"We thought Gabe had driven off," joked Frieda.

Marcia and Donna sure were sorry they hadn't been better helpers looking after Gabe and me like they were supposed to. Mom and Dad would never shame us, but they must have given Marcia a look or a shake of the head for talking Donna into leaving us behind because she was sulking. I figured it was like finally getting a ticket for speeding; she was way overdue. She was annoyed because she got caught, not because she cared. Donna appeared genuinely sorry, but her expression changed as soon as Dieter was introduced to her and Marcia.

Carl ran his hand above the grill grate and peered into the firebox.

"Do you swim or eat first, Uncle Carl?"

"By all means, swim, Dietrich, swim!"

Dieter slipped off his shirt. A big gold cross hung on his chest. Frieda folded the shirt, and Dieter slunk the long chain into her palm for safekeeping. The sides of his swim briefs had shiny racing stripes like some kind of space ship fabric.

I stripped down to my new one-piece Catalina and beat him into the water. I was always the first in and last out, with raisin fingertips before noon. I splashed out and dove under, and when I came up he was nearby.

"Can you swim to the raft?" he asked.

"Sure."

Lines tethered to floats stretched between two anchored rafts, marking the boundary of the public swimming area, and we took off for the near raft. Dieter must have held back to stay by my side. He hoisted up onto the raft. I took the short ladder. We sat facing the lake. He shaded his eyes and looked out to its only island.

"I understand Île de L'eau refers to the island and to the lake," he said.

"Check."

He smiled. "And there's really water on the island?"

"From a spring. The lake has springs, too. They're all around here."

"Have you ever been on the island?"

"Sure, every time I went to camp. It's across from the other side of the island, and we rowed over to hike the trails. Lots of people do."

"Does anyone ever swim to it?"

"Yeah, pretty often. From the camp side, it's close enough. If somebody swam from anywhere else, I never heard about it. Everybody would have."

He nodded.

Well away from the *No Wake* sign, an inboard with a wheelhouse headed up to the North Shore Restaurant and Marina, off to our right. They were tucked where the lake met the mouth of the Sherburne River. The Marina gave Tedeschi's a run for its money, renting motorboats and providing gas and pump-out, but the Marina's pier, off to the river side, was only used for docking. Whether boaters rowed or motored the Sherburne, they had to be careful, since people fished off the bridge just upriver. I'd heard a tale or two.

"How's the competition," asked Dieter, lifting his chin toward the restaurant.

"It's nice. I like eating there."

Outdoor umbrella-covered tables overlooked the boardwalk connecting to the Marina, and the food seemed to taste better when boaters docked and just hopped off to dine, but even when you ate inside, all the tables had picture window views of the lake.

"How about the food?"

"Really good. It's regular."

"What's regular?"

"American, even though the Georges, who own it, are Greek. Dad and Carl call it three squares."

"Check," he said.

It was my turn to smile.

We eyeballed the rest of the lake. Lakeshore Drive circled Île de L'eau, but once past Grand Central on this side, the road was hidden by trees. The only thing to see were miles of irregular shoreline full of interesting coves and points and the crowds at the other end of the town beach.

Nobody else had shown up at our end yet. We turned around to see what our group was up to. Dad was wading into the water holding Gabe, Carl was tending the grill, and Donna and Marcia and Mom and Frieda were setting out covered dishes.

"It looks like there's time to swim to the other raft and back before we eat," said Dieter.

I jiggled my legs in the water, hemming. "Maybe you can."

It was rare for me to give up a swim, but I didn't want to hold up lunch for everyone. Being as it was my first time in the water for the summer, I'd need a breather at the far raft, and I'd be a lot slower than him to start with.

"Will you spot me?"

"Alright."

He dove and passed several floats before he surfaced, and then he sped through the water with a crawl stroke until he reached the other raft. Several people were on it, and by then, everyone was spotting him. Somebody reached out their hand, and he tagged it, reversed direction, and did the back stroke a good part of the way. When he got near and switched to a breast stroke, I jumped back in, and we glided to Dad. Gabe's feet were in the water, and at the last minute, I dove under and came up to surprise him. He just about flew out of Dad's arms, screaming for joy.

Dad let Dieter take him, and he lowered Gabe so he had enough freedom to slap his hands against the water. He twirled him in a circle. Gabe caught on naturally, kicking his legs and squealing the whole time, especially after his diaper slipped off and sank. I retrieved it and Dieter floated Gabe to shore, where Mom nestled him in his soft warm blanket. Frieda was snapping away with Dad's camera.

We toweled off and gathered around the two picnic tables pushed together. Frieda asked Dieter to say grace. What with his big gold cross, I figured we were in for something, but it was what we always said.

"Bless us, oh Lord, and these thy gifts, which we are about to receive from thy bounty, through Christ, our Lord."

"Amen," we all said.

As usual, there was a lot of bounty to be grateful for, and today's theme was in honor of Dieter. Carl had made his famous Coburger Bratwurst, grilled it over the traditional beechwood and pinecone fire, and served it with his sauerkraut and crusty rolls. Naturally, that was just the main dish.

Dieter was wowed. "This bratwurst rivals any I had in Bavaria," he said. "Everything is excellent. You'll spoil me, but I appreciate that you're willing to take me on for a few weeks."

"It's our pleasure, Dieter," said Dad.

"And we can always use more waitstaff in the summer," said Mom.

"We're absolutely thrilled you're staying with us," said Frieda. Carl nodded.

"How come you've never been here before?" asked Donna.

"I have been here, several times, but I was young. I went away to school, and my father has been opening new offices ever since then. Time flew." He glanced in my direction and added, "These things happen."

Check. Getting away for more than a few days was hard for any of us, too. Following the war, my mother and father, Isabelle Benoit and Raymond Durand, had married in a double wedding with their best friends, Frieda Norden and Carl Meyer, and all of them poured everything into an inn they bought, which they named The Neston Arms.

We Durands lived across the street where the family had for generations, long before the inn was built. Carl had grown up around the corner, and now he and Frieda lived in a wing of the top floor of the Arms in the owners' quarters.

Everybody wore more than one hat. Carl and Dad were hands-on chefs and bakers who also oversaw food and beverage operations. Mom developed menus and conferred with the front of house manager on service. That was just the restaurant and banquet side of the business. Frieda supervised the accommodations side, and as the accountant, kept the Arms in the black. Some years had been better than others, but with repeat customers and referrals, she said the bottom line was really improving. But probably not nearly as high as her brother's, who was Dieter's father.

Dieter sure wouldn't spend his summer relaxing. Except for the time in early spring known as mud season, there was always something to be preparing for and working on and cleaning up from. Being June, wedding season was in full swing, and there were vacationers all summer. The Arms was almost completely booked through Labor Day.

"Where do you go to school?" asked Donna.

"The Avon School."

Donna didn't ask where that was. Apparently everybody else knew, but all I knew was that when a school is called *The*, it's a private school where the boys have to wear ties and blazers with an emblem on the pocket over the heart.

Expecting her next question, he said, "I'm a rising senior."

"And aquatic champion," said Carl.

No wonder he swam over and back so fast.

"Which is why he'll have to leave at the beginning of August," said Frieda.

"That soon?" said Donna.

"I've got final practice drills for a competition," said Dieter.

"Not just any competition," said Frieda. "The 1964 Summer Olympics qualifying trials."

Everybody was so surprised, it took a minute before Frieda could deliver the punch line. "They're in New York at the end of August. If he qualifies, he'll compete in Tokyo."

"Tokyo!"

Personally knowing someone who might be going to Japan rubbed off in a big way, but after another minute, Dieter cut the hubbub short. "Until then, Île de L'eau is my lap lane."

Well, not for the next thirty minutes, anyway. We weren't allowed to swim after eating, so we settled into lazing, which was just as well, since it gave us time to ruminate on that news.

Marcia was also entering senior year, so I wondered if she would cozy up to Dieter, but she only had eyes for Audrey Hepburn, who was modeling some famous designer in the latest issue of *Vogue*. In between flipping through the pages of *Seventeen* and *American Girl*, Donna sized up Dieter. Eventually, she tossed the magazines aside and grabbed Marcia's copy of *Mademoiselle*.

"What are you doing," said Marcia flatly.

"I'm just going to look at it," said Donna.

"And wrinkle it," said Marcia. "Now put it back nicely."

"Fine." Donna grabbed her dog-eared copy of *To Kill a Mockingbird*.

Dieter moved to sit next to her.

"That's a favorite of mine, too," he said.

"Really?" said Donna eagerly.

She and Dieter got to talking. I hadn't read the book they were talking about, but I guessed I would before it was required. I stretched out on a towel in the sun and started the first book of a series I planned to read over the summer.

Mom and Dad formed a tunnel on a blanket, each cupping a cheek in one hand so they could face each other. Dad held Gabe's keys over his head and shook them. Cushioned on both sides, Gabe pulled himself up into a standing position a few times, and Dad let him grab the keys. He had started saying Dada and Mama, which thrilled them every time, even if he said dadadadada to Mom.

Frieda and Carl took a walk. Holding hands, they headed down the beach, swinging their arms and splashing like kids.

Eventually, Dad got up and checked how many exposures were left on his camera.

"Can I take some pictures, Dad?"

"You think you're ready?"

"Yes."

"It's not a toy."

"I know."

"Alright then."

He sat in a chaise and patted his hand on the seat. I sat in front of him, and he put his arms around me, holding the camera. He slid the strap around my neck.

"Okay, you hold it, both sides, just like this."

It was heavier than I thought it would be.

"Before taking a picture, make sure the lens cap is off, and the film is advanced, like this, until it stops."

He advanced it half way and I finished.

"Now focus on something."

I pointed straight ahead.

"I'm looking at the raft, but it's fuzzy."

He guided my hand to a dial, and as I turned it, the focus turned clear.

"This number tells you what shot you're on out of the number available on the roll."

"It says six."

"When you're ready, press this button."

I took a test picture of the raft and advanced the film again.

"You've got it. There are twelve exposures on the roll, so you've got another six left. You want to take them?"

"Yes."

"Just keep the camera dry."

My first real picture was Gabe. He was stretched over Mom's shoulder, facing backward. After he turned around, I got him and Mom and Dad, all in profile. Marcia cocked her head, but Donna had gone back to reading with a smile on her face, or maybe she was just daydreaming with the book in front of her. When Carl and Frieda came back, I took a full body shot of them standing at the water's edge. Carl set up a game of chess, and I got Dieter thoughtfully considering a move.

From time to time, he exchanged a few words in German with his aunt and uncle. A lot of people in Neston, including us, spoke French in the home, as well as at work. Being so close to Quebec, it just came with the territory. Obviously, German was spoken as frequently by the Nordens as by Carl and Frieda, except that they also spoke it on their frequent trips to Europe. I'd heard Frieda mention that Albert and Penelope went at least once a year, another reason they didn't have time to come up to Neston from Connecticut, and it was also the reason that Dieter, who was as all-American as they came, had what she called The Continental Effect. I'd seen it enough times at the Arms to know there really was something to be said for it.

I advanced the film. It kept going.

"Now we have to load a new film," said Dad.

We moved to the deep shade at the table, and Dad showed me how to finish winding, store the film cannister, and catch the new roll. This was a careful process that I only watched.

"You think you could do this next time?"

"If you're with me," I said.

"How about if you drop off this roll for processing tomorrow and pick up some more?"

Big smile. "Okay."

He showed me how to store the camera in its case.

"How about some beach ball?"

"Yeah!"

Beach ball was the only sport we all enjoyed together any more, and we tossed the ball back and forth to see how many times we could pass it without it touching the water. Marcia, Donna, Dieter, and Carl played against me and Mom and Frieda and Dad, who held Gabe in one arm and hit the ball with the other, which got Gabe pretty excited. He took a swat, too. As usual, Donna never missed a pass and came out the winner. She would have won anyway even if she wasn't trying to impress Dieter.

Everybody retreated to their blankets and chaise lounges.

"Are you coming back out?" Dieter asked me.

Now that I knew for sure he was a champion swimmer, I felt less confident about going out to the raft with him again, but I guessed he had already figured out that I loved the water like he did.

"Will you show me how to do a back flip?"

"I will."

We swam to the raft again, and I watched while he demonstrated a couple of flips. I tried imitating him, but my practice tucks were too straight and shallow.

"Mind if I position your arms and legs?"

Except for accidentally swishing him earlier, I'd never gotten close to a boy before, and if I had known the lesson involved him touching me, I never would have asked him. I could have said no, but I asked him to show me, so said "alright."

I needn't have given it a thought. It was like getting fitted for new shoes. First, he showed me how to stand, and then he gently guided my elbows and knees into better position.

"That's it. You're getting the angle."

He knelt down and stretched his arm behind me.

"Now bend just like you're doing the limbo."

Getting the small of my back to curve over his arm took all my focus, until the corner of my eye caught Donna drifting nearby on the tube, watching us like a hawk. I tensed up.

"Stay loose, relaxed." He stood. "Try a practice lift."

I tucked and leaned back and bounced a couple of times.

"You're ready."

I teetered backwards over the edge. "Lift off!"

It was over so fast, I swam back and clung to the platform.

"I flopped over a little," I said breathlessly.

"You did great. Try again?" I did. Well, we did together.

He was a fast swimmer, but when it came to diving and flipping, it was all in the technique, and my being small and light worked almost as well as his being tall and strong. I did tire out sooner, though. When my body began to feel heavy climbing the ladder, it was time to dry off and get changed.

Dad waded out and put a big towel around me. "That was something, Ette."

Everybody except Marcia was impressed.

"Maybe you can show me next time," said Donna.

"Sure, I'd be happy to," said Dieter.

I wondered if he would figure out that she already knew how. She and Kimmie Hart were tied for Neston's favorite cheerleader, and she could bend better than Gumby.

Dieter and I headed to the Beach Bun. As soon as we got near, Debbie ran over, followed by her younger brother, Larry.

"Hi, Ette."

"Hi, Debbie. Dieter, this my best friend, Debbie Fortin. Debbie, this is Dieter Norden."

"Like Skeeter?" said Debbie.

"Different spelling. Short for Dietrich."

"How come you swim so good?" said Larry.

"Well," corrected Debbie. "A good swimmer swims well."

Larry scowled.

"I'm training for the Olympics."

That raised a ruckus again.

"Where?" Brenda Pratt shimmied up close. Her raccoon eyeliner covered more skin than her two-piece.

Dieter looked away. "School."

"Where's school?"

"Connecticut."

"Too bad."

Dieter couldn't even get into the bathroom without pushing through, and Mr. Fortin, who was a history teacher at the high school, intercepted the crowd.

"Alright, alright, give him some air," he said, and he stood near the door so Dieter wouldn't be hounded.

Debbie went into the ladies' side with me. "What's he doing here?"

"Visiting. Frieda—Mrs. Meyer is his aunt." Frieda and Carl weren't relatives, even though they were just like them, but they were the only adults I ever called by first name. "And working, too."

"For the summer?"

I gave her the scoop.

"Zowie!" she said.

"I know. Isn't that something?"

"Are you still biking on Thursday?"

"We said we were. Or going to the library if it rains. Can't Paula go?" Paula Bouchard was my other best friend.

"Yeah, she's coming. I just thought maybe you'd be busy with, you know."

"Dieter?"

"Yeah."

"Not when we already made plans."

When we came out, Dieter was surrounded. He called out, waving. "Etienne!"

"Dietrich," I hollered back. All of the kids left except Larry, who must've figured he had a pass since Debbie was sticking to me.

Dieter leaned close. "Do you have any money?"

"Yes." I made it a policy to carry my plastic squeeze coin purse, which was perfect for the beach because it didn't matter if it got wet. You never knew when you might want some coin, especially when you were in the vicinity of Tedeschi's, and sure enough, here I did. Or, I should say, he did.

"I promised to send postcards. It's a tradition."

"I've got plenty. They're cheaper by the half-dozen."

"Good, then that's what I'll get." He smiled down at Larry, who was all but hanging on to him, and said, "Catch you later."

Larry looked grateful as Mr. Fortin took him back to their table.

We went into Tedeschi's Bait & Tackle.

"Sorry about that," said Dieter.

I wasn't sure if he meant the money or the commotion. Either way, I shrugged.

I turned the paperback book rack while he did the same with the postcard rack.

Old Mr. Tedeschi rang up the vintage cash register for the smallest of sales. Like always, he'd seen and heard everything. Whatever he didn't gather from his stool parked next to the screen door, he got from customers.

"Good luck, kid," he said.

"No luck to it at all, sir. Just hard work and prayer. The outcome is in God's hands. But thanks all the same. I appreciate it."

Mr. Tedeschi squinted at him as dubiously as The Rifleman eyeballed rascals.

Maybe Dieter was churchy after all. Paula's parents would like that. Reverend Bouchard was the minister at the Meetinghouse, and Mrs. Bouchard was from Georgia.

Once, when I was picking through the final markdown bin in Woolworth's basement, I overheard Mrs. Pierce and her daughter Shirley in the next aisle over saying Mrs. Bouchard was churchy. To me, it would make sense if the minister's wife was churchy, but they must have been gossiping because they said it like a swear word. I thought Mrs. Bouchard was nice, so I wasn't sure why churchy would be bad in her case.

Marcia called a lot of things "outside the norm," things that weren't really abnormal, but they weren't completely normal, either. I guess Dieter was outside the norm, since regular boys weren't Olympic contenders, they didn't wear big crosses, and they didn't say things like he did to Mr. Tedeschi. Besides, he must have been looking forward to having other boys to pal around with all day, but he didn't switch allegiance because Etienne turned out to be a girl and Gabriel was a baby.

I didn't expect it would last. Plus, if Donna had anything to do with it, today would definitely be the first and last time.

Chapter 2

THE RACKET OF THE lawnmower and vacuum woke me out of a sound sleep at 9:30, a sure sign I was tuckered out from all those back flips, and that being on summer vacation had sunk in.

The Lacroixs were hard at work. They named their mom-and-pop business *In 'n' Out* because they worked on the inside and outside of people's homes and because they finished everything faster than most homeowners would. For years, Mr. Lacroix had been keeping up the yard, plus doing all kinds of handyman work, but Mrs. Lacroix had only started last year. After Gabe was on the way we needed the extra help, and with our improving bottom line, we had enough money to hire her. Mrs. Lacroix laundered the linens, dusted and vacuumed, what-have-you. My sisters and I had always done chores, and still would, but I don't know how Mom had also done all Mrs. Lacroix did before she came on board.

She switched off the vacuum when I went into the hallway.

"Everybody's gone to work," she informed me. "I said to your mother, 'Go, she'll be fine with me.'"

"Thanks, Mrs. Lacroix. I won't be in your way."

I went into the kitchen and found Mom's note propped against the napkin holder.

Precious Ette, I hope your dreams were sweet. Did I ever tell you that you're a neat sleeper? See you later. Love, Mom.

She hadn't. She saved things like that for her notes, and I saved all of her notes.

There was a note from Dad, too.

Ette, there are three rolls of film in the paper bag on the hall table and enough cash to pay for prints that are waiting and a couple of rolls of film. And now that you're a photographer, how about if you pick out an album you like? Thanks for being a big helper. XO, Dad.

Notes from Dad were much less frequent, and this one was a really good surprise.

I ate and did the breakfast dishes, thinking the next family splurge we saved up for should be an automatic dishwasher. After I took a bath, I finished putting away my school things for the summer and walked over to Putnam's Art & Photography.

Putnam's walls promoted their photography services with enlargements of portraits and special events, mostly weddings, and pushed art supply sales with its own Fine and Folk Arts Gallery, which displayed artists' watercolors and oils for sale alongside all sorts of wooden hand crafts. I scanned the latest rotation in the gallery and moved on to the photo albums when the cashier charged by the end of the aisle.

"You get out of here!"

"I'm just looking."

I could have sworn the other voice was Sammy Fortin, Debbie's oldest brother.

"You're not buying, either. I'm not selling any glue—to you or your friends, so you can tell them to quit loitering."

"I'm just—"

"Get out now, and if you come back, I'll report the lot of you to the police."

"Alright, alright. You don't have to holler."

It *was* Sammy. My heart pounded.

The cashier closed the door behind him and stood there, waiting for Sammy and his friends to leave.

"You did the right thing," said a customer to the cashier.

"Pain in the neck," he said. "Mr. Putnam had to pull it from the floor."

What had Sammy done? I tried to think of who his friends were. Mr. Fortin would have a fit if he knew Sammy had been thrown out of a store.

I took a deep breath and looked at photo albums until I found one I liked, and when I went down the model kits aisle, I saw a sign. *Model glue available at the counter.*

I paid for our prints, more film, and my album. While I was filling out the envelope for the rolls to be processed, I asked, "Why is the glue behind the counter?"

"The kids are sniffing it."

"How come?"

"To get high."

"What's that?"

"A feeling."

"Oh." The only time I got a feeling was from some cough syrup, but it made me feel low, not high.

"Ran us out of inventory. Not any more."

Mr. Fortin would do more than have a fit. And if Sammy had seen me, and then Mr. Fortin found out, Sammy would think I tattled. An icy stab hit my stomach. I looked both ways out the windows, but he and his friends were gone.

I hightailed it home and left the bag with the pictures and the change on the sideboard, plus the album, so Dad could see what I picked out. I was tempted to look at the prints, but it was more fun to look at them with Dad.

Even if I had been there when it was taken, I missed things until I saw them in the picture. It was funny how the photographs could make me see things for the first time. Sometimes Dad did, too. Like he said, not even the eye of the beholder always saw what was there.

I took the short cut to the east service entrance of the Arms. Gabe had a play pen at Carl and Frieda's, and Mom was working at a table next to him.

"Baby Gaby!" I picked him up and did an Eskimo kiss.

"Ahh," he said.

"Somebody's wet."

"I changed him fifteen minutes ago," said Mom.

That happened a lot.

"You can bring him in here," said Dieter. "I'm just finishing the postcards."

Marcia and Donna and I had slept plenty of times in the room where Dieter was staying. I laid out the changing pad to protect the blanket. On the nightstand between the beds I noticed a big black Bible with gilt pages and *Dietrich B. Norden* embossed on the cover, and next to it was a framed three-by-five formal of a girl with dark brunette hair flowing over her shoulders.

Frieda came to the door. "Now's your chance to escape the ogre," she said to Dieter.

"You're hardly an ogre," he said, licking a stamp.

"All the same, you gotta git while the gittin's good."

She turned to Mom. "He was out the door at eight o'clock to swim before the crowds arrive at the beach."

After he got back, she explained, she'd given him the full tour and overview of the Arms, and then handed him over to the *garde manger*—the chef who oversees cold foods, for hands-on practice for the dinner service.

"I put him through the paces," she said, "but he passed with flying colors. He's ready for the floor tonight."

When Dieter had set foot on the property less than forty-eight hours earlier, André Michaud, the *maître d'*—the restaurant and wait staff manager, had claimed Dieter as FOH—front of house material. Mom and Frieda agreed completely.

Gabe was happy as a clam after I changed him. We came out.

"So you've got a of couple hours to paint the town," said Frieda.

"Etienne, if you're not busy, will you show me around?" said Dieter. "If you don't mind. I don't want to put you on the spot."

I obviously was not busy, but everybody else was, including Donna. I guessed this was just his way of being friendly, and after all, he had shown me how to do a back flip, so I could return the favor and show him something I knew.

"I don't mind. I'll be back right around 3:00," I promised Mom.

Dieter and Frieda exchanged *deux bisous*—kisses on both cheeks.

"There, I'll be a princess for a couple of hours," she said, "and you're going to miss it."

Chapter 3

I FIGURED WE SHOULD start at the beginning, so we crossed the common to the museum, which takes up the whole third floor of Ward Memorial Library.

We dropped a donation in the box and signed the visitor book. Two couples also had also signed in, both with the last name Thompson, one out-of-state, the other local, and from the looks of them, the men were brothers. *Our first visit*, wrote one in the comments section, and *Ours, too*, wrote the other.

Polly Racine, the white-haired docent, was chatting with the couples. They, and Dieter, were in for a treat. Mrs. Racine was a volunteer, but she was a real pro, a walking encyclopedia.

"Welcome to the Neston Historical Society Museum," she said, starting the tour. We stood before the mural-sized oil landscape of early Neston and viewed the details she described.

"The history of Neston started like other places in Vermont with virgin forest. It was settled as a logging town. Land had to be cleared if it was to be colonized, and the area's most abundant resource provided Neston with homes and commerce from its earliest days. Sawmills built on the bank of the Connecticut River received the horse-drawn timber out of the wilderness, which stretched west past our own great Lake Île de L'eau."

She paused in case anyone had a comment or question, and since no one did yet, she went on.

"In time, rough logging roads branched south beyond Hinton Ridge and north to the Canadian border. The potash industry followed soon after. Potash is, literally, the wood ash left at the bottom of an iron pot, and is used in making gunpowder, glass, dyes, soap, and fertilizer. It was a valuable and lucrative commodity. And so, cradled between water and wilderness, Neston quickly became prosperous, if not populous."

The couples smiled and nodded. We looked at saws and tools on our way into a round room covered with paintings.

"This cyclorama of pastoral oils illustrates the changes that nature underwent. The locale was a natural migration for French-speaking Quebecois. Neston grew as sheep farmers moved onto cleared tracts, and the lumber industry flourished to the point that the hills were razed."

The middle of the cycle of paintings showed eroded hillsides, and the couples shook their heads, but there was a happy ending to this part of the story, and we came to it.

"Eventually, long rolling acres of hay, corn, oats, and potatoes were planted, and cattle and horses grazed. Game and fowl returned with the regrowth of the forest."

In the center of the next room was a case containing business ledgers with perfect script, musket balls, and a drum. On the wall was a signed full-length color engraving of a man. Standing on a porch with one foot on a step, he looked down at us.

"Like most places, Neston has been touched by war. Much of what we have to show for the era of the War of 1812 comes from Neston's most controversial character, Chauncey Smith." She indicated the engraving, and after a good look, the couples crowded the document next to it, a warrant for his arrest. It was always good for a gasp. Dieter was interested, too.

"Neston, as well as other towns along the border, was opposed to the war and simply did not stop doing cross-border business—not until forced to do so. The Sherburne River empties into Lake Île de L'eau, and it was an important and profitable trade route between Quebec and Neston, particularly for Mr. Smith, who is pictured here at his lakeshore tavern and trading post. He was highly successful and therefore had the most to lose. But lose it he did, and only the site of his homestead remains."

Unsurprisingly, there were more gasps.

"He, however, was never served the warrant for his arrest, and many speculate that he took the river into Quebec. These artifacts and the Chauncey Smith Historic Site provide a small glimpse into some of the enormous difficulties people faced at that time. Opinions remain divided on Chauncey Smith, however, so if you take sides with him in public, be forewarned." She raised one eyebrow.

Everyone chuckled.

"Where's the site?" the visiting Mrs. Thompson asked.

"On Lakeshore Drive, past the town beach. It's marked, so you won't miss it."

Dieter nodded, realizing where it was. Of course, I'd seen the sign for the historic site, which was next to a park, but I'd never gone to either one.

We entered another room, and the roped-off tableau took the visitors' breath away. Spotlights shone on stuffed cotton mannequins.

"Meet the Lamberts. The clothes and implements were their own belongings, and the backdrop is an authentic reconstruction. You see them as they looked and as they lived."

The couples said what everybody said: "They were so small."

Mrs. Racine stood aside while we examined everything.

They say a picture is worth a thousand words. At the museum, placards placed next to the artifacts, landscapes, portraits, and photographs identified the subjects and objects of Neston's past, but I'd seen the items enough times that they spoke for themselves.

Eliza Lambert's decorative combs lined up in a case made me imagine her arranging them in her hair for one of their barn dances before her husband went off to the Civil War.

Behind their replica figures, a hearth contained a cast iron cauldron and andirons, with a long rifle over the mantle. The table held a shallow bread kneading bowl and pewter plates, a butter churn sat next to its stool, and a log splitter and rusted scythe leaned against the wall, all original from the farmhouse.

"Eliza kept the farm going," I said to Dieter. "The Lamberts still run the dairy. We get all our milk and cream from them."

"Oh, yes, I saw the Lambert name on the cartons."

"She raised six children, too, and they had lots of kids. Luc Lambert—he's a couple of years older than me—he told me his mother showed him Eliza's diary where she wrote she wouldn't bury her husband in his uniform because he paid for it with his life. That's how the uniform ended up here. There's a hole on the back side where a bayonet went through. He got an infection."

Dieter stared wide-eyed at me.

"What?"

"You've got quite the insider information," he said.

I shrugged.

"I've read that disease took more soldiers than the war itself," he said. "It's sad, but the personal history is fascinating."

"Yeah, I asked Luc if his family was going to give Eliza's diary to the museum, but he said his mother couldn't part with it yet. I told him I thought they should have pictures taken of it, at least that page. That way they could keep it and it could still go on display here."

Mrs. Racine took us into a room with broadsides lining one wall.

"Unlike most places, Neston is the epicenter of the greatest collection of springs in the state. At one time, Wortham County flourished as a destination for those seeking the curative powers of the waters. The heyday of the mostly homespun resorts declined when other areas more easily developed eclipsed the remote region, although a lakeside gilded age colony has survived."

Several broadsides advertised the springs and guest houses. A tall glass case dividing the room contained everything from needlework to account logs. Its prize possession was a communal snuff box.

"This single object recalls William Ward's prominence as the founder of the First Bank of Neston, from whose largesse Ward Memorial Library is named," said Mrs. Racine. "Indeed, we could say everything here evokes the dreams and daily lives of the people who once wore the clothes and wielded the instruments essential to daily life."

She and I saw things the same way.

"There's a big Ward wedding this Saturday," I said, when Dieter and I took our turn at the Ward snuff box.

"Aunt Frieda told me, but it would be hard to miss all the preparations. It will be quite the reception."

It sure would.

We moved to a large room with exhibits on the war years up to the present.

"After a decrease for almost a half-century, the population of Neston revived when waves of Europeans sought mountains and seasons that reminded them of home before the Great War. To the immigrants, the natural springs offered more than external healing and year-round sources of solace. As a haven for their weary souls, Neston was their Little Switzerland.

"Among them was Walter Eckert. He had amassed a fortune in the old country and was determined to build a palatial abode with a commanding view over a turn of river reminiscent of one he was particularly fond of in his homeland. He settled for the corner of Stony Brook Hill overlooking Île de L'eau. The formerly denuded landscape had grown in, but it took much less effort to clear the land of its second growth.

"His mansion, built with native wood as well as granite and marble quarried from other Vermont counties, took four years to complete. Neston boomed, in part due to the financial backbone the bank provided. The Wards promoted commerce. The next generation of skilled labor apprenticed in the mansion's construction, and thereafter, a large staff was required to maintain it and provide all its comforts.

"During that time, Eckert built his sphere of influence and looked for a wife. He courted Marie Best, direct descendant of the timber baron who had gone on to found Bestbury some miles south of here. The colossal house was the venue of their wedding and reception. Its prime acreage was the backdrop of the honeymoon, which spanned what by all accounts was a glorious summer. Their important friends continued to flock to the house. They came as much to enjoy being treated as royalty as to enjoy the simpler pleasures, such as plumbing that piped spring-fed water.

"Eckert was a genius photographer with a passion for moving pictures, and he documented the construction and celebrations himself, right up to the late fall of that year, 1929, when the Eckerts left for parts unknown."

Mrs. Racine paused, expecting another exclamation, which came on cue. Everyone knew the stock market crashed in 1929.

"These curated copies of his photos tell the story of his mansion up to that point. All the rare originals and the films are secure in the special collections bunker of the Ward Memorial Library downstairs.

"Like most towns, Neston suffered after that, the more so as the taxes on the Eckert estate could not be collected. Eckert had been a first-generation immigrant with no local family, and it was not possible, as the Best remnant uncontestably asserted, to extract blood from a stone. Even if they could have been held culpable, they too had nearly been wiped out. However—" she led us to the next section of the exhibit, which was chock full of brochures and photographs.

"The mansion was rescued when it was turned into a sanatorium. Its luxury was a bonus for the wealthiest—and sickest—who sat bundled in the fresh freezing air on its balconies and verandah. They came for the waters, too. The springs had never entirely lost their allure. While their mineral powers could not be directly credited with curing tubercular lungs, they did wonders for digestion and complexion, so with improved health, many people were considered healed when they left. Certainly, medical professionals who otherwise never would have considered venturing so far north settled in."

The local man elbowed his out-of-state brother, who tried not to smile.

"When the sanatorium closed, the mansion was shuttered, but in less than a year, the Driscoll brothers of Portsmouth came in, modernized it, and renovated it as The Neston Inn. Now, there's not much debate over the fact that the Driscolls had better investment sense than sound management practices. They claimed its spring was a fountain of youth, and people from around the world flocked to the inn. But after a nearly fatal group case of food poisoning, a class action lawsuit was brought over the failure of the claim. They went bankrupt, and the doors closed again."

The visitors murmured and shook their heads as they looked over the memorabilia.

"This is an unusual chapter in the building's history," said Dieter.

"Yeah," I said. "I used to think it was icky, but I found out it's been good for business. When the Driscolls turned it into an inn, some of the rich people who had been at the sanatorium came back. Their families still do. You see these pictures *Courtesy of Armand and Nicole Papineau*? At first, they gave them to us to display, but when the Historical Society opened, we gave them back to the Papineaus, and they donated them."

Mrs. Racine moved us along. "Neston declined further when many of the former Europeans' offspring went back to that continent to fight in a second war. The names of those who did not return are inscribed on the large monument on the town common, and the remains of those who did rest under their markers and headstones in the cemetery behind the Meetinghouse. Naturally, with a reduction in its work force, the saw mill industry declined.

"Soon, another entry was recorded in the phases of the Eckert estate, all of which are in the records of the tax division at the Town Clerk's Office and in the minutes of annual town meetings, but like most Neston history, are widely although unofficially attested in the considerable trove of well-preserved and often trustworthy oral tradition."

That brought another round of chuckles.

Mrs. Racine should know. She had been the Town Clerk for thirty years. She looked at her watch. I'd have to tell Dieter later.

"Today, the estate is known as The Neston Arms. This postcard was made from a photograph taken on opening day by one of its owners."

In fact, Dad. Dieter stepped close and saw the placard. *Courtesy of the Durand and Meyer Families.* He smiled. I knew just how he felt.

Four flags with the families' coats of arms waved at the entrance: Durand, Benoit, Norden, and Meyer. In the middle, the American flag flew.

"It's beautiful," said the visiting Mrs. Thompson.

"We've got dinner reservations for tonight," said her sister-in-law. "It will be our first time there, too."

I'd let Mr. Michaud know, and he'd alert the front desk. We went out of our way to encourage first-timers to look all around the public areas. After visiting the museum, the Thompsons would enjoy the Arms' history even more.

"The name change to The Neston Arms did more than distance the inn from its previous owners and failures. Arms captures its character as a distinguished hostelry and the people who make it that way."

Mrs. Racine didn't have to add that last part. I thought so too, but it was a really nice thing for her to say.

"How the two couples managed to buy it and turn it into a showcase destination is private, but the banners of the arms are public, and no doubt they are the semaphores that spark thousands of conversations."

I had taken the tour enough times to know semaphores sent messages, in this case, through flags. She was right. Our coats of arms did start lots of conversations.

The next part was what always got me, though. It explained why she talked so much about Walter Eckert's mansion.

"The Neston Arms has driven progress just as its predecessors did. Several visitors only too happy to trade urban decay for open land with pristine air and water, despite the long and cold winters, saw Neston as good place to stay year-round."

This time, the local brother said, "See?"

Mrs. Racine paused, as the other brother said, "Long and cold, alright," and the rest of us laughed.

"But we wouldn't trade it for the world," the first one added, and his wife nodded.

"Naturally, progress brings change, some wanted, some not. Forestry remains important to Neston's economy, but only one major wholesale saw mill remains. However, several small businesses have filled the need for retail lumber, veneer, and other wood products, and furniture manufacture has replaced potash production.

"Changes to the land also took place when the state widened and repaved the old Neston Road. Renamed Neston Avenue, it runs north of Main Street, making it part of the east-west route running all the way from the Connecticut River Road to the interstate highway. The New District it spawned ruffled some feathers, but those disgruntled Nestoners saw opportunity on the flip side of the coin. They petitioned the government, and the heart of the town was designated a historical district, preserved from development. The New District and the Historic District bring many people into Neston, both regional residents and tourists."

She paused and took a breath. "And today," she concluded with a smile, "Neston is a prosperous town, population 6,717."

Mrs. Racine got her standing ovation. She deserved it. We all thanked her. The couples stayed behind, but Dieter and I left.

Chapter 4

WE WENT DOWN TO the second floor and passed by the children's library. At the main circulation desk on the first floor, Dieter applied for a temporary lending card. With his address being The Neston Arms, he identified himself as Frieda and Carl's nephew and said they could vouch for him staying until August. I did, too.

"Are you the swimmer?" asked Miss Harrison. Dieter smiled. "Yes, I'm the swimmer."

My, that news spread even faster than usual for Neston.

Miss Harrison blinked and issued the card.

"We offer reader advisories if you want assistance finding something," she said.

"Actually, I could use some. I'm interested in primary sources on Neston, especially postcards."

"We have many materials for in-house viewing." She made a note. "Let us know when you'll be in, and we'll retrieve the postcards to have them ready for you."

"I'll do that. Thank you."

We went out. The Meetinghouse carillon started tolling, and we stopped to hear the time. We had fifteen minutes left.

"I didn't exactly show you around," I said.

He looked surprised. "It was perfect, Etienne. You bring so much to it. You could be a docent one day."

"People might think I was trying to drum up business."

Half the placards said *Donated courtesy of the Durand and Meyer families, proprietors of The Neston Arms.* The photographs were credited to who took them—Walter Eckert, Willard Putnam, who photographed the inn when it was owned by the Driscolls, a few others, and Dad—but credit for donating was a whole other matter.

"Descendants telling their stories isn't a conflict of interest," said Dieter. "They're the most interesting stories."

"I'll think about it." I had years before they'd let me. "At any rate, I know everything is safer there. Before we donated the originals, they were in the big file cabinet in the office next to the kitchen. I just hope Mrs. Lambert keeps Eliza's diary in a safe place. I sure would like to read it."

"Did you ask your friend?"

"Luc? No. We're not friendly enough for that."

But maybe I should.

"I had no idea how important the history of the Arms has been to Neston," said Dieter.

"I think it's interesting."

"Extremely interesting, and an advantage to have it so well documented."

"Some people think Neston is boring."

I felt the comfort of belonging to generations of Durands in Neston, but a lot of the high school kids were leaving permanently after they graduated.

"Do you?"

"No, I love it." Besides, I couldn't imagine leaving Gabe before he flew the nest. "I want to stay here."

We strolled under the awnings on Main Street. When we crossed the street to the post office, I pointed and said, "The *Neston News* office is that way, in case you want to give them the scoop straight from the horse's mouth."

"And deprive them of hoofing it? No, they know where to find me."

"Okay, but the society page runs on Thursdays, so I'd be on the lookout if I were you."

"So noted."

Dieter had a tremendous interest in all the architecture, especially how the town had modernized without compromising its history. Lehmann's department store and Woolworth's hid in old red limestone, cheek by jowl with the gray granite block's bank and police station. Except for modest signs, the buildings with everything from attorney-at-law offices to tailoring services to a music shop looked no different from the nineteenth century residential houses they had taken over. I gave him the scoop on a couple of them and paused to retie my shoelace in front of one. He took the bait.

"That house—Uncle Carl lived here."

"Check."

He rubbed his chin. "So, the old Meyer homestead is Wortham Realty now."

He was all smiles as he looked it over. "You know, I remember when Oma Meyer finally convinced me to go into the root cellar with her. I noticed it was cooler than the basement, and she gave me my first real lesson in architecture. I couldn't have been more than four or five years old, but I remember it clear as day. Grandfather Meyer was alive then, too."

He paused to remember. "I knew Uncle Carl held on to the house, but I didn't know what became of it. This is wonderful. Aunt Frieda must be pleased."

"Yeah, the Frohlichs—the people who run the business—are friends with Frieda and Carl. They used to live upstairs, but they built a new house and moved out. It's been empty since then. Carl says you've got to have just the right kind of tenant when there's a business downstairs. You could go in. If Carl doesn't have time, the Frohlichs would show you around the whole place. They're a hoot, just like Frieda."

"Thanks for the tip. I have such happy memories of the time I spent in the house, I was hoping I could see it again. I will ask him."

We moved on slowly and he said, "The Historical Society information was very enlightening, Ette, but I'd have missed out on the best part if I'd gone by myself. Your background knowledge is incomparable. I'm thrilled you had the time to show me. Thank you so much."

I never had a compliment that nice. "You're welcome."

We continued toward the Arms when he said, "You didn't have to walk me all the way back."

"I live right up there."

We went to the corner, and I stopped in front of the house.

"This is your home?"

"Yes."

"It's one of the best examples of Federal I've ever seen."

"It is?"

Most of the houses in this section were alike, two or three story white clapboard with black shutters, but I guessed he would know his Federals, being from Connecticut.

"Oh, it's extraordinary," he said excitedly. "Door fanlight and sidelights, and a center attic window with three panes."

"The attic window is one of my favorite spots. There's a cushioned seat built in under it. But I like the new breezeway, too."

He craned his neck as we walked around to the driveway. The little barn connecting the house to the big barn had been renovated with a mudroom and lots of windows. It was more like a giant sunroom than a breezeway, and the big barn's arched carriage doors now disguised a garage. The rest of the barn had two floors of storage.

Mom saw us and came out, and after *deux bisous*, Dieter said, "Whoever did the work did a great job matching the look of the original."

"Yes, it's a requirement," said Mom. "The Historic District rules are very strict."

"And now there's no more clearing ice off the car all winter long or lugging groceries in through rain and snow," I said. "That's why I like it."

"Definitely improvements," he said, although I doubted he did much of those things. It was the height of luxury to me.

"I know you must get back, but please, come visit us when you have time," said Mom. "You have a standing invitation."

"I would love to, Mrs. Durand."

I would have shown him where to cut through the arborvitae to the service entrance, but I was the only one who could fit through the low opening any more, and once I got around to growing, I wouldn't either.

Chapter 5

WITH THE WARD-COTE WEDDING three days away, the groom and his family and other out-of-state guests would start checking in any minute. They had fully booked the inn.

Claude Cote came from a line of bankers in Providence, and the bride, Eugénie Ward, of the line of Ward bankers, was Neston's own debutante—its last one, according to Mrs. Bouchard, who said they weren't making them this far north any more—and if that wasn't enough, the *Neston News* had already run a story on President Fred Ward, Sr. and the trustees of the First Bank of Neston naming Mr. Cote as Second Vice-President. Fred Ward, Jr. was First Vice-President, but if anything happened to him, a Cote married to a Ward worked just as well to keep everything in the family. People said it was a classic merger.

Tonight, the informal dinner was in La Terrasse, the Arms' dining room, and tomorrow, the dress rehearsal dinner for the wedding party would be in the Excelsior Room upstairs. The reception on Saturday would fill the Cullinan Ballroom, spill across the space between the grand staircases, and overflow into the dining room and through its French doors to the outdoor terraces.

La Terrasse had one table that wasn't bad but it was always reserved for the earliest seatings. The banquette surrounding half of Table 14 curved in the corner nearest the entrance to the kitchen, where the main wait station was. A full floor-to-ceiling wall muted the noise, but the table saw all the wait staff traffic coming and going. It was where families with young children were seated, with parents on the ends and children nestled in the middle of the curve. Getting out caused as much commotion as crossing a row of people from the wall seat to the aisle at the Bijou movie theater. Children, when they dined at La Terrasse, were supposed to be seen, but not noticed more than their parents, and certainly not any other adults.

Some fancy restaurants banned young children altogether, but the Arms was an inn, so of course families with young children stayed and ate, and La Terrasse was open by reservation to the public. Our patrons usually had well-behaved children, but when a parent or nanny quietly whisked a child away, other customers were reassured. More often than not, they smiled forgivingly. The next generation of fine diners was developed, and their good manners turned to our advantage. I heard patrons say this was a place where things were as they should be, as they used to be when they were growing up. As somebody put it in the guest book, *Civility and decorum still exist at The Neston Arms.*

Gabe was subject to the same rules, but babies were often the quietest of the kids. Maybe it was the classical music or candles that calmed them. When we could, we ate at Table 14, either before or after the dinner rush, which is when most families with youngsters had the sense to eat. When we couldn't, occasionally we went at off hours to a table in a corner of the kitchen, where we could at least see Dad and Carl, and they might even sit for a minute. We stopped taking Gabe to the Arms at all when he had begun teething, but he was in a lull before the next eruption, and there was no more school in the morning, so we were in the clear.

With or without Gabe, we got the same service as any other customer, and except for locals and perennial repeats, people in the dining room didn't know we were the owners. We dressed as formally as every other patron, we stopped and gave our reservation name, we were taken to our table and seated, we signed for the bill and tipped well.

Table 14 had two early reservations tonight, so Frieda, Mom, Gabe, and I took 8:30 under our reservation name, the Alcott party—my choice. It was very risky, having Gabe when it was smack in the middle of the rush, and the wedding group was in the room, but there was another reason we broke our rule.

Mom and Frieda wanted to see how Dieter was doing on the floor. Not that the rest of us didn't. Not that just about the whole dining room didn't.

He was on Caesar salad tableside service, and Caesar salad was selling like hotcakes. The diners blabbed with him like I'd never seen them do with any other waiter.

"It's a shame he can't be in two places at once," said Frieda. "He ought to be working the Excelsior Room tomorrow, but he's too valuable selling on the floor to work the fixed menu."

"I think some of them will be disappointed," said Mom, with a nod toward the wedding party table, "but André and I saw it the same way."

According to Mrs. Bouchard, it's practically a law at finishing school that debutantes don't pay attention to waiters, but if she'd been here, she would have said the bridesmaids coveted Dieter more than Scarlett O'Hara wanted Rhett Butler. Not even garlic, another no-no, was an obstacle. About the only ones not fazed were the bride and groom.

"What else is tableside this week?" asked Frieda.

"Steak Diane tomorrow. Trout Meunière on Friday."

"Are we running Chateaubriand again Saturday? We've got a lot of anniversary bookings."

"Yes, we're running it often," said Mom.

That was one of the Arms' most expensive items, only served for two. We always had it on Valentine's Day, Christmas, and New Year's. Practically all the waiter had to do was cut and sauce the meat, but the show was fun.

"I think we should hold off training on desserts," said Frieda. "He'd be better off spending the training time on entrées."

"*Absolument.*"

Ditto. Crêpes Suzette and Bananas Foster were also prepared tableside and they had better markups than salad, but they didn't fall into the expensive category like entrées did. Caesar salad was just a way for Dieter to get his feet wet with the least amount of time invested in familiarizing him with service. After the wedding reception banquet, Mr. Michaud would add regular wait service to his tableside preparation service.

We ordered the Caesar salad.

Gabe took seeing Dieter in stride. Mom was holding him, and like the first time he recognized Dad and Carl making appearances in their toques, he just waved his free hand. He was already acclimating to the dining room. He'd seen Marcia and Donna often enough that he only followed them with his eyes. He would nod off soon, but Dieter came to the table prepared.

"I've been expecting you, Gabe. Here, I've got something special just for you." He reached for a napkin on the cart and unfolded it with a waiter's presentation flair.

"Zwieback," he said. "Only for VIPs."

Mom took it. "This is very thoughtful, Dieter."

It was a dangerous moment, but Gabe just grabbed it and turned it to mush.

Dieter carried on with us as inconspicuously as any tableside waiter was supposed to, putting the service focus on stylish preparation, with more attentiveness to the diners than the other way around. We were the only table that let him.

Chapter 6

WE LITERALLY GOT BY on the skin of Gabe's teeth because he started crying early in the morning. Mom dipped her left pinkie in cool water and ran it over his gums, which soothed him and let her find more nubs emerging. I knew better than to try that myself. I distracted him by gently bouncing him on my hip while I carried him around the house, looking out the windows and talking about what we saw, but he smiled through his tears when he saw the squirrels racing up and down the trees. That didn't last long, but Mom had her tried and tested remedies ready, cold carrots or teething ring, and if all else failed, oil of clove. He liked cool rubbing the best and calmed down.

It hurt to leave him, but the day was just as nice for biking as my friends and I had hoped for, so I rode to the parsonage to head out with Paula.

"Come on in, Ate," said Mrs. Bouchard, giving my name her Georgia pronunciation.

I did, but I stayed on the rug inside the kitchen screen door with one hand on the handle. If we didn't make a quick exit, Mrs. Bouchard would sit me down for sweet tea and penuche fudge so sugary it made my teeth hurt.

"And what do you young ladies have planned on this glorious morning?" she asked.

"We're biking to Debbie Fortin's first," said Paula, "and then taking Stony Brook Road to the Durands' and back again."

"Bicycling on unpaved roads? Do young ladies find that amusing nowadays?"

"Yes, Mother."

"I had no idea, Paula. I thought we gave up that sort of thing when we no longer had to. It's rather dirty."

"Not very, Mother."

Hadn't Paula told her we planned to bike around Lakeshore Drive?

"All the same, do take care for your hands."

"Yes, Mrs. Bouchard," I said.

Mrs. Bouchard was fixated on the proper care of her hands, which really was important since she played the church organ, plus they did look nice. She had a shoe box full of nail polish, and every Thursday she and the pianist, Mrs. Taylor, got together and gave themselves manicures, which is how we figured it was the best time for Paula to get out of the house.

"And traffic," she called out after us.

I took the lead. We crossed Main, took Prospect to South and went halfway up Maple.

The Fortin house was humming. It always was. Debbie was the fourth of six children, and the Fortins' was the gathering place for the kids' friends and their families. I had slept over a lot. With all the extension leaves in and the end seats doubled up, the dining room table sat fourteen, and I'd been there when a children's table was set up, too.

Mr. Fortin's summer project was replacing the porch floorboards, and he and Sammy, Bobby, and Larry were setting out sawhorses. Mrs. Fortin was hanging whites on the laundry line. In the kitchen, Cathy and Peggy were already assembling sandwiches for lunch.

"Hi, Ette! Hi, Paula!" said Peggy. "What are you going to do today?"

"None of your beeswax," said Debbie before we could get a word in edgewise.

Debbie used to look up to Peggy as the oldest daughter and her big sister, but as soon as the year between them really began to show, she was none too pleased about living in her shadow. It wasn't just having to wear Peggy's hand-me-downs. All the Fortin children had auburn hair and russet eyes, but Peggy's hair had gone all copper, and she was the only one of the children who didn't have freckles.

We went upstairs to help Debbie put fresh sheets on the girls' beds, which had to be done before she could go out. A barrette, hairband, and three missing socks were recovered in the process, which we completed in record speed. She grabbed her collapsible cup, and we were all set.

"Wait a minute," she said. She shuffled through her desk drawer.

"What are you looking for?" I said.

"My penknife. I just bought it."

A penknife came in as handy as a plastic squeeze coin purse. I should have thought to bring my own.

"It's not here," she fumed. She took everything out of the drawer.

"Do you remember where you used it last time?" said Paula.

"I picked a knot out of Larry's sneaker lace. But this is the only place I put it. I just bought it," she repeated.

Paula and I checked under the beds. Nothing. Debbie pulled out the other desk drawers and slammed them shut.

"Sammy," she said venomously. "I'll bet he has it. He's not even supposed to come in here."

We went out to the porch, and sure enough, Sammy was using it to lift loose nails.

"Sammy stole my new penknife, Daddy! Right out of my desk. And look, he half wrecked it."

Mr. Fortin raised his eyebrows, but he was fair.

"Is that Debbie's penknife, Sammy?" he asked.

Owning up in front of Bobby and Larry would have been hard enough, but having his dirty laundry flying in front of Paula and me was a good reason to get it over with lickety-split.

"Yes, sir."

He had bent the blade and had a hard time closing it before he handed the penknife to Debbie.

"And you *stole* it from *her desk*?"

"Yes, sir."

"You know you're not allowed in the girls' bedroom unless they ask you."

Sammy dug a sneaker toe in the ground.

At school, Mr. Fortin had no tolerance for kids messing around in his home room students' desks. Marcia got a deten   tion for it once, and a lecture on how the property in a home room desk was private, even if you sat in their seat for his history class. And everybody knew it was an ironclad rule that the girls' locker room was completely off-limits for boys.

Now, right here, under his own roof, his son, the eldest, who was supposed to be setting an example for the others, was sneaking in the girls' bedroom and stealing from his sister's desk.

"And what are you using a penknife for, when I showed you how to pry the nails out with the claw end of the hammer?"

Mr. Fortin was annoyed now.

Sammy shrugged. "I don't know."

"We have some things to discuss later. For now, you have something to say to your sister."

"I'm sorry," he said to Debbie. "I'll pay you for a new one."

"And?" Debbie was outraged.

"I won't go in your room."

"Alright," said Mr. Fortin. He handed Sammy the hammer. "Let's get to work."

We got on our bikes and charged up Maple Street. Debbie didn't stop for breath until the pavement ended at Wheeler Farm, but she was holding in whatever she had to say, so we turned onto Stony Brook Road.

It was the most beautiful road in Neston, with the brook running its length, maples on both sides, and long southerly views down the valley below and up concave Hinton Ridge on the opposite side. The Wheelers took their huge Percheron horses along the road to tap the maples in the sugarbush and do some logging. Thanks to Walter Eckert, Arms acreage was the western end of the road. People from around the world came to take pictures in the autumn, and the ones who could afford it stayed at the Arms, and if they couldn't they stayed at the Riverside Motor Court.

We rode wavelengths back and forth on the hard-packed dirt, free for the summer. Bypassing civilization, we turned off and rode single file on a foot bridge over the brook and onto the thin trail that ran through the woods behind my house to the stick hut we'd built in a clearing. Leaving our bikes in the shade there, we kicked off our sneakers and hobbled over the stones in the brook.

"I dare you to wade to the birch without falling in," said Debbie.

"Alright," said Paula. "Let's hope I don't break my leg."

She got that right. It was easier to step stones in this stretch of Stony Brook than to wade in it. The water wasn't deep, but the current was tricky and the biggest underwater rocks that looked the safest to step on were slippery.

"Well, at least it's clean," said Debbie. "Just watch your hands."

"Very funny."

If there was anything Debbie liked, it was winning, but this time she miscalculated. I had home court advantage. Durands had been wading Stony Brook for ages. Every spring at the first sign of thaw, I went to see what had changed. I knew where a rock had moved or the shoreline shifted. Under the surface, I knew where slate was tilted, as slick as a playground slide, and I knew where to gain traction on thousands of granite pebbles.

I played along.

After Paula had two close calls, she surrendered. Like they say, it was the right thing to do.

I was ahead of Debbie in nearing the birch that arched over the brook. Lurching to keep her balance, she did what everyone did who didn't know Stony Brook like the back of their hand: after each step, she looked down through the transparent water, reading the lay of the brook bed. Standing still in the fast-moving water was like holding snowballs in your bare hands.

"My feet are turning blue," she said.

I kept going. "Giving up?"

She wouldn't say it.

"Second place," she conceded.

She clambered out with legs as stiff as Frankenstein and silently thawed while we dried our legs on the grassy bank.

"I've been thinking about where we should go next week," said Paula. "Let's start on the far side."

"Yeah, by the campgrounds," said Debbie.

"Sounds good to me." Seeing as we knew that stretch well, it was a safe strategy for our first leg around the lake. "And let's bring lunch, since it will take a while."

"Yeah, and I can get away from my crummy brother," said Debbie.

She finally spit that out.

"What's the matter with Sammy?" I said.

"He started hanging around with Brenda." "Pratt?"

"Yeah, after baseball games, and one time I saw him pushing her up against the gym wall outside the high school."

"What?"

"Was he hurting her?" said Paula.

"I wasn't sure at first, but they were just kissing."

"Eew," said Paula. "I mean, not Sammy. It's just, Brenda's only going into eighth grade. Daddy probably won't let me date without a chaperone until I get to college."

"They're not dating," said Debbie, "They only see each other, sometimes."

"Brenda lives with her uncle," I said.

They nodded. He was known around town as a drinker.

"But how could she be kissing already?" said Paula.

"You would too, if it was Ringo," said Debbie.

Paula blushed. "I wish."

"Yeah, I'd kiss George if I could," said Debbie.

They had started going boy crazy as soon as the Beatles landed on American soil. Brenda and Sammy were fuel to the fire.

They looked at me.

"Don't look at me," I said. "I don't even like the Beatles."

They looked at me anyway.

"You never said so before," said Paula.

"That's weird, not liking the Beatles," said Debbie.

"It's all that screaming I don't like. When they're on TV, you can't even hear them. Girls act crazy everywhere they go. I don't see what's so great about that."

The screaming was most of what I remembered. We only watched television at Carl and Frieda's, since their apartment was high enough to receive a signal sometimes, but what with it snowing that night, the picture had been fuzzy.

"You could listen to the records."

I had to. "Marcia and Donna are always playing them, and Dad's always telling them to turn it down. Besides, they're on the radio all the time, everywhere you go."

The songs were okay. I just thought some of them got kind of monotonous. I didn't want to hold anybody's hand, not even one of the Beatles. Well, except Gabe's.

"The radio is the only way I hear them," said Paula. "But never at home. I'm not allowed to listen to any rock and roll at home."

"But you like it," said Debbie, "don't you?"

"Of course. I've never been allowed to see any Elvis movies, either. I don't see all the fuss. But Daddy always says, 'I can't have my daughter doing that.'" She mimicked Rev. Bouchard.

She wasn't just saying that so Debbie wouldn't think being the minister's daughter made her weird. She really meant it.

"So, Ette," said Debbie, "if you don't want to kiss one of the Beatles, then what about Dieter?"

"What?" How would I know? I hadn't ever thought about kissing a boy.

"Who's that?" said Paula.

"Dietrich Norden, just a certain dreamboat staying at the inn all summer," answered Debbie for me. "Wait till you get a load of him."

They eyeballed me again.

"He's going into his senior year," I said. "I'm just a little kid."

So were my friends, but that didn't stop them from wanting to kiss Ringo and George, so I knew it wasn't a good answer, but Paula chimed in, "Anyway, I wouldn't want to be trapped against the gym wall when I get kissed, no matter who it is. Didn't Brenda push Sammy away?" she asked Debbie.

"Not until she saw me, and then he turned around and yelled at me, and he's been giving me dirty looks ever since then."

"But why would he steal your penknife?" I asked. It made no sense to me.

"Other than GPs? Probably just to let me know he'll get back at me if I say anything. You have no idea what he's like."

I did have an idea. She was the one who didn't, and neither did Mr. Fortin. He was obviously not aware that Sammy was in so much trouble. Sammy had two more strikes against him besides Debbie's penknife: Brenda and Putnam's. If he pushed a girl up against a wall to kiss her, and he got back at Debbie for seeing it, who knows what he might do to get back at me if he found out I knew he was barred from Putnam's? I shivered inside. I sure wasn't going to say anything.

"Well, that's too bad," said Paula. "I'll bring cookies next week." She offered what she could for comfort.

Paula truly had no idea. Timothy Bouchard was a model big brother and son. But she did know what it was like to have her room invaded. Although Rev. Bouchard's office was in the church, people were always in and out of the parsonage, including women who had the roam of the house and seemed to think popping their heads in her bedroom door was sociable.

I also had an idea of what it was like to live with a Sammy. Sort of. Gabe and I were too far apart in age to ever come to that, but a crummy sister was like a crummy brother, just in her own way. I felt for Debbie. I always thought the Fortin kids stuck together.

Chapter 7

AFTER LUNCH, I WENT to work. Legally, I was too young to be employed, but that never stopped me or any of the other underage kids I knew from working at their parents' businesses. There was always something kids could do, especially the farm kids, who worked regular and overtime. If their parents ever had to pay them, they'd go broke.

Sometimes I put the duplicate checks from La Terrasse in numerical order. Among other things, each number sequence of the dupes corresponded to a specific waiter, and Mom reviewed them with Mr. Michaud to see which waiters were selling, not just taking orders. Since finding ways to offer new dishes or lighter adaptations of the rich cuisine was her constant pursuit, she had a particular interest in seeing those menu items sell. That made me a regular in-house Guinea pig, a job I loved.

As soon as I was old enough, I'd start at the bottom, literally, in the Arms laundry, then I'd move upstairs as a *femme de chambre*—room cleaner, and then as a *plongeur*—dishwasher. Eventually, I'd work every possible position in the dining room and inn. We used the French Kitchen Brigade terms, which make every position sound good. There was a pecking order, but everyone respected it and each other. All the jobs were hard, and each one was important.

In the meantime, mostly I helped by folding napkins. I'd folded mountains of napkins in my day. I could see piles of them ahead of me. The lobster fold was all set for the rehearsal dinner, but we couldn't have enough extra empire folds for the reception. Each napkin would get a rose in its own stem holder tucked into the fold.

The Wards were going all out. But that wasn't why we needed so many extras.

For some reason, people were very extravagant with napkins at weddings. Napkins made dandy blindfolds and shoeshine buffs, got dipped into club soda to remove stains, dabbed under teary mascara or runny noses, and occasionally doubled as emergency diapers, but the most unique use we saw was an entire zoo of napkin animals. After napkins were unfolded and placed on the lap, they often slipped off of satin skirts, as well as the trousers of toast makers who forgot they were there when they stood to raise a glass. A lot of napkins ended up under the draped tables.

I went up to the Meyers' quarters and tapped quietly on the door. I was expected, but you never knew when somebody might be catching forty winks. A siesta was standard practice. They couldn't endure the grueling hours otherwise.

Frieda answered. "Enter and sign in, please," she said, like the host did to the contestants on the game show *What's My Line?*

I laughed.

"Hi," said Dieter, who sat down at the table with two piles of napkins on it. "I heard you can help me get the hang of this."

"Sure, it's easy."

Frieda left me to show Dieter the fold, and we were neatly stacking our folded batches into one of the clean cardboard boxes on a stainless cart when she returned.

"Did you get out on your bike ride this morning?" she asked.

"After Gabe settled down. He's teething again."

"Better this morning than last night."

"Yeah, he's pretty perfect."

"Give him time."

She watched us for a minute. "I haven't seen a good speed contest with mixed age and sex and weight classes since I sat for the CPA exam."

We cracked up.

"You don't need me," she said and went down to the office.

When the work got routine enough to fold and talk at the same time, he asked, "So, you went bike riding? How was it?"

"Good," I said, but my face flushed when I remembered Debbie's question. I wished she hadn't said it. I really didn't want to be thinking about kissing, especially not with Dieter right next to me.

"We only went back and forth on Stony Brook Road. Next week, we're going on Lakeshore Drive. We're doing sections this summer until we go all around it."

"Sounds like fun. I'd like to myself. Maybe next year."

I guess Frieda's nephew was planning to return. We stopped from time to time to fit more batches into the box.

"Do you have any brothers and sisters?"

"I have one sister, Stefanie. Her name is German, the feminine form of Stephen, just like Etienne is Stephen in French."

"Is that why you said Etienne's a great name?"

"It's one reason. Also, Stephen is one of my favorite people in the Bible. Names are important in the Bible. Yours means crown, the kind that athletes won, so that's another reason I think Etienne is a great name. Why did your parents give you the masculine form?"

"They didn't. They were visiting friends in Saint Anne de Bellevue before the holidays, and I came along early, so I was born in a Montreal hospital, and the name was a mix-up with another Durand family."

"Relatives?"

"Not that they knew of, not close ones anyway. There are a lot of Durands in Quebec. Around here, everybody knows Etienne is a boy's name, so I have to explain, but they get used to it, most of the time."

"It suits you—as a girl's name."

Well, I was glad somebody looked at it that way. I made a mental note to read the Stephen story.

"What's the B in your middle name stand for?" I asked. "I saw it on your Bible."

"Bonhoeffer."

"I've never heard of that name."

"It's a surname."

"He was a Sir?"

"S-u-r name. It means a last name. I'm named after Dietrich Bonhoeffer."

"Who's he?"

"He was a lot of things, a German theologian—"

"What's that?"

"Theo means God, so it's God philosopher. He was a pastor and teacher as well."

"Your parents must be very religious, to give you that name."

"Not very, just what you'd call regular. I think their main reason was his courage. Bonhoeffer was controversial."

"How come?"

"He always opposed Hitler, and that was dangerous. When the Nazi buildup took over the church, he worked to form a new one. Eventually, he became a military intelligence officer, but he was actually spying."

"Wow."

"What really made him controversial was his direct involvement in plots to assassinate Hitler."

"Like President Kennedy was?"

"Different motives, I'd say. Kennedy wasn't guilty of the Holocaust. And very different methods. Bonhoeffer believed that pacifism wasn't the answer to the Nazis and that taking personal responsibility to end the evil was the best response he could make. He saw it as a Christian action."

"Did he get into trouble?"

"He did, after the plots failed. He was put in prison."

"Oh. For how long?"

"Eighteen months."

"Then what did he do?"

"He was hanged in 1945, literally days before the end of the war."

"That's sad."

"In some ways, but not because he lost his life. He counted it the cost of being a disciple, a follower of Christ. Many people do."

"Do you like being named after him?"

"I do. I consider him a hero."

"Well, at least your name wasn't an accident."

"Neither was yours. It just wasn't given to you by your parents. What's your middle name?"

"Roy."

"It could have been a given name or a surname, but in any case, in French, *roi* means king."

"Yeah." I knew that much, but it didn't make me want to advertise my middle name.

"If you put your names all together, it comes out something like crowned king forever."

"I never thought about it that way. That's not so bad."

"Not at all. It's an allusion to Jesus."

"Are you sure?"

"Positive."

"But a lot of names are hand-me-downs."

"They are, and Roy might be, but that doesn't change what yours means. I think it's very special. It's a hymn of praise all in itself."

Well. I chewed on that for a while before I asked, "Is your sister older or younger?"

"Older. She's married to Sidney Randall. Their son, Sidney Junior, just turned three, and she's expecting another baby this fall."

The picture of the girl on his nightstand looked too young to be his sister.

"So you're an uncle."

"I am."

I expected him to say more. "Don't you like it?"

"I do, but they live on Long Island, and since Junior was born, I haven't seen him that much. They came to the house for Christmas last year, but the nanny had to keep after him so he wouldn't break any antiques. This year we'll be going there. The baby will be born, but they have a nursery and playroom. It'll be easier on everybody."

"What does Mr. Randall do?"

"Real estate. That's how he and Stefanie met. She had a listing, and he showed it to a client. Real estate is what all the Nordens do. The family has been in business since the late eighteen-hundreds."

"Is that what you'll do?"

"After college."

"Do you want to?"

"Yes, very much."

"What are you going to study?"

"Architecture."

So that's why he was so interested in Neston's buildings.

Carl came in and patted my shoulder. "You are learning from the expert, Dietrich," he said.

"I am."

I smiled. After Carl left for a soaking bath, I said, "Frieda's a Norden, and she didn't go into real estate."

"It was the plan, but she bucked tradition and went into accounting."

I wondered what would have made Frieda not join the family business, especially when it was so old, but then, Dad hadn't followed in his father's footsteps. Frieda's choice was good for us, though. We might not own the Arms if she hadn't made it, or be improving the bottom line so well.

Just then, she returned. "We had record sales of Caesar salad last night," she said.

"Well," Dieter shook his head, "I hope I can deliver on Steak Diane tonight."

"So do I," said Frieda. "Otherwise, we might all turn into wabbits."

Chapter 8

THE REHEARSAL DINNER HAD gone really well. Mom's gazpacho was a hit with the bride and her bridesmaids, who were thinking of fitting into their gowns, and of course Steak Diane was the hit it was predicted to be in the dining room.

Sticking to the tradition of keeping the bride and groom apart before the wedding, the men had gone to Île de L'eau for the day, and the women strolled in and out of Neston's stores and wandered the Arms' grounds. The bridesmaids would be thrilling to more tableside service tonight, while the groom and groomsmen would chow down at the North Shore Restaurant.

I finished the first book in the series I'd started and went to the library. Dieter was sitting in the reading area at the big front window, but he was only looking out and watching people. He saw me come in and held up his index finger. I waited at the door to the stairwell while he returned a magazine to the rack.

Miss Harrison was at the circulation desk. As he came toward me, she looked to see who he was smiling at, which was too bad because she missed him look toward her as he passed, smiling at her as well.

He closed the door quietly. "Hi. How are you?" He kept his voice low and motioned for me to go first. He probably could have run up the stairs three at a time.

"Good. Did you swim?"

"Yes. It's excellent. I leave at eight if you want to swim with me, any time. You'd like it."

We went on in silence to the second floor. Actually, I would love it. During the three years I had gone to summer camp, morning was my favorite time. I thought about the possibilities for swimming with him next week.

We went into the children's library, and I introduced Dieter to Mrs. Farnham. She and I went way back.

"Do you need any help today, Ette?"

I didn't. I dropped my book in the slot and checked out the next one in the series. On our way back down, Dieter said he had reserved a room to look at a collection of old postcards that didn't circulate, courtesy of his advisory request.

"Do you want to join me?"

I did. Dieter signed a form with rules about carefully handling the book, and Miss Harrison looked all business as she unlocked what everyone called the fish tank room because it was glassed in.

"Lock the door behind you and return the book directly to one of us at the desk when you're done," she said.

I'd never been in the room before. It's not as if everyone stared the whole time at the people in there, but I wasn't the only one who liked watching the silent movie inside. It seemed they must be doing something important, but they were kept an eye on for hanky-panky, too.

As soon as I went in, I understood why the people I had watched inside never stared back out. Outsiders could look in, but if insiders looked out, the outsiders would know they were checking on how much attention they were getting.

I sure didn't want any attention. If anybody I knew saw me in there, shoulder to shoulder with Dieter over the book of old postcards, there'd be no end of it. We were sitting so close I could smell his aftershave. It had citrus and something else familiar in it but I couldn't remember what.

Right away, I could see why he was so interested in postcards. The illustrations and photographs on them went back to the middle of the nineteenth century. Many scenes and buildings remained recognizable, but there were big exceptions.

"Paula's parents have this one with the original Meetinghouse in it, before it burned," I said, "but I've never seen old Neston Road before it was paved," as I admired a watercolor winter scene of the route with a horse and sleigh. "But a lot of farms still use sleighs. The Wheelers give rides on Stony Brook Road when the snow is deep. Some of the guests go."

"Have you gone?"

"No, I only watched." It sure looked fun, though.

Many of the postcards showed life before cars or street lights or electric signs.

"Do you think it felt different then?" I asked.

"Good question. Connecticut is changing fast, and I notice differences just traveling between school and home during breaks. Some towns have changed so much, I've wondered if that's one reason why it's said you can't go home again."

"It would be sad if I could never go home to Neston again. Plenty of people want it like the old days they remember."

"I'm nostalgic, too. Finding things as they were is as close as you can get to being in the past. Like this building," he indicated the Neston General Store. "Exploring the oldest structures is like going back in time, and I'm looking forward to shopping there at least a couple of times."

"Everybody likes to go there. It has regular things for sale, plus what tourists want to buy, and kids really like the big penny candy counter. Maybe I should be more of a tourist. If I went on one of those sleigh rides, I could find out how it felt way back when."

"Neston has done its best to keep its past, but as you say, things have changed anyway."

"It just grew up," I said. "These are its baby pictures."

He laughed. "At least you can recognize the adult from the baby. In these postcards, you can see the past in the present, which isn't true of many places, and it won't be for the areas of Neston that aren't preserved in the Historic District. That's what makes it so valuable. Once it's gone, it's gone forever."

"I wouldn't like that," I said. "We live in the baby pictures."

He smiled. "*Carpe diem*."

"What's that?"

"Latin for seize the day, grasp it. In this case, enjoy it while you can."

"Oh."

We got to the end of the album of postcards.

"Are you doing this for school? Or is it just for fun?"

"It's definitely fun, but I've been thinking about using this kind of research for my senior thesis."

"What do you mean? I thought the thesis was the main idea."

"It is in one sense, but it's also used in another sense. A senior thesis is a major paper required for graduation. They're more common at colleges, but some high schools, like mine, also require them."

"We don't have senior thesis here, but now that I've seen these postcards, I'd like to do a regular paper on the differences between the olden days and now for Mr. Fortin's history class. Maybe this fall, if I get him."

"Debbie's father?"

"Check."

"I thought you said he taught high school."

"Seventh grade."

"I shouldn't have assumed—I didn't think you were old enough to enter junior high school."

"I just finished fifth grade, but junior high isn't like kindergarten, where you have to be a certain age."

He connected the dots before I could explain. "Then you're going to skip sixth?"

I nodded. "I think so. I have to decide."

"It's a big decision."

"Mom and Dad have been talking to me about it all year."

"What do they think? If you don't mind me asking."

"They think I'm ready, but we have to meet with Mrs. Richardson—she's a guidance counselor—so she can ask some questions, especially since I already skipped a grade."

"You're exceptionally intelligent, to skip two grades."

"I don't think so. The first time was only second grade, and I skipped because I knew everything that got taught from the books and papers Marcia and Donna brought home, two years in a row, plus, Donna used to play teacher with me. It wasn't that hard."

"Seventh grade might be."

"I hope so. My teachers were always worried I was bored."

"Were you?"

"Yeah, sometimes. Anyway, I followed everything Marcia and Donna did up until they went to high school, and then I couldn't any more, so this would be the last chance I have to skip again."

"How will you decide?"

"Make a list, for and against. Think about it some more. See what Mrs. Richardson says. What would you do?"

"The same, but I'd add a third column to my list. I call it the God column. And I'd pray about it."

"What's a God column?"

"It's where I consider a decision about my life from God's point of view, to see if it's something he wants."

"How do you know?"

"If it's something that's wrong to do, then there's no point in making a list. But when a door opens, then I look at where it might lead."

"Like what?"

"Swimming, more than anything else. God gave me the talent and plenty of opportunities, so I think it's an open door, but it was a big decision for me to go for the Olympic qualifying trials."

"So what made you decide?"

"Well, like you have Mrs. Richardson, I have a coach, more than one, actually, and they encouraged me, and my parents were all for it, so then the decision was left to me."

"What if they said no?"

"I wouldn't compete at the trials."

"Even though you're good at it?"

"If my coaches said I couldn't make the cut, I'd need to do some serious explaining why I thought I knew more than their expert opinion, but I trust them to tell me if I'm ready or not. If my parents said no, I wouldn't give it any more consideration, not for this round."

"Even if the coaches said yes?"

"I can't really see myself disagreeing with my parents when I wouldn't with my coaches. I might not know my parents' reasons as clearly as I do my coaches', but I trust that God guides them in ways I never see. What my parents say is just one of the ways God opens and closes doors for me. You recognize them when you see them."

"Would you help me make a list?"

"I will. You talk and I'll write."

I didn't think we'd do it right that second, but he put the postcard book aside, slid the stack of scrap paper to himself and took a stubby pencil. He numbered a scrap 1.

"Okay. I'll learn new things."

He scribbled fast and pushed the scrap aside.

"I already know sixth grade."

He numbered 2 and scribbled *know 6th gr* and added it to the pro stack.

"I'll have to take the bus. But I would have to later anyway."

He numbered 3 and started a con pile.

"Marcia won't like it."

Con.

"Mom and Dad say it's okay."

Pro.

"Unless Mrs. Richardson says no."

He added a question mark at the top and put it aside for a third pile. He kept up scribbling.

"I'll miss my friends an awful lot.

"But they'll be there in another year.

"And I'll make new friends.

"What if I don't do well? I don't want bad grades. I never had a bad grade.

"But I could get help.

"The other kids are bigger than me. They might pick on me."

Getting picked on by Janice and Tina is what was really on my mind, but it could happen anyway.

I thought for a minute. Dieter kept his head down, pencil ready.

"I guess that's all for now. I don't know what to put in a God pile. I never thought about that before."

"You do have a question. This is a good start."

"I like the pieces of paper instead of a list. I can sort them better."

"That's true. You can rank them a number of ways."

We thanked Miss Harrison on the way out.

"Let me know if you come up with anything," he said. "I'm booked tomorrow, but will I see you in church?"

What with Sunday being the day after the wedding reception, and brunch, and almost all the guests checking out, we wouldn't be going to church as a family. These things happened often, so we attended inconsistently and hadn't been at all since before Gabe was born. But nothing was stopping me from going with Dieter.

Chapter 9

IT WAS THE DAY of the big wedding, and except for Mom letting me follow her while she did the early walk-though of the Cullinan Ballroom, the Arms was off-limits for me. I sang *Old MacDonald Had a Farm* to Gabe, acting it out as I pointed to the pictures in the book. He did a pretty good moo and flapped his arms like duck wings along with me.

He fell asleep peacefully. I had my book to read, but I kept looking up to watch him. The bottle slipped out of his mouth and I took it away. Except for the plastic bottle we used for outside the house, we still used glass bottles. Mom thought the plastic changed the taste of what was inside. I tried it with water once. Mom knew best.

She said Gabe's teething spell had been unusually short. After two days of fussing, last night his lower gums had begun erupting. But he had only cried during the worst of it, which Mom said, at least for the moment, indicated a high threshold for pain. Only time would tell if it lasted.

And all that arm movement, which he did awake and asleep. Would he always be an arm-moving sleeper? Would he grow up to use his hands? Or was he just dreaming of make-believe driving, turning and turning the wheel, or being a duck? Like Mom said, we'd find out. Only time would tell about any of it. I didn't mind at all. Everything about Gabe fascinated me.

Sometimes he made sounds while he slept, but I couldn't understand his private language, and he wouldn't be able to tell me later. He'd forget it. Maybe he'd make up a new language. I heard about kids who did that. I don't know how the French and English got sorted out in our brains when we were growing up, but somehow they did. I always understood both. Including his own, Gabe might be dreaming in three languages.

His dreams must be made up of the things that had gone into his experience of life so far. I wished they could all be happy things, like being rocked and lullabied, and splashing in the lake as he had for the first time just a few days ago, but it wasn't possible. Already he knew crying for hunger and wet diapers, and sometimes just wanting to be cuddled, and now he had felt pain from teeth cutting through his gums. I might not be able to spare him life's sorrows, but I would never add to them.

When he grew up, what would he say were his happiest childhood experiences? Almost more than anything, I wanted to be part of what brought Gabe sweet dreams and memories. I wondered what his first memory would be.

I thought of my own. The earliest vivid memory I had was Mom releasing me to take a few steps on my own toward Dad. We were in the yard next to the row of daffodils, and I could feel the cool grass through my socks.

I read and dozed off a little myself, waking just as Gabe did. I smiled down at him as his eyes fluttered. I always hoped the security of waking to me would be planted deep in his brain like it was with Mom and Dad.

"Gabe," I said quietly.

"Ahh," he said. He reached out his arms.

I let down the drop side of the crib and nestled my head so he could mash my cheek. He knew the routine. I nibbled his fingers. "Mmm, Gabe so good." He jabbered and slapped me while I changed him.

Afterward, I held him up so we could look out the window and watch Mom at the mailbox, talking to the mailman. Suddenly he started crying. She heard him and looked up to the window. We met in the kitchen.

"Gabe's hungry," I said.

"Yes, with new teeth, he will be."

Mom had never been in a hurry to supplement breast milk with bottles or with the introduction to solids, which should really be called softs, but she said each of us had our own timetables, and if Gabe's teeth hadn't been indicators enough, Gabe himself had let it be known all along when he was ready for more.

I had an idea. "Mom, what if I make a French omelette? It wouldn't take any more time than to cook oatmeal."

"That would be very special, Ette. But don't finish with the extra butter."

A French omelette is not the same as an American one. At the inn, we quickly served up mountains of puffy half-moon omelets made to order, and they're good, but the purely egg and butter French version that Mom's family made is cooked at a lower temperature and has an entirely different shape and creamy texture. The delicate membrane containing moist soft scramble is all in the technique. We had a special pan just for omelettes and crêpes, and since this was only my third attempt, Mom continued her careful supervision.

It was an oddly violent process, but that helped me remember it. Crack the eggs, stab the yolks, add a pinch of salt to the wounds—to the wounds was my addition—and a tiny bit of water, and beat it until the yolk and white run together. The hardest part of the cooking technique was the swirl and jiggle in the hot buttered pan, and since I had to be cautious about how much butter Gabe could start out with, keeping the eggs from sticking was extra hard. Then I had to get a clean lift at the edge to roll the omelette into the classic cylinder shape, like a scroll.

Mom forked off an end and tasted. "You have the touch, Ette. Do you know why?"

"I made it the way you taught me."

She put her arm around me and kissed my forehead. "That's part of it, but it takes more than that. Practice makes perfect, but so does patience. It's the secret ingredient, Etienne, and you are very patient."

She took another piece. "See, the outside is as delicate as lace, and the inside as soft as marrow. They only come by waiting on the low heat."

"Hear that, Gabe? You ready?"

He was a long way off from the need to play with food to get him to eat, and I doubted he ever would. He was ready.

He loved it. If he didn't remember it, I would.

I walked to Putnam's for the prints of the photos I had taken at the picnic, and on the way back, I stopped on the common across from the Meetinghouse. The big event had taken place, and I joined the throng waiting to gawk at the newly wed Mr. and Mrs. Claude Cote. It was like a ballgame. The crowd went wild.

The couple proceeded out of the church onto the common. Several times members of the wedding party waved to people they knew in the crowd who had not been invited to the wedding or the reception, but Eugénie's sister Lisa, who was near my age, turned her nose up at me.

Never mind that we were putting on the most impressive reception extravaganza Neston had ever seen, this day the Durands worked for the Wards, Lisa's attitude said. If I acted that way to all the kids of the people who were employed at the Arms, I'd have a lot of snubbing to do. Besides, the hospitality business is all about the opposite, being nice, so I smiled back, but that only seemed to irk her.

The groomsmen went up onto Neston's grand gazebo and the bridesmaids stood on the step below them. The maid of honor spread Eugénie's long bridal train over the steps. Claude situated himself next to his bride while the photographer set up a tripod. He took shot after shot. The wedding party stepped down, the Wards and Cotes took their places, Rev. Bouchard took his turn standing between the bride and groom, on and on it went with combinations.

Meanwhile, the ruckus continued. Mrs. Bouchard blazed away on the carillon. Girls in crinoline and white patent leather ran amok with boys in miniature tuxedos. Senator Perry, who was with his wife and state politicians and their wives, shook hands as they worked through the crowd toward the gazebo.

The finale was so crowded it made the floorboards creak. The maid of honor lifted the bride's train again, and the whole group proceeded to the Arms.

I saw Paula holding open the side door of the church, and I went over.

"Hi."

We were intersected by florist assistants hurrying to transport arrangements and a colossal bower up to the Arms, where it would be set up around the five-tier cake for more photos.

"Isn't that beautiful?" she said.

"Yeah."

"Just like a fairy tale."

"I guess so," I said. Real was fine with me.

"Did you see the bride? Isn't she gorgeous?"

"Yeah, she looks really nice."

"Mother says long trains make for long marriages."

I pictured the double wedding photograph I knew so well.

"Mom and Frieda wore dress suits when they married Dad and Carl. They only had on hats."

"Oh. I'm sorry, I didn't mean they won't, too."

"I know, that's okay."

"Did you see her ring?"

"No, I was too far away."

"Yeah, neither did I, but I heard it's big. I want a big ring when I get married. Mmm." Paula sighed like diners at La Terrasse did when they tasted our tournedos with foie gras. "Don't you?"

I hadn't thought about it, but before I could answer, Mrs. Taylor interrupted next.

"Everybody's out now," she said.

It was Paula's signal to pitch in with the cleanup crew.

She did errands around the church like I did at the inn and had seen a lot more wedding parties than I'd seen, but I had reasons for being blasé other than the fact that, unlike her, getting married was the furthest thing from my mind.

A wedding was a wedding. There was only so much individuality in a traditional church ceremony, but a reception, now that had a personality all its own.

Marcia called this one inflated. The politicians had VIP tables right next to family in front of the head table. The Wards knew where to butter their bread—and the aftermath for the Arms was bound to be enormous. It wouldn't make any difference to the Meetinghouse.

Chapter 10

BEFORE CHURCH, I SAT in the third floor window seat, where I looked up Stephen in the Bible. He starts out as a helper but he also preaches, and does miracles, too, which I'd like to see. Some people spread lies about him and get him into trouble, and when he gets to defend himself, he gives a long speech. At first, everybody thinks he has the face of an angel, but it ends with him saying all they ever do is resist the Holy Spirit. That gets them really angry, since they can see he's full of the Holy Spirit himself, but when he says he sees Jesus in heaven, they've had enough and they stone him to death.

I was not expecting the ending, which is probably why this was not one of the Bible stories I remembered hearing before. Usually happy ones were told. Once, when I saw a book with drawings of martyrs tied up with fires set all around them, I closed the book. I wanted to forget what I saw. It took a while, but I had, until now.

Stephen was a martyr, but they weren't just from a long time ago. So was Dietrich Bonhoeffer. According to Dieter, people were still put to death for their faith in Jesus. The picture in my mind shifted to how he saw them as heroes. If it hadn't been for that, it would have been hard to think of Dieter and myself being named after martyrs.

Reviewing the scrap papers was my other task. When he tucked them into my library book, Dieter had stacked the pro pile on top of the con, but when I laid them out in number order, it was like seeing a motion picture of my thoughts when we made the list.

Either way, they ended up being almost equally for and against, with Mrs. Richardson as a question. That wasn't helpful, but with more than one way to slice the cake, maybe I could sort my thoughts better if I arranged them differently.

I ordered most to least important, and it seemed to me that the first thing I had said was also the most important: learning new things. I put Mom and Dad's approval second most important, but then I decided it was first after all. I had their approval, but if they had said no, the door would have shut. The meeting with Mrs. Richardson wouldn't even have been made. I saw Dieter's point. I kept ranking. Doing well academically was also very important. Taking the bus wasn't. The cons were things I was afraid of.

I hadn't mentioned being called Eddie, I guess because I was so embarrassed to say it to Dieter. It may not have been written down, but it was on my mind. I felt more anxious about being taunted than anything else.

It's not that Eddie was such an awful word, all by itself. It was just plain disrespectful, and an excuse for more, who-knows-what. If it wounded me in grade school, it would be fatal in high school. I'd be branded and shunned from the start.

I thought of what I'd heard over and over. Take things one at a time. Don't put the cart before the horse. You can't cross a bridge until you get to it. So I made a timeline order. Mrs. Richardson came first. Then there was taking the bus on the first day of school, going to classes, doing well, making new friends, and hoping I fit in. Some worries were here and there, but a couple came in last, not even worth listing.

It just depended on Mrs. Richardson. She was the question scrap, but she might as well be in a God column.

Every night when I went to bed, I prayed for God to keep my soul and for Gabe and Mom and Dad, but I had never prayed about a decision before. Everything was always clear-cut, but this time was different. I'd give it a try. It seemed to work for Dieter. Besides, it was Sunday, and that seemed like the right time for an extra prayer.

"Hi, God, it's Etienne. I think the door's wide open to skip sixth grade and go to junior high school, but if it's a bad idea after all, please make Mrs. Richardson close it. Amen. Oh, thank you."

Chapter 11

DIETER WAS WAITING FOR me to walk to church with him. He must have hardly slept, but he smiled and said, "What a day. The air is so pure here."

"Yeah."

As we went, I told him about how I came to my decision. "The scraps of paper really helped."

"I'm glad," he said, and after a pause added, "Now is when it gets interesting. I'll pray for you."

I didn't mention that I had prayed.

We entered the vestibule and took a bulletin from one of the greeters. I was prepared to let Dieter sit where he wanted, let the chips fall where they may. This time of year, summer residents and visitors and campers were in attendance, and some of the year-rounders got out of whack if they didn't sit in "their" seats, but as we entered the sanctuary, he said, "Where do you usually sit?"

"Up front," I said.

In fact, we didn't have usual seats. The front row was always the last to fill in, if it did at all, and since we Durands, as occasional attendees, had learned our lesson about bumping seats, that's just where we ended up.

"Ladies first," he said.

We went up the center aisle, passing the Fortins in the rear. Larry hissed "Dieter!" as we went by and was promptly shushed by his father. The congregants sitting in front of the Fortins turned around and echoed the shush. It spread like wildfire.

Eyes turned to see what the conniption was about, but by then all there was to see was Dieter and me walking the gauntlet. Green-eyed Miss Harrison cupped her hand to Shirley Pierce's ear. Tina and Janice threw poison darts.

Mr. and Mrs. Ward, Sr. also turned. A lone bridesmaid was with them. That was it for the wedding party. Usually, more guests staying at the Arms went to church, but the reception had run very late. Dieter nodded to them, and they obviously recognized the waiter who had served their table. Their masks slipped a little when they saw he was carrying a large Bible, but the reception had been a home run out of the park, and you couldn't take that away.

We slid in next to the Bouchard children, who sat alone right under the watchful eyes of their parents. Just then, Mr. Richardson came up behind us and put his hand on the opposite pew to indicate the seat to his wife. They must have gotten bumped. Mrs. Richardson glanced over at us as she entered the pew. I always liked her soft-looking red hair, and her pleasant expression had a look of mild interest. Of course, that didn't mean anything. She always looked that way.

I did the introductions.

"Dieter, this is Paula and Timothy Bouchard. And this is Dietrich Norden."

"Seriously?" said Dieter. He shook hands with Timothy.

"You get it," said Timothy.

"Of course."

I only got the point because Paula explained it to me once. Paul is the main writer of the New Testament, and he gave a lot of instructions to Timothy. He loved him like a son. So, Paul—Paula, Timothy. It seemed like a lot for her to live up to, especially because he was older.

"Can I talk to you after?"

Timothy nodded.

"We have to clean up," said Paula, bug-eyed at Dieter.

"I'll help."

The bells rang ten, indicating the chitchat stage was over. I guessed I'd be helping, too. That was fine with me.

The church smelled good. Tall sprays of flowers were placed at the foot of the lectern, where Rev. Bouchard asked the congregation to turn to hymn number 295.

The choir let out when school did, which was too bad, because the summer people never got to hear it, but Mrs. Bouchard tuned us with a prolonged organ note of "Near to the Heart of God," and Mrs. Taylor joined on the piano. Most everybody knew the song, including Dieter.

I wasn't surprised to see that the sermon reading was from Psalms. Like last year and the year before—I couldn't remember before that—Rev. Bouchard preached from Psalms. He always had light fare on the menu in summer, just like we did at La Terrasse. After all, a lot of people were on vacation.

Dieter held his Bible so we both could read it. As if that wasn't enough, I was prepared to follow a lot more closely than usual. If the Bible was that important to him, then I wanted to find out what was so interesting because it hadn't ever seemed that way to me, including the Stephen episode, which felt more disturbing than inspiring.

The sermon was "God Is My Rock and My Salvation." Rev. Bouchard explained the comparison was most often to mountainous rocks or cliffs, where David, who was a shepherd who became the king of Israel, hid in caves to escape his enemies. Rev. Bouchard said God is still a defense and refuge from the enemies we encounter today. According to the Psalm, liars and people who made mischief were the ones making life hard for David.

Like the mischief makers sitting in the pews behind me? If Tina and Janice weren't lying name callers bent on making my life hard, I didn't know who was.

Rev. Bouchard kept the message upbeat, though, and as soon as he got to the prayer about trusting God at all times, Dieter bowed his head and leaned forward with his forearms on his thighs.

"'Pour out your heart before him,'" quoted Rev. Bouchard.

This wasn't the same as praying for an answer, like I had earlier. How could you trust God to defend you from what already happened? I had no idea how to make God my rock or salvation. Wasn't he already supposed to be?

Besides, caves were there for the taking, first come, first served. With mountain hideaways all the way to the border, for centuries Wortham County had provided as much protection for dodgers, bootleggers, and smugglers as for abolitionists guiding escaped slaves. Except for Chauncey Smith, the Historical Society Museum didn't mention that tidbit of common knowledge, and of course, neither did Rev. Bouchard. It also occurred to me that instead of hiding in a rock, Stephen was killed, by stones no less. It wasn't clear-cut how things would turn out.

But I'd think about it.

There was the future to consider.

After the service, Paula and I took one side of the aisle and Timothy and Dieter took the other, cleaning the pews of crumpled bulletins and tissues, putting the odd glove and Matchbox car in the lost and found bin, and arranging the hymnals and Bibles in order in their slots. Timothy and Dieter hit it off, and Paula was more interested in what they were saying than talking to me. We kept pace opposite them and caught snatches of conversation about the Red Sox and Yankees, running and swimming, junior and senior year, pre-med at Vermont U and architecture at Yale.

Just as I suspected, Mr. and Mrs. Bouchard were happy to meet Dieter. A kid who carries his own monogrammed Bible is way outside the norm but guaranteed to be right up their alley.

"You boys must get together," said Rev. Bouchard.

"I'd like that," said Dieter. "What's your schedule, Timothy?"

Timothy and Dieter figured out that their summer jobs were opposite hours, except for Sundays.

"In that case, won't you join us today?" said Mrs. Bouchard.

"Well—" he hemmed.

"Yes, do," insisted Rev. Bouchard.

He and Mrs. Bouchard would have had Dieter at their home for the rest of the day if they could, but he only agreed to their repeated offer of "at least mid-afternoon supper," a Sunday tradition in this part of New England.

Dieter wasn't being rude. He was exhausted. The Ward wedding week had been the most demanding ever, and it was his first.

For a minute, I was afraid I might lose the morning swims Dieter had offered me to Timothy.

Chapter 12

WHEN THEY CAME IN from working brunch, Marcia and Donna went straight to their room and closed the door. No radio, no record player. They had worked late last night and gone back early this morning. Dad came home hours later, looking dog tired, but like always, he took a shower and sat with Mom. I crawled around on the den rug with Gabe, playing hide and seek so they could talk.

When he and Mom came in, Dad had the album and the old and new batches of pictures, which had been sitting on the hall table until there was time to look at them.

"Good choice, Ette," he said, flipping my album's empty pages.

"I wasn't sure if it cost too much."

"You made the right choice. You have to pay more for the better material, but it holds up much longer than the cheap stuff. You want the best to keep your memories, right?"

"Check."

"Have you looked at the photos?"

"No, I was waiting to look with you and Mom."

"How about if we just take a peek at them?"

I knew he was too tired to label them, especially since he had some catching up to do.

He sat between Mom and me and held them up, one by one. The oldest ones were only from months ago, but it was a wonder seeing Gabe so tiny.

"Look, Gabe," said Mom. "That's you."

Dad held the picture out of Gabe's reach.

When we came to the pictures Frieda had taken at the picnic, you could really see the differences in how he had grown. Then there were Dad and Dieter and me in the water, Dad dipping Gabe, Dieter swirling him, Mom nestling him in the blanket. We were all wrapped up in reliving the happiness when the shot of the empty raft appeared.

"There's your first photograph," said Dad enthusiastically.

I looked at it. It seemed kind of stupid, just an empty raft, as blank as an Etch-A-Sketch turned upside down and shaken.

"It was only a test shot."

"Oh, but the water is sparkling," said Mom. "It's beautiful."

"I guess," I said, looking at it again.

A path of luminescent gold stretched across the water. And suddenly I was in its spotlight on the raft with Dieter, soaking up the views and talking and diving and doing back flips. I imagined the raft at night, the shine of the moon's silver light reaching for it, clearing it off so it would be ready for new scenes.

Mom and Dad went wild over the next photo. There was Gabe, on Mom's shoulder, his amber eyes round as a doe. He and I both had that unusual color, which we got from Mom, but Gabe still had a rim of white skin around his eyes.

They went wild over all the rest, too.

"These are terrific, Ette," said Dad. "All of them. You've got talent."

Well.

"We should have extras made to give as keepsakes for the day," said Mom. "Albert and Penelope would especially appreciate them."

I knew Mom and Dad wouldn't praise me that much unless the shots really had come out well. But it wasn't just my talent. Gabe was so adorable it almost hurt.

"What if I take a picture of Gabe every week?" I said. "In front of the growth chart."

"That's a wonderful idea," said Mom. "It's time to start."

Years ago, Dad had tacked a fabric measuring tape to the pantry wall, and Mom had regularly marked and dated our heights on the wall. Marcia and Donna didn't want to get measured any more, but I still did, which mostly revealed that, compared to them at the same age, I was lot shorter.

"So it is," agreed Dad. "How about if we get started now?"

We crowded into the pantry. I got down on the floor and focused Dad's camera. Mom and Dad propped Gabe upright. It took several attempts, since he either bobbed up and down or wanted to crawl to me, and we were laughing hilariously before I got any pictures I thought would turn out okay. Dad insisted on taking a shot. That was fine with me. We went into the kitchen and I sat on the step stool with Gabe on my lap.

Donna came in yawning and flipped through the stack of photos, echoing our oohs and ahs. She perked up at the ones of herself and Marcia. They took after Dad with his gray eyes, which were also unusual because they changed hue a little bit depending on their surroundings.

According to Marcia, we all had mousy brown hair, but I saw different shades, like a bowlful of mixed nuts in their shells. Dad's hair was straight and medium, like a pecan, Mom's was a lighter walnut, and wavy like its shell, too. What with our round amber eyes and wavy walnut hair, which we also got from Mom, you could hardly tell Gabe and I were related to Marcia and Donna, but that wasn't the only reason. Marcia had started tinting her hair as dark as a Brazil nut so she'd look like Natalie Wood—and less like the rest of us. Meanwhile, Donna, whose hair was already as light as an almond shell, was using a lemon rinse and drying her hair in the sun. She was the more photogenic of the two, but I saw she noticed, like I had, that the shot of grouchy Marcia, sitting in the shade, had a more dramatic look, moody like the models in her magazines.

When she got to the end, she lingered over the picture of Dieter.

"We're getting copies made," I said. "Extras to give to Dieter's parents...and everybody."

As that sunk in, she tried to hide her happiness.

"At least they'll see he had some fun this summer," she said, "since he didn't bring his own camera."

I could have told her he didn't need to. For places, he bought postcards. For people, everybody else would photograph him, with or without others. Really, Donna just wanted him to have a photo of her as much as she wanted one of him. But he already had a girl on his nightstand.

Chapter 13

I LEFT A NOTE FOR Mom and Dad.

Gone swimming with Dieter. Love, Ette.

I didn't need to add anything else. That was the full scoop.

Dieter came out the service door of the Arms, and his face lit up when he saw me. I was relieved, but he said, "So you're finally going to join me."

"Well, it rained."

It was just like the Wards to have the rain hold off until after their daughter's wedding. Things went that way for them.

"It did," he said.

"I had a dentist appointment Tuesday," I said, although it was late enough that I could have gone. I didn't make any excuse for Wednesday, which was another beautiful day. I could have gone all three times.

"Do you swim in the rain," I asked.

"It depends. Not if it's coming down hard or there's thunder or lightning. I swam on Monday, though. The rain was very light." He looked down at my sneakers. "Good shoes. We have to walk. I'll understand if you change your mind."

"No, that's okay. The beach is less than a mile away." We passed Neston Elementary School.

"Can I ask you a question?" I said.

"Of course."

"It's kind of personal."

"Thanks for the warning, but you can ask me anything." "You said you'd pray for me about skipping sixth grade."

"I am."

"What do you pray?"

He thought for a minute. "Can I get back to you on that?"

"I guess." I shrugged, obviously disappointed.

"It's not a secret. I keep a prayer journal of requests and answers. I'll give you a copy of what my requests are for you, but if I were you, I wouldn't read it until after you get your answer."

"Well, okay," I said, although it threw me for a loop.

He could see it. "You'll understand why then," he said.

When we got to the short stretch along Neston Avenue, it was noisy with traffic, but as soon as we turned onto Lakeshore Drive and it got quiet, Dieter said, "I looked for a path down from the Arms but I never found one."

"No, it's too steep."

"That's why switchback trails are used in the Alps."

"What are they?"

"Trails that zigzag instead of running straight up a mountain. The distance is longer to hike, but switching back and forth is much easier going up and down because the incline isn't steep. Unless a person is a rock climber, it's the only way to hike many mountains, and they make it possible to bicycle some as well."

"If we had one, wouldn't just anybody climb it?"

"You probably couldn't prevent some trespassing, but if it was well posted, I think most people would respect it as private property of the Arms."

"Especially if a fine for trespassing was posted."

He laughed. "Yeah, that might help, too."

The smell of bacon wafted from the North Shore Restaurant, where the breakfast crowd was out it force, but the George family did a hefty business all the time.

We stayed on the shoreline and walked the length. Except for Old Mr. Tedeschi's son, who was sweeping the store porch, we were the only ones on the beach. He waved us over.

"Mr. Ted, this is my friend, Etienne Durand."

"Oh, I've known Ette forever," said Mr. Ted. "My Sophie is close in age, but she's gone to camp in Maine."

"Hi, Mr. Ted," I said.

"You think you're going to keep up with the champion here?" No."

"Well, you kids have a good time. Be safe."

"Always," said Dieter.

He set his duffel on a picnic table directly in front of the raft closest to the store and the Beach Bun, so I did too. It was the Central in Grand Central, where I never sat unless I was visiting the Fortins. It was their favorite spot like ours was the opposite end.

We stripped to our suits and walked into the edge of the water, where Dieter stopped. I thought he was praying, but maybe he was listening. I heard a thrush singing. I could feel the ripple of the sand on the soles of my feet. We must have stood there a whole minute, until it was quiet enough to hear the gentle lap that restored the beachline every night. Just as smoothly as possible, we walked out. When the water reached my chin, instead of diving under, I started gliding, and we went noiselessly to the raft. We just held on to it. I wasn't winded at all.

"I'll spot you," he said, almost whispering, and I knew why.

Voices carry over still water.

"But—"

"Right beside you."

"What if I don't make it?"

"You're a good swimmer, Ette. You'll make it. But you can stop and hold the float line if you need to."

I looked down at the far raft.

"I'll be with you."

I took a breath and let go, following the float line on my left. Dieter's side stroke was enough to keep up with my turtle's pace breast stroke.

I made it just fine.

"I knew you could do it," he said.

"I didn't."

"Now?"

I knew he meant "And now that you do know?" but I said, "Now I'll go to shore and spot you on the way back."

He swam halfway to shore with me and gave me a head start walking on the beach, and then he went back along the float line and took off so fast I almost had to run to keep up.

When he came out, I clapped.

"You're the one who deserves applause," he said.

I wrung the water out of my hair, which was just long enough for a pony tail.

"If I had a cap," I said, "I could do the front crawl stroke," and then we both said, "Tedeschi's—"

"That reminds me," he said. "I owe you."

We dried off in the sun, just watching the water.

Eventually, he said, "How do you feel?"

"Fine. Why?"

"It's just something athletes have to pay attention to. A small thing can turn into an injury. If you notice anything, let me know."

"Check."

"Do you need to get back?"

"Not right away. Do you?"

"No. Mind if I take a couple more laps?"

Me, mind? "You've got to practice."

Several people had arrived, and I felt better knowing that others were keeping an eye on him, too. And of course, they did, just as amazed as I was at his smooth speed.

He came up out of the water and was reclining on his towel, drying off in the sun again, when a man approached.

"George Congleton," he announced, as if he was reminding Dieter of a connection, and stuck his hand out.

Being a gentleman, Dieter stood up to shake it. "Have we met before?"

"No, no, Congleton Agency."

George appeared to expect a response, but Dieter waited.

"Boston?" He delivered that clue to jog Dieter's memory, and when it didn't work, he clarified. "Modeling agency."

"Nice to meet you," said Dieter, not surprised, and not offering any information. Apparently, these things happened, to him anyway.

"My agency is always looking for great talent. We could use a man like you."

"Thanks, but I'm already booked."

"Hmph. Mind if I ask who you're working with?"

Dieter put on his shirt. "I really can't say."

George Congleton was prepared. "Well, you take this anyway." He handed Dieter a business card.

"Thanks." Dieter picked up his bag. George got the hint, and this time we went to get changed without being hounded.

We went into Tedeschi's Bait & Tackle. Tedeschi's outfitted the casual beachgoer as well as the serious angler. It was chock full of hats, sunglasses, flip flops, snorkel gear, life jackets, towels, suntan lotion, you name it, plus convenient dry goods. I looked over the swim caps while Dieter picked out more post cards. He sent them to everybody.

I joined him and held up a pink cap with a rainbow of metallic coin-sized sequins. "What do you think?"

He burst out laughing. "That looks like something Aunt Frieda would wear as a gag."

I held up another one I'd been hiding behind my back. "What about this one?" It was covered with red, white, and blue rubber daisy petals.

"Very patriotic," he said, still laughing.

"It's like jewelry, a cap for every occasion," I said. "Okay, I'll go get the real one."

"Let's see if I can pick it out."

"Alright."

We went back to the display, and he went straight for the white cap with a low nap wavy pattern.

"Causes the least amount of drag," he said, "and matches your bathing suit."

He was right, and it was no joke on me.

Chapter 14

AN HOUR LATER, I was ready to hop on my bike as soon as Debbie swung by, and we caught up to Paula, who was tying down a red-checked tablecloth in her bike basket. Mrs. Bouchard and Mrs. Taylor were already into their manicures, so we got a clear getaway.

Neston Avenue was busy. We crossed the Sherburne River bridge and turned onto the western entrance to Lakeshore Drive. The stretch of road to Neston Campgrounds was familiar to all three of us. The week we had attended camp at the same time was when we got to be best friends.

We passed by slowly. It was tempting to go in, just for a quick look around to see if anything had changed, to remember what fun we'd had. Suddenly, going back felt easier than going forward. All the fun had been handed to us on a platter, but now we had to make our own.

Other than a couple of station wagons loaded with gear roped onto roof racks, traffic dropped off after that, but we stayed close together in formation on our side of the strip of grass in the middle of the dirt road. Eventually, we turned onto Leeward Lane, an offshoot marked as having a boat launch and picnic tables. With a clear view of Île de L'eau Island, it was the perfect spot for lunch.

A pickup truck towing an outboard backed down the ramp for a nice day of father-son fishing, although from the tackle boxes and ice chest loaded in the boat, you could tell they were stocking their freezer. We watched the boy tie the boat to a piling while his father parked the truck. I would have said hi, but he acted like we weren't sitting right there.

So did his father. "That's not the right way to knot the line," he snarled. "It could have slipped off."

"Sorry, Dad."

"You never listen to me." He got in and the boat rocked.

The boy looked terrified. The father started the engine and angrily swerved away from shore.

We silently unpacked our lunches. Debbie and Paula ate the crusts around their peanut butter and jelly first, saving the best for last, and I peeled back my waxed paper bag and ate out of it.

"Whew, that smells," said Paula. "What have you got?"

"Tuna sandwich." Technically, it was a slice of Pan Bagnat.

"What's all that stuff in it?" said Debbie.

"Capers, olives, anchovies, garlic."

"Eew," said Paula.

As promised, she brought cookies, and I begged off, saying I was too full.

"You always say that," said Paula.

"It's true. I am full." Also, I didn't want to offend Paula, but I don't like sugar cookies.

"She never eats dessert," Debbie informed Paula.

Meals at the Fortins often ended with a large portion of pie and ice cream, but turning it down there was met with somebody gladly claiming "more for me."

"I do sometimes," I said, "just not that often."

I was easily tempted by Charlotte Russe, but I had faced the facts: my friends were fried chicken and mashed potato people; we were Coq au Vin and Pommes Anna. Except for desserts I found too sweet, I was fine with whatever they served, but when they came over to eat, it didn't work the other way around. We adapted. Mom learned to cook some American dishes we never would have eaten otherwise. Considering that my family's livelihood—and that included me—revolved around a deep appreciation of food, it seemed too bad that I couldn't share that with my best friends. They say breaking bread together brings people closer, but food itself divided us. And even if they were usually the ones who didn't like what I did, I was always the odd one out. Oh well, friends can't have everything in common.

"I like strawberry rhubarb pie," I said. It seemed there was a rhubarb plant growing in every yard. That struck the right nerve.

"We're going strawberry picking tomorrow morning," said Debbie. "Want to come?"

"It's sorting day for the thrift table on the Fourth of July," said Paula.

"We're going to the beach," I said.

"You're going with Dieter, aren't you?" said Paula. "When he came to Sunday supper, he told us he goes swimming almost every day."

"You've been swimming with him every day?" said Debbie.

"Just this morning."

"And tomorrow," said Paula. "And you were at church together."

"That's practically dating," said Debbie, incredulously.

Not that direction again. I stuck with my original argument. "Do you think he would date a little kid?"

"But you went out alone with him."

"Not that kind of going out. He's a family friend."

"I've never seen anybody that good looking," said Paula. "Don't you think so?"

"I guess." Everybody else did, with modeling agency offers to prove it.

"What did you talk about?"

I thought for a second. "Not that much, really. We swam."

But when you added it up, it was a lot for the short amount of time he'd been here, and some of it wasn't regular at all. A little voice inside told me I shouldn't say anything about the Historical Society Museum or Tedeschi's and especially not about the fish room at Ward Memorial Library.

"You must talk about something," said Debbie.

"Oh, yeah, we talked about a kind of hiking trail. If the Arms had one, people could go right down to the beach instead of going around, and it would be easy to climb back up."

I squashed my wax paper bag into a ball and deliberately missed the trash can so I could get up. I hoped every Thursday wasn't going to turn into girls and boys talk. In general, I wasn't interested, and in particular, I didn't want Dieter turning into another thing that divided us, like food did.

"This isn't as far as I thought it would be," I said right away. "Let's go there," I pointed over the water to the next tip of land visible past the woods, "to Mallard's Head."

"Alright, but if I'm not back home by 2:00, Mother will call a deputy to come looking for me," said Paula.

"You're kidding," said Debbie.

"No."

"I wouldn't be missed until I have to wash the dinner dishes."

"Sure you would," I said. I didn't believe that's what the Fortins were like. "Besides, there's plenty of time."

It wasn't as if we had never taken the long way around Lakeshore Drive to get home from camp or for a Sunday drive, but it had always been in a car with one or both parents, and that made it unfamiliar enough that biking it felt like jumping in water over my head the first time.

This section of road was less traveled and shady. There were old houses with year-round residents, but most of the young people had left, and more and more, places were rented out for visitors to "go to camp," whether they were staying in a rustic cabin or a cottage with housekeeping or farmhouse. The permanent and vacation homes had two things in common: back side to the road and front to the lake, and labeled with artsy signs like *Perch Ants* and other names you had to figure out.

The turn into Mallard's Head was as plain as any other, with only numbers on the mailboxes, no personal names. A couple of lanes as thin as capillaries led to hidden houses.

Debbie came astride. "Are you sure this isn't a private road?"

"It would say so if it was," I said.

In a minute, the road took a rounded turn to an opening with a mirage. Four houses in a semicircle overlooking the water led to a tapering strip of beach. And smack in the middle of the yard was a swimming pool with some kids in it. There was actually a striped cabana and adults sitting under umbrellas.

"Yeah, well, it's a private party," said Debbie, wheeling around, but a girl in the pool waved and hollered, "Hi! It's me, Theresa."

Paula and I stopped and Debbie came back.

It was Theresa George, of the Georges of the North Shore Restaurant and Marina. She was a year ahead, like Debbie's sister Peggy, but we all knew each other. She seemed nice, although I thought of her family as competitors, even if they did serve regular food.

She was across the lawn in no time.

"Hi, Theresa," I said.

"We didn't mean to interrupt you," said Paula politely.

"It doesn't matter," she said. "You rode out all this way?"

"Yeah, but we stopped once already," I said.

"Come on, meet my family. You must be thirsty."

We looked at each other. We were deer in the headlights.

"Okay."

We laid our bikes on the soft emerald grass—they must water it—and followed her, trying not to stare at her bathing suit—she didn't shop for that in Neston. It was black with built-in bra cups that she was already filling out, and it matched her silky black hair, which was so thick her page boy hung from the weight of it, as perfect as if she'd just come from the hairdresser. Her olive skin was already tan, and summer was just starting.

The men and women looked at us inquisitively, but she trooped us to a couple who looked about a hundred years old who were seated in the shade of one of the umbrellas, just like the ones on the wharf at their restaurant. Although it was hot out, the woman was wrapped with a beautiful white lacy shawl. If I didn't know better, I would have said she was grandmother Janou in *An Affair to Remember*, except her husband was still alive, sitting next to her, with white hair like Einstein and wearing baggy linen long sleeves and pants. Their bony veiny hands touched.

"These are my grandparents," she said. "Pappouli and Yaiyai, these are my school mates," and she introduced us with our full names.

The king and queen nodded and murmured approvingly, and Theresa moved on.

"These are my Papa and Mama," she said, and she repeated the introduction. They smiled and smiled, but no one spoke until she finished. "And these are my brothers, Tony, Gregory, and Nikky, and their wives, Maria, Doris, and Lina, and my nephews and nieces."

Except for the baby on Lina's hip, who looked about Gabe's age, the slew of kids had all gotten out of the pool and stood so close that the water dripping off of them splashed onto my ankles. She was formal with the adults but didn't name the kids. Her brothers were much older, and you could tell she introduced them by age order, just like the men came first every time. Once she finished, all commotion broke loose as the kids jumped back into the pool.

Theresa was expected to be the little hostess. She used silver tongs to get cubes out of the ice bucket and poured from glass Kool-Aid Man pitchers of iced tea and lemonade with real lemons. Papa and Mama asked questions in thick Greek accents while the rest crowded around to hear what we were saying.

"You are from near by, yes?"

"You know our Princess from school?"

Yes. Yes. Princess?

"Mr. Fortin is a history teacher," said Theresa.

They gave long and serious nods.

"History is very important," said Papa.

Debbie looked down and picked at a cuticle, but Paula showed her manners and said, "My father is the minister at the Meetinghouse."

They crossed themselves.

"Oh, he's not a priest."

No matter. They crossed themselves again.

I broke the reverence. "We own The Neston Arms."

"Oh," they said one after another in long drawls, with more nodding, and quite a bit of chin stroking.

But they couldn't have been nicer. The table was loaded. Debbie and Paula looked at the spread like it was Martian food, but I knew that accepting the Georges' hospitality was the greatest compliment to them. These were my kind of people.

Debbie eyeballed Theresa sullenly and then turned to squinting at the kids in the pool. The lemonade and tea were far too sour for Paula, just like the smell of the dips repulsed her. She and Debbie only ate watermelon, but so as not to insult the whole family, I explained. "We just ate lunch," and speaking for myself, said, "but I'd like a taste. What are these?"

On a small plate, Theresa put different kinds of olives, slices of cucumber, a dollop of white dip with flecks and chunks, and toast points cut like little pizza slices with a Dijon-colored dip. I smelled each before tasting.

Pappouli and Yaiyai looked on with their upper lips pursed into deep creases, and everybody else, including Debbie and Paula, watched to see the slightest rejection.

The olives were very tasty and salty. The white dip was sour in a good tangy way that you don't get very often, and the tiny cubes of cucumber and minced dill were fresh.

"Mmm, that's bright," I said.

Both the white and yellow dips had garlic in the background, and the yellow dip had lemon and a swirl of olive oil over a main ingredient I'd never tasted before.

"And this one is smooth as velvet."

"This girl, she understands food!" cried Mama. They clinked colored aluminum cups and toasted in Greek. The commotion came back to life.

I had tasted a lot, but nothing like those two dips. "What are they?"

Mama rattled them off, and Theresa spelled them out: tzatziki and hummus. I'd have to look them up, since I knew better than to ask for the recipes.

Debbie hadn't stopped jerking her left leg, all antsy like she was the one who was under deadline instead of Paula.

"We have to get going now," she said.

"Thank you very much for everything," I said.

"Yes, thank you," said Paula.

"You are going to ride?" said Papa, as if bicycling were as dangerous as swimming after eating.

"Yes, we have to get back on time," said Paula.

"But we just meet our Princess's friends," said Mama.

"We give you ride in the truck. Plenty of room for the bikes."

It took repeated promises that we were fine before they'd let us go.

"You come back, bring bathing suit," said Mama.

"Thank you, I'd like to," I said, and Paula said, "Me, too," but Debbie was already pedaling.

Safely out of range, she said, "Did you see how old her brothers are?"

"Yeah," said Paula, "and they call her Princess!"

That was it for chitchat. Biking from home to the boat launch on Leeward Lane had been a hop, and Leeward Lane to Mallard's

Head only felt like a skip, but put them together, and we had to hightail it to jump back in time. If Paula was late returning home this first time out, there wouldn't be any other times.

Chapter 15

MY EYES WERE GLUED shut. I'd slept really late again, but it didn't matter. That was one of the great things about being on vacation. I took my time waking up slowly and gently rubbing my eyes open.

I had missed swimming with Dieter. He'd understand. I could explain later, while we were folding napkins, that I had overdone it swimming and biking in one day. I wouldn't be doing that again.

Plus, the bike ride had taken longer than I thought it would. I rolled onto my side and looked out the window at the oak branches. The usual flock of crows was cawing, and that helped me figure out where I had gone wrong. I had eyeballed Mallard's Head from the boat launch as the crow flies.

I needed a map of the lake. That was easy enough. Tedeschi's had lots. And I needed to start wearing my watch. I'd only worn it for show before, but now I had real reasons keep track of time: to see how long it took us to bike a certain distance and to budget our time so we got back when we promised we would.

It sure had been fun, though. Well, Debbie hadn't liked being at the Georges, but I had. I thought about what she and Paula had said about Theresa and her brothers. It was true. Theresa's brothers were a lot older. Although their own children were under school age or just barely reaching it, strictly speaking, any one of her brothers was old enough to be her father.

Talk about a surprise baby. But I doubted if Mom and Dad expected Gabe more than decade after me, and he was wonderful, you could see that already. That gave us a boy in the family. Except for taking a lot longer, it was just the same with Theresa. Her parents must have been shocked to have another child when her brothers were completely grown up, but they finally got a daughter in their family. No wonder she was their Princess.

I would have figured they lived near their business, just like the Tedeschis did and we did, but I never would have guessed they lived on the lake in a compound, like the Kennedys.

Among those who lived year-round at Île de L'eau, the Tedeschis were old timers who had bought and built when it was dirt cheap. So had the Buckminsters, who owned a gas station and a fuel business.

Nowadays, if and when it became available, waterfront land wasn't a bargain. If William Ward hadn't bought himself a whole peninsula way back when, Claude Cote would have been the latest to pay, but his father-in-law, Fred Ward, Sr., built him a house on it, just like he had for his son, Fred, Jr. They sure stuck together.

What with businesses at one end of the lake and houses on Mallard's Head, even if they had bought before prices went up, the George estate had to cost a fortune. It was the Head on Mallard's Head. I hadn't even known about it. Good thing we rode by. I wished I could see the inside of her house, whichever one it was. Actually, I wished I could see all four of them.

The Georges stuck together even more than the Wards. The whole kit and kaboodle lived together and worked together—or did they still work together?

I had seen Gregory outside at the Marina plenty of times. We weren't regulars at the North Shore Restaurant, but we ate there often enough that I recalled seeing Doris or Lina hostessing or Maria running the cash register while Mama and Papa strolled around talking to people, patting shoulders and laughing. I guessed Tony and Nikky worked back of the house and kept the books.

So how could they all get away? It didn't add up. It was a Thursday during the summer lunch rush. The entire clan was home, having fun at their in-ground pool, and they could have gone swimming in the lake if they wanted. On the surface, they didn't seem so different from us, but those were big differences. Forget about the pool, we'd just managed to have a picnic day all together ourselves, although it was rare and took a lot of planning. Another day like that might be long in coming, if it did at all for the rest of the summer.

However they did it, I wanted to find out.

Chapter 16

MISS HARRISON WAS ON greeter duty at church.

"So nice to see you again," she said, smiling up at Dieter as she handed him a bulletin.

Apparently, I was wearing my invisible costume. Fine. One bulletin was enough for the two of us anyway.

"Thank you," he said. "It's good to be here."

"Oh?" she fished, but of all the people, the Armstrongs arrived directly behind us, and she had to give them bulletins.

I was bound to see Janice up close sooner or later, but I was surprised at how shaky I felt when I did. After all, I wasn't the one calling her a name, but it hurt. I was still confused over why it started, and I was afraid of the damage it might do.

Dieter motioned ladies first and we passed the Fortins. Larry was watching for Dieter, but we passed by without incident. On the other hand, Paula looked like she wasn't expecting to see us again, but she got over it quick enough, hanging on to Dieter's every word.

"I saw Baltimore delivered it on the chin to the Red Sox," he said, ribbing Timothy about his favorite team.

"They'll make it up this afternoon," said Timothy. "Anyway, stats don't tell the whole story."

"Don't I know," said Dieter, "but Pedro Gonzalez took the Yankees over the White Sox one-zip in the eleventh inning. Now that's a stat that tells the story."

"The season's not over yet," said Timothy. "Not by a long shot."

They both grinned.

Paula had plenty of reason to smile, too. Saturday had been another wedding day. Except for July Fourth, every Saturday was, up until the middle of August.

The church smelled good again, although the flowers in front of the lectern weren't like the big spray that had been left after the Ward-Cote wedding. And at the Arms, none of the wedding parties would take over the inn and the ballroom and the restaurant like that one had.

But between yesterday's wedding and the couples celebrating their June anniversaries, there were love birds everywhere. If couples weren't holding hands, husbands had their arms draped over their wives' shoulders. It was nice enough to make anybody smile.

We belted out "A Mighty Fortress is Our God." I made a note to look up bulwark.

Rev. Bouchard tied it into his sermon. "Martin Luther, who composed the words and music of this song, calls God his mighty fortress, a bulwark never failing," said Rev. Bouchard. "He certainly needed one. In order to escape arrest and trial and almost certain death at the hands of religious leaders for his biblical beliefs, Luther arranged for friends to make it look as if they kidnapped him."

We reacted to kidnapping like we were at the movies.

"They took him to a castle, where he hid for close to a year."

That was an unexpected plot twist.

"We can see how he was influenced by Psalm 18, a song composed by David, who writes, 'The LORD is my rock, and my fortress, and my deliverer; my God, my strength, in whom I will trust; my buckler, and the horn of my salvation, and my high tower.'"

Dieter nodded emphatically. I made a note to look up buckler.

It was another rock sermon, but eventually Rev. Bouchard went in a different direction.

"In his song, Luther refers to the devil as the Prince of Darkness, the ancient foe seeking his woe. In life, Luther said the devil was the spirit who spoke through his enemies."

I heard a sound behind me like when Larry got shushed. No wonder. Those comments were not light summer fare. Rev.

Bouchard was almost in over his head, and he must have known it because he brought the sermon to a quick close.

"God's name means I Am, the one who was and is and will be. And that is why Luther wrote, 'from age to age, God is the same, the rock that never fails.' Let us pray."

If what he said was true, that meant the devil could speak through churchy people. They went after Luther to kill him—and they succeeded with Stephen. It only made their stories scarier than ever.

Although I thought Janice and Tina were my enemies, I didn't believe the devil was speaking through them. Name calling wasn't the same as killing. But high school didn't have rocks where I could hide from classmates bent on mischief. It seemed God really was the only one who could protect me, so I prayed about that again.

Chapter 17

AND I WENT SWIMMING with Dieter again. Now that he'd shown me that I could make it to the raft raft without difficulty, I wanted to complete the lap.

"I wish I could do the crawl stroke like you, over and back," I said.

"Have you been swimming much this summer?"

"Only at the picnic and with you."

I thought he would say it was too much to expect, but instead, he said, "From what I've seen, you're a natural in the water. I think you're a strong enough swimmer to make it. The key is focusing on consistent strokes."

Which was the nice way of saying my form needed work. Which was true. I had passed all my swimming lessons on the first try, but my instructors had told me the same thing.

"And it'll make me go faster."

"Speed's not your goal at this point. Take your time making sure each stroke is properly executed. The risk of injury is higher with improper strokes. You may pick up a little speed, though. Consistent strokes save time and energy."

We went out slowly to the raft and from there, I focused on doing each stroke the correct way, each one the same. Right arm, left arm, right arm, breathe, left arm, right arm, left arm, breathe. With my face under water so much, I relied on the line and Dieter on either side to keep from veering off, and I didn't try to speed up at all, but the pace felt so smooth that when we got to the far raft and I wasn't out of breath, I turned around and we swam back.

"You're a quick learner," he said.

"Thanks. You were right about paying attention to the strokes."

"The more often you practice, the farther you'll be able to swim before you tire out, but you shouldn't push yourself too much, especially at first."

"Yeah, I should stop now." I'd accomplished enough.

I glided back to shore, where the hot sun felt good on my muscles, but I was okay.

I watched Dieter while he did his laps. His arms and legs clicked like a metronome, and he reset it faster with each lap. He stroked through the water so cleanly and uniformly, all he saved in energy he made up for in speed.

I realized I hadn't looked up the words from the song yet, so after he sat down and relaxed, I asked him, "Do you know what buckler means? And bulwark? They were in the song we sang yesterday."

"A buckler is a small round shield used in hand-to-hand combat."

"I can picture that."

"And a bulwark is a thick defensive wall. As Rev. Bouchard said, Martin Luther's friends took him to a castle, where he hid for close to a year, and like any good castle, it was a mighty fortress with bulwarks built on high mountain rock."

Now we were cooking with gas.

"So that's why the song has both. One's for up close and the other is for far away."

"Exactly."

"Thanks. I meant to look them up. We had vocabulary lists every week at school, and I never noticed most of the words before I got a list. But once I learned what a word meant, I noticed it a lot. So now, I try to pay attention and notice new words even if I don't know what they mean yet." I still liked reviewing the lists, but I would never admit that to any classmates.

"You may not see bulwark or buckler very often."

"That's okay, I'll remember. Anyway, I guess David helped out Martin Luther with the words."

"I think Luther was inspired as much by his surroundings as he was by David calling God his high tower. It so happens the fortress Luther hid in was originally constructed as a tower."

Interesting architecture point.

"Did you study it at school?"

"No, my parents and I toured castles last summer. We saw where Luther stayed. It's undergone quite a bit of work over the centuries to stand today, but many castles have completely gone to ruins. Their bulwarks really did fail. But God is the bulwark that never fails, and that's why ever-lasting salvation is from God alone."

It was starting to make sense. "What was Luther's castle like?"

"It's beautiful now. Wartburg was—"

"Did you say Wartburg?"

"In German, it means observation point, like a watchtower, which any fortress had."

"Check."

"It was a royal hunting castle when Luther was there, although he was secluded in a prison room."

"Oh," I said, disappointed that his rock was a prison. I hoped this wasn't going to be another martyr ending.

"It didn't sound that way in the song."

"No, but he wasn't in a dungeon. The room even has a window. It was built for knights taken prisoner, so it was better than most people lived in. He kept up the charade by calling himself Knight George. People in the castle never knew it was Luther."

While I was chewing on that, Dieter added, "Even if it were a dungeon, I'd trade places with him in a heartbeat if I could do what he did while he was there."

"How come? What did he do?"

"He began translating the New Testament so Germans could understand it in their own language. That made it available to the common people for the first time, and he didn't want people to just hear it, he wanted everyone to learn how to read it. And he used his time to write. One of the most important things he wrote was that no one can buy God's forgiveness or earn their way to heaven. Salvation comes through faith. He changed the world."

"I guess changing the world is worth being locked up in prison."

"The salvation of a single soul is worth it."

Dieter already had big ambitions, and it seemed like this was another thing, actually, the most important thing to him.

If what he said was true, he thought I was worth it. Although I didn't think he talked to me any differently than he would to anybody else who asked him about God things, he must have seen that everything he said had an impact on me.

I didn't get it all, but it was probably like swimming laps. You had to take them one stroke at a time and build up over time.

Chapter 18

DEBBIE WANTED TO TAKE the eastern side this time. If she had noticed we had gotten pushed for time last week, she didn't say anything. It was fine with Paula and me, especially considering the opposite side was the only other choice anyway. I suggested we check out the official point of interest. Potash Park was next to it. The distance was perfect for lunch half way, and exploring the site should be interesting.

We passed the North Shore Restaurant and Beach Bun and Tedeschi's, full of confidence as we entered less familiar territory. This was a fun ride.

Well, the scenery was. Sections of the road were overdue for grading. Potholes are nature's speed limit. So is a washboard surface. They're as hard on bicycles as on cars, except if you hit a pothole too hard, you can get thrown off a bicycle. Debbie and I moseyed single file behind Paula, keeping plenty of distance and watching where she swerved.

We had agreed to say or signal any time we wanted to stop, so when I hollered "dismount," we walked past *The Old Homestead.* The Tedeschi farmhouse was farther away from the water than most of the others, and the barn was close to the road. Back in the day, cows crossed the road to the pasture on the other side. The last of the working farms had cleared out from around Lakeshore Drive, but cow crossings were common all over the rest of Wortham County, sometimes sheep and goats, too.

"Sophie told me her grandfather and father were born here," I said. Just thinking about it was interesting. Old Mr. Tedeschi and Mr. and Mrs. Ted still lived here, raising Sophie and her brother Ted the Third.

"They'll die there," said Debbie.

As if lots of people hadn't been dying in the houses they were born in for most of history, which she of all people should have known.

"So what?" I said.

"Old Man Tedeschi probably never left the state."

As if there were something wrong with that.

"He did so. I saw him on the World War I float on Memorial Day. He probably fought overseas. He maybe traveled all over."

"Well, well."

Paula glanced over to me like she had the same thought I did: what was with the bee in her bonnet? Sammy, still?

Debbie took the lead. Before we reached the Buckminsters' house, she pointed her left arm down at the elbow with her palm facing us, the signal to stop. Their house name was one of those clever puns so common around the lake, but like the Tedeschis' sign, not a water theme. *Deer Haven* hung below enormous pairs of antlers. Hunting still ran in the family as much as fishing. They were always getting big catches.

I guessed Debbie and Paula's fascination with the house ran in another direction from mine. "Bucky" Buckminster was thirteen but looked older. He'd been an item of interest to the girls on the playground for the past two years. We passed the house in slow motion.

"They opened a new gas station," said Paula. "I saw Bucky washing the windows."

"Really? Where?" said Debbie.

"Connecticut River Road, near Leo's Pizza."

That was a smart location for a new business. They would get the north-south traffic customers, who wouldn't have to turn off onto Neston Avenue to gas up at their filling station there. It made sense, too. Everybody already used Buckminster Fuel Delivery and Service. If they kept it up, Bucky wouldn't have a reason to leave Neston either, but I wasn't about to burst Debbie's bubble. Apparently, her favorite Beatle had competition. At any rate, she snapped out of it.

When we couldn't drag it out any longer, I took a cautious lead, thinking how Neston was changing before my eyes. In fact, how long would it be before a regular hotel went in—or worse, another inn somewhere nearby? Or more restaurants? We could get hit from two directions.

Competition was even harder on the gas stations. They were pretty much the same, so another one was a direct hit. All they could do to get ahead was multiply. I felt good for the Buckminsters. They were getting the leg up. But that was just because I liked them. There were two sides to every coin. You just wanted your coin to land on the side you called.

We passed a grouping of summer cabins situated close to the water. I caught signs for *Shade Shack, Runaway, The Hat Box, Bearfoot Den*. It was like a little town. People of all ages were out in force for the single purpose of having fun. Just like us.

A ways on, we stopped at an opening with a scenic view across the water to a house at the end of a small peninsula.

"That's where Lisa Ward lives," said Paula.

"No, it's not," said Debbie. "It's the old man's house."

I knew it was, although nobody called Fred Ward, Sr. old, like they did Old Mr. Tedeschi.

I looked at the map I'd bought. "It's called Point Droit," I said.

"Like, French for on the east side?" said Paula.

"No, east would be *est*," I said, although the peninsula was on the east side of Île de L'eau.

In fact, east side would be *côté est*. The marriage to a Cote had to be a coincidence, but it was just another one of those things that always worked out for the Wards. I thought for a minute. They owned the biggest inboard on the lake, called *The Starboard Side*, which is the right side of a boat, so right point must also mean on the right side. Or maybe in the right. Either way, it summed up the Wards, although they really had given a lot to Neston.

"But it's sort of the same," I said, leaving it vague.

"Want to see it up close?" said Debbie.

"Nuh uh," said Paula.

"Can't," I seconded.

Point Droit Drive was posted coming and going as obviously as Burma Shave signs: *Private, No Trespassing, Hunting Prohibited*. Lisa's house and the new home of the Cotes were visible between trees, and the historic Ward house was more visible at the end of the peninsula, but we'd never see it up close.

"Well, maybe by boat," I added.

Debbie took a binocular case out of the knapsack in her bike basket. "That's what you think."

"Ooh," said Paula.

I had to hand it to her, bringing binoculars was a smart idea—but not for this.

Debbie found her focus. "It's the Taj Mahal," she said." She whistled. "Old lady Ward and Fred Junior's wife are out sunbathing."

"Let me see," said Paula.

After a minute, she said, "Whew, you're not kidding. Here, look." She tried to hand me the binoculars.

I shook my head.

"Don't you want to see it?" said Debbie.

"I can see it from here."

"Not like looking through binoculars." Paula held them out to me again. "Here."

"No, I don't want to."

"Why not?"

"It's snooping."

"You were already looking," said Debbie.

"Anybody can see it from here. That's just sightseeing."

"Suit yourself," said Paula.

"What a prig," said Debbie.

"Don't call me that," I shot back.

"If the shoe fits."

"Well, it doesn't. Just because I think using binoculars to watch people in their own yard is snooping doesn't make me a prig. Look it up."

She shrugged. "Maybe I will."

That was it for an apology? And what was up with her language?

"Let's go," she said. "I'm getting hungry."

Paula and I exchanged another what-was-it-with-her look.

Whatever it was, she didn't have to take it out on me.

The historic site was a couple of miles away, and the section of road to it ran close to the water, so the views were a good distraction. We came to the historic marker.

CHAUNCEY SMITH SITE TRADER AND TRAITOR

Chauncey Smith (b. 1776) built on this site in 1799
and ran Smith's Tavern and Potash Works.
Opposed to War of 1812 sanctions on commerce,
Smith and others continued trading,using the site for
cross-border smuggling. A warrant for Smith's arrest
was carried out on August 9, 1815. Local militia found
the site deserted. Smith's goods were confiscated
and the dock and buildings burned to the ground.

"Are you telling me there's nothing left?" said Debbie.

"There's got to be something," said Paula.

But the pickings were slim. Mound outlines indicated where the foundation of the tavern had been, but old stone fences marking the property lines remained.

Debbie threw up her arms. "We came out here to see nothing? First we crash Theresa's party and now this."

"What difference does it make?" I said. "We would have come here no matter what." Which was true. It was the most logical stop on this leg.

"We might as well look around," said Paula.

We walked our bikes to several boulders half in the water.

"You just have to picture everything that happened here," I said. "The boulders must have been part of the potash works. It takes a lot of wood and water, and there's plenty of both here. And with a dock, all that the merchants who traveled by water had to do was sail or row in, load up, and pull out."

Admittedly, this might be the least visited historic site in the state, but it was no wonder Smith chose this location. It was a beautiful wooded spot on a beautiful, spring-fed lake, with a boulder furnace provided by nature for a good moneymaking business.

Plus, the story made it all the more interesting. I wasn't sure I blamed him or the others. What can you do if your ability to provide for yourself and your family is taken away? And it's not as if making potash was a bad thing in and of itself. Without it, a whole bunch of things must have gone missing, like that time the entire shelf of bread was empty because of a late delivery, only it would have been a lot worse because a lot of things were made with potash, and they might have been short for who-knows-how-long.

"This is boring," said Debbie.

"It's not what I expected, but the park looks nice," said Paula optimistically.

We walked the few feet along the shoreline directly into Potash Park. The grove of trees had several picnic tables speckled with shade. A fire pit had been built next to some waterside picnic tables. We sat down.

"Too bad we can't roast marshmallows over the fire pit," said Paula.

"We've got a fire pit," said Debbie. "We roast wienies and marshmallows all the time."

"You do? Since when?" It must be new or I would have noticed.

"Since last month. Mom wanted it for her birthday. It keeps us out of her hair."

"You get to roast marshmallows whenever you want?" said Paula longingly.

"I'm sick and tired of them."

That stung, but Paula didn't bite back.

"Yeah, it is nice here," I agreed with Paula, and not just to hold up my end in turning the conversation around. I would have said that eating *al fresco*—in the fresh air, especially waterside, was my favorite way to dine, but Debbie said, "We got a kiddie pool, too," and added bluntly, "It saves on baths."

Well, we tried. Swimming saved me a few baths myself, at least when it was early and the water was fresh. Once people swam nearby, you couldn't trust how pure the water would be. But it wasn't anything I was going to mention.

I bit into my Cornish pasty. "What's it today?" said Paula.

"Meat pie. It's a good way to use up leftover roast."

"If you've got any," said Debbie.

The way I remembered it, Mrs. Fortin always cooked enough for an army. All our moms planned for leftovers. Those growing kids must be eating the Fortins out of house and home if they were eating hot dogs all the time.

"I wish this place was more like Fort Ticonderoga," she said.

"Is it like Santa's Land?" said Paula. "I loved the Sweet Shop."

"No, it's a lot bigger," said Debbie. "It's all about history, which is why Daddy wanted to go, but the people are dressed like olden times and there are all kinds of things to see. We're going to Plimoth Plantation in August, and that will be even more fun."

"They sound interesting," I said.

At least she was happy about something—and she didn't call her own father the old man. The Chauncey Smith site could stand to be beefed up, but I wouldn't want crowds flocking to Île de L'eau like they must to big tourist attractions.

"I haven't been to Fort Ticonderoga or Plimouth Plantation," said Paula.

"Me neither," I said. Not even Santa's Land, but Mom and Dad had taken Marcia and Donna. There were photos of Donna petting Rudolph and Marcia squirming off of Santa's lap. They both smiled when they posed on the train, though, so that looked like it would be a lot of fun, but I didn't think it was a good enough reason to ask to go. I had a bone to pick with Santa.

The first major fight I had with Marcia was when she told me Santa wasn't real. But she was right. Santa was a hoax. His story wasn't like regular fairy tales. Nobody spent weeks every autumn convincing you Cinderella was real. But you wrote real letters to the North Pole, and left real milk and cookies for Santa, and then you got real presents. What was the point of telling kids about Santa if you only had to disappoint them later?

Gabe would be a little over a year old this Christmas, and even if none of us said anything to him about Santa, Gabe couldn't miss him. Santa was on many of the dozens of cards we strung up over doors, his tiny elves hung on our tree in our living room, and out on the common, life-sized painted wooden cutouts of Santa in his sleigh, pulled by all nine reindeer, were as brightly lit as the nativity scene out in front of the Meetinghouse.

All that was just the tip of the iceberg. I had a feeling Jesus might have a thing or two to say to Santa about Christmas. The least I could do was tell Gabe that Jesus wasn't a fairy tale.

Not that I was against make-believe. The Chauncey Smith site was entertaining enough for me. All I had to do was fill in the blanks with some imagination.

For the longest time, all Debbie and Paula and I did was make-believe. One day, we were moms bottle feeding our baby dollies, the next day we were princesses dressing for a ball, and the day after that explorers searching for a treasure island. The stick hut was our home or our castle or our ship.

I guess those make-believe days were gone, but that didn't mean we couldn't imagine. The story of this place was already here. You just had to picture it.

Chapter 19

GABE AND I BOTH went down for the count. It started with him crying. He'd eaten and burped, his diaper was clean, everything was the same as always except he wouldn't go to sleep. He pushed the bottle away and cried.

I perched on the wooden flip stool next to the rocker while Mom tried to comfort him, but he wouldn't have any of it. He just kept on crying. He never cried this much before. I couldn't stand it. I wanted to cry myself.

"What's the matter, Mom?"

"I think he has an earache."

"How can you tell?"

"He's scratching his left ear."

He swatted so much, I hadn't noticed that in particular.

"Will you go get the ear drops? Run the bottle under hot water until it's warm. I'll need your help."

I didn't move. Ear drops? He could be dying.

"And the heating pad."

"Maybe we should go to the doctor."

Mom felt his forehead. "He's not running a fever, so I don't think he has an infection. It's probably just a little wax buildup." She reassured me with a smile. "These things happen."

But I was afraid for Gabe. All that crying couldn't be normal for a little earwax.

"Maybe you better check me," I said.

She felt my forehead. She looked me over, undecided. "How do you feel?"

"I think I have an earache, too."

She looked in my ear. "It's a bit pinker than usual. Well then, why don't you get the thermometer also?"

Gabe was fit to be tied while I held him in position in the crib and Mom put one drop in his ear, but she just acted like everything was regular. She plugged in the heating pad, put it on low, and sat in the rocking chair again with the pad slung over her shoulder.

"There, there," she said over and over, trying to keep Gabe's head against the heat while not fighting him at it.

I shook down the thermometer and showed it to Mom.

"Good. Sit still while you take your temperature. No, Ette, not crouched on the stool. Sit back in the club chair. Relax."

I stuck the thermometer under my tongue and gave it a good five minutes before I handed it over. Sure enough, I was a hair over 99.

"That's almost a hundred. I think we better go to the doctor," I said. "Before the office closes for the weekend."

Dr. Lewis had been our family doctor since Marcia was born, so we'd known each other my whole life. I didn't much like the shots I had to get, but otherwise, he was nice.

He saw Gabe first. I was too wound up to read, so I found all the hidden pictures in two issues of *Highlights* and was working on finding six differences between two cartoons when I heard Gabe crying in the hallway. I jumped up.

"He's okay, Ette," said Mom, bringing him into the waiting room.

"Are you sure?"

"Yes. You go in and I'll tell you afterward."

The doctor can keep you waiting, but you can't keep the doctor waiting, even if you are shook up.

"Well, hello, Etienne," Dr. Lewis said cheerfully. He always acted as if it was a pleasure visit, but I don't know how he could, when Gabe just came out of there crying to beat the band.

"Just one moment, and you can have a seat."

He swiveled away from me on his low round stool and attached a funnel-shaped tip to a silver instrument.

The nurse was just as happy. She pulled a fresh sheet of paper over the examining bed. She patted it and I stepped up and sat.

He swiveled back around.

"So, tell me what's happening."

"My right ear hurts."

"How long has it been hurting?"

"I didn't notice it until this morning."

"What a coincidence, you and your brother both getting ear aches."

"I guess."

"Any other aches? Headache? Toothache?"

"No, I haven't got a toothache. Well, not since a couple of weeks ago, but it was just a molar coming in."

"Good, good, let's take a look at your ears."

A small beam of light came out of the tip of the funnel instrument, which he used to look into my right ear.

"Mmm hmmm, mmm hmmm. Let's just check the other ear, as long as we're at it. Mmm, hmmm."

He popped the tip off the instrument.

"Seems you've got a case of otitis externa in your right ear."

"What?" That sounded serious. "Will I go deaf?"

"No, no, it's a mild case of infection in the outer ear, better known as swimmer's ear."

Swimmer's ear!

"Do you get it from swimming?"

"Usually, when the ears are immersed in water repeatedly, but the infection isn't from swimming itself, it's from moisture left in the ear. Have you been swimming recently?"

"Yes. I was planning on going a lot this summer. This doesn't mean I can't go, does it?"

"No, no, but not for a few days until this clears up. I'll prescribe some drops, but you'll need to keep your ears dry thereafter, or an infection could return."

I only nodded. I wore a cap when I was doing laps, but when Dieter took off by himself, I usually took off my cap and spent some time floating or bobbing above and below the surface. The moisture must have gotten in. How can you keep your ears dry when your head is under water?

Chapter 20

GABE WAS UP AND rambunctious before the count of five. His earache was a combination of a side effect of teething, and, like Mom said, some ear wax, which Dr. Lewis had flushed out in the office. She assured me he'd been crying when they came out more because he didn't like the flushing than any other reason.

I, on the other hand, stayed down for the full count. I woke up Saturday with my ear feeling worse, and I knew the medicine needed time to work, which I guess is why a sick person is called a patient. I went to bed with the heating pad set on high pressed to my ear. We had the hot water bottle in case Gabe needed it, but he seemed to like grabbing it more than anything.

I lazed all day. I finished another book, and since I wouldn't get to the library for the next one in the series until Monday at the earliest, I thought of asking Donna if I could borrow that book she was rereading, if she was finished with it, but then I decided, if she didn't like Dieter showing me how to do back flips, she wouldn't want me horning in and reading one of their favorite books. At least not her copy. It was better to let sleeping dogs lie. I made a note to start checking out more than one library book at a time.

I reviewed all of last year's vocabulary lists, which was just as well, since I'd forgotten a few words that I hadn't seen anywhere else yet, and that tided me over until dinner. After Gabe finally went to bed good and quiet, Mom and I played Monopoly.

I wanted to make up for the last time we had played, when I'd landed on utilities but hadn't bought them. Mom had, plus she'd put houses on Mediterranean and Baltic, and I'd landed on them so often that she had enough money to buy Boardwalk and Park Place. Then she had more houses. Normally, the game took a long time, but it hadn't taken me very long to lose. And now, I lost in no time flat.

"Last time I lost because I didn't buy. This time I lost because I did. How come I lost again?"

"You had no cash margin."

I knew that. You lost when you ran out of money.

"But this time, I thought you would land on one of my properties, and I'd get some money."

"Oh, so you gambled on that."

"Well," I grumped.

Mom didn't pull any punches. "You lost both times because you did not calculate your risks against your benefits. You must always do that. The last time, you didn't invest your capital, so you had no assets and received no income. This time, you overcompensated and spent all your capital. With no operating funds, it is not possible to meet expenses, and eventually, the assets are lost. That is how many people go out of business. Bankruptcy is what caused the Driscolls to lose The Neston Inn."

I'd heard Mrs. Racine say so during tours of The Neston Historical Society Museum, but I was always so focused on the inn becoming The Neston Arms that it hadn't sunk in. It did now. Bankruptcy was a word I'd never forget.

Sunday morning, my ear pressure opened and closed a couple of times. I wasn't sure if I was talking too loud or not. I wasn't going to risk singing way off key at the top of my lungs at church. And an extra day with the heating pad couldn't hurt if it meant getting back in the water sooner. I'd doggy paddle if I had to.

But I wouldn't. After the brunch service, Dad came into my bedroom to see how I was feeling, and I learned that Frieda and Carl and Dieter had just left for Montreal. They planned to come back Wednesday. This was all the vacation the three would have together, and the only vacation all summer for Carl and Frieda. Maybe Dieter would have one when he went back home, but I doubted it. He'd be in the thick of training with his swim coaches.

Dad didn't need to tell me their time off meant double duty for Mom. The *sous-chef* stepped in for Carl or Dad when needed, the *maître d'* handled dining operations if Mom was away, and guest operations and housekeeping were good to go for a few days without Frieda, but when it came to money, Frieda ran a tight ship. Each department reported directly to her, and Mom was her accounting backup.

"I'll help," I said. "I can look after Gabe by myself, and when he's sleeping, I can sort the dupe numbers." There wasn't a lot I could do for Dad.

"That would free up Isabelle. I'm sure she'll appreciate the offer, but the decision is hers. How about if we see what she says?"

"Okay. I can always fold napkins."

That only helped the waiters, but even when Dieter and I both folded, they still had plenty more to do. Mr. Michaud always kept them on their toes making sure their tables were picture perfect, plus we were coming up on Independence Day, so they had to prep extra supplies for all the wait stations.

"Are we doing the sailboat fold again this year for Fourth of July?" I asked.

"You think we should?"

"Yeah. Everybody likes it because of the sailboats on the lake." A lot of boats were on Île de L'eau for the fireworks.

"Good point, but ask André first."

"Okay." Mr. Michaud usually liked my napkin folding suggestions.

"I'll be up and Adam tomorrow morning."

Dad's moustache tickled when he kissed me on the forehead.

"When was the last time I told you I love you?" he said.

"Yesterday."

"That long ago?"

He set a small brown glass bottle on my nightstand, one just like the ear drop bottle.

"I have it on good authority this prevents swimmer's ear," he said. "Just don't get it in your eyes."

I opened the bottle and jerked my head back as soon as the dropper got near my nose. Isopropyl alcohol.

"I won't," I said. "I promise."

Gabe and I were on our own after we ate lunch. The plan for the next few days was, if he wasn't fussing, I'd burp him, read to him when I put him down for his nap, and play with him as long afterward as possible. Mom was still his favorite food, and there was only so long he would go without her.

It wasn't really different from what I'd been doing, but there was more responsibility since it was just Gabe and me. Mom said she trusted me, seeing as I kept such a close eye on him. If there was a problem, a call could bring her home almost as fast as if she were only coming up the stairs. So far, so good.

Donna was around enough to bump into us on our own, but she said babysitting was good experience to have and didn't try to boss me.

Marcia was working like mad, and when she finally noticed, she said, "You *are* getting paid," in a tone that meant she had a hunch I wasn't.

"No."

She shook her head and rolled her eyes. At least she didn't call me dumbbell. She walked out of the room before I had a chance to answer.

Mom had offered to pay me, but I said I wouldn't do it for money. I didn't want to get paid for babysitting Gabe; I wanted to look after him because I loved him. To me, it wasn't a job, even if it was good experience. But if it helped out other people with their jobs, and the Arms benefited, all the better.

Chapter 21

WE SKIPPED THE NEXT bike ride. The Fortins were going away for the Fourth of July holiday weekend, and the Bouchards were going to a day-long barbecue hosted by friends.

It was just as well. That would give Debbie time to get over her disappointment, and maybe she'd be in a better mood next time. She was getting to be like Marcia, firing off her cannon before anyone even took aim at her.

I was in a great mood. My ear was better, I'd been busy all week, and Gabe and I'd had a grand old time, but then, I was always in a good mood this time of year. The days were at their longest. Even if the light was losing minutes day by day, you didn't notice it for months because it was also the warmest time of year.

And I was back in the water. It also had gotten much warmer, and Dieter and I spent twice as long swimming. Afterwards, he showed me how to use the alcohol dropper.

"Same time tomorrow?" he asked.

"Check."

We met as usual. By now, I always looked forward to walking and swimming and talking, but I did today more than ever.

A quarter-page picture and lengthy write-up of the Ward-Cote wedding and honeymoon destination had been in yesterday's *Neston News*, and except for quite a few pictures and notices of silver and golden wedding anniversaries, the rest of the page was taken up by a photo of Dieter, smack under the American flag with The Neston Arms sign in full view, followed by an article, "Olympic Hopeful Summers in Neston." It was a banner day for the society page.

I was surprised, since he hadn't mentioned it, but maybe surprise was the point. After we were on our way to the lake, I said, "You didn't tell me you got interviewed."

"I didn't think of it. I've been interviewed several times."

"Because of training for the Olympics?"

"Yes, but they started when I began winning competitions."

In other words, he'd been interviewed a lot. He was being modest.

"Mom and Dad said it was an interesting piece," I said. Donna had clipped it for her scrapbook.

"It's well-written, and fairly, too. There have been other articles that leave out what I always say is the main point."

"About swimming for the glory of God?"

"Yes, My life verse is, 'whatever you do, do it all to the glory of God.'"

I'd never heard of a life verse. "That must be from the Bible."

He nodded. "From First Corinthians. I don't swim for glory for myself, although I get plenty anyway. I won't say I don't enjoy some of it. It's just that my glory isn't the point."

"Well, your pose gives a little glory to the Arms."

He smiled. "And the American flag, since I'm swimming for the United States. I told the reporter that where I'm working for the summer is part of the story. If I weren't at the Arms, I wouldn't be practicing in Île de L'eau."

"It was interesting what you said about losing."

"I really don't look at not winning a medal as losing, but I've learned that it's important to explain why because a lot of people don't see it that way. Of course, I train to win, but just making it to Olympic qualifying trials is a major achievement. One of my coaches said he felt that way when he did."

We stopped for traffic turning onto Lakeshore Drive, but he stopped again before we got to the beach and said, "Hold up a sec," so I did.

"Listen," he said seriously. "Publicity is good if you want to bring home the gold for the USA, but being under the microscope all the time comes with it. Do you see that crowd ahead?"

Grand Central was already filling up.

"That's way more people than usual."

"And I'm pretty sure some of them are reporters. Now that the local angle is out, other news outlets can't afford to miss a story on someone who might become an Olympic athlete."

"Check."

"People may want to take your picture, too, Etienne, not just mine."

"Mine?"

Gawking at Dieter was the norm, so I'd gotten a taste of being the sidekick they sized up, but this was different.

"I'm sorry, I should have warned you. I'll walk you back if you want."

I exhaled through my mouth.

Suddenly Dieter bowed his head and said, "Lord, please bring clarity." And then he looked at me.

"It's sink or swim," I said.

I thought for a second.

"Let's go swimming."

He smiled. "Let's."

Sure enough, there were reporters who started taking pictures as soon as Dieter came into view. Like Frieda said, he was under more surveillance than a Soviet submarine.

It turned out the crowd was Fourth of July vacationers, early birds eager for every second on the beach, but the reporters attracted them like crumbs to seagulls. I hung back and blended in with their circle around Dieter as he answered questions, and after the reporters photographed him under the American flag hanging at Tedeschi's, he handled the gawkers like he had the first day he had come to the beach. He posed for a couple of pictures with kids and thanked the people for their support, but this time they didn't disperse, and I had to come out of hiding. I wasn't used to paring down to my swimsuit in front of spectators deliberately watching, like Dieter was, but I figured they weren't looking at me.

I was wrong. They stared me up and down. We stuffed our clothes in our duffels and were splashing into the water when one of the reporters noticed me.

"Who's the little lady?" he called after us.

But we dove so his radar couldn't reach.

Chapter 22

A CLOUD CAME OUT of nowhere and burst over the Independence Day parade, but the show went on, and the quick downpour only made things more interesting, which proved Marcia was wrong; she hadn't seen everything before. Viewers crowded under store awnings or framed tents lining the common, where I stood in front of Dad. Donna left her spot with us to be with Frieda and Dieter, who was incognito in Carl's old fishing hat.

The Miss Maple float had a fake tree canopy, and the politicians had rolled up the roofs on their convertibles and waved from the windows, but the World War II and Korean War veterans marched on in the shower. Dad whistled and waved. The cheers went up louder than ever when the float with World War I veterans went by. Sure enough, Old Mr. Tedeschi was on it.

Uncle Sam, who was on stilts, slipped on the wet pavement, and at first it looked funny.

"Whoa," the crowd gasped as he tried to regain his balance, but turned to screams when he fell. Mr. and Mrs. Fred Ward, Jr., driving behind him in their robin's egg Thunderbird with the round backseat windows, would have hit him but he rolled toward the curb of the common practically in front of us.

Following behind, the high school band faltered, but the band leader struck them up again and they marched around the stilts, their instruments dripping wet and the majorettes dropping their batons.

Thankfully, the fire trucks were next in line and some firemen jumped off, grabbed the stilts, and hauled Sam onto the grass for first aid.

Or maybe not so thankfully.

"Serves you right," said a boy with a mop top. "Killer!"

"No war! No war!" The chant picked up.

Dad pulled my back to him and kept his hands on my shoulders.

In seconds, several firemen were almost butting chests with a handful of kids who looked like they were college age.

The new police cruiser squeezed in front of Wheeler's Percherons with its lights flashing and siren wailing and the horses neighed and veered away, sending a wave of people to hop backwards, smack into the crowd behind them. The boys from Future Farmers of America came forward and helped control the horses while Mr. Wheeler reined them in. Three police officers rushed out of the cruiser and inserted themselves between the kids and the firemen.

"Okay, let's stay calm here," said one.

"We're calm," said the mop top.

"They're the violent ones," another one said, pointing at the firemen.

"We save lives!" yelled a fireman being held back.

"Nobody's violent, we're all just being peaceful today," said the cop. "Now let's just live and let live, or you can go on your way."

The kids grumbled and decided to go on their way. They shot dirty looks at Uncle Sam, who it turned out hadn't broken anything, and most of the onlookers clapped when he stood up.

The Grand Marshal and the dignitaries with him had turned the corner and didn't know about the ruckus behind them. The FFA boys regrouped in the gap that had opened up, flanking the normally calm Percherons.

I could feel Dad relax as we watched the old tractors that brought up the rear of the parade, but he took my hand when the crowd dispersed. Donna and Frieda and Dieter met up with us.

"What happened?" asked Frieda.

"War protesters," said Dad.

"Are you okay?" asked Dieter.

I wasn't. I'd started crying.

"I didn't know there was a war. Will you have to go?" I said to Dad.

"No." He knelt on the grass and thumbed away my tears. "I've already served, with Carl, remember? You don't need to worry about that. And I'm too old," he added, trying to make me smile.

"But there's a war?"

"It's not official, but trouble has been brewing for a long time."

"Is that why President Kennedy was shot?" I still didn't understand that.

He thought for a second. "President Kennedy—that was a different thing," he said, but he didn't sound convincing.

"How come I didn't know? They didn't tell us in school."

"Well, this conflict is reported in national newspapers and magazines. You don't read those at school, do you?"

"No."

That explained why I hadn't seen it in the local paper. The *Neston News* had an international section, but I skipped over it to read the funnies and Dear Abby, although if something about war had been on the front page, I would have noticed.

"Where is it?" I asked.

"This one is in southeast Asia."

"So it's not here?"

"Halfway around the world, in the Far East."

"Then why would we fight there?"

"A lot of people are asking that question."

"Like those kids."

"Yes, but some people think we ought to get involved, like we have before in other places."

"Do you?"

"That's a tough question, Etienne. Nobody wants war."

I'd have to look into this. I heaved a deep breath.

"You okay now?" I nodded.

"You want to go home?"

"No."

"What's your pleasure?" said Frieda. "Ring toss?"

I shook my head.

"Potato sack race?"

"I wouldn't do that if I were you," said Dieter. "It's a good way to get injured. It's harder than it looks."

"There's always the glutton for punishment contest."

"That's disgusting," I said.

"Agreed," said Dad.

Frieda knew how we felt about the pie eating contest. She was just cheering me up.

"Mom said I could see if there was anything for Gabe at the thrift table."

"I second that motion," said Dad. "He's growing like a weed."

Donna wasn't much interested but went along with us to the tent in front of the Meetinghouse. After all, she was spending time with Dieter; she had dolled up for the occasion. She sifted through the costume jewelry while Frieda and I picked over quickly outgrown baby clothes and Dieter and Dad browsed books. Alongside hand-knit booties, mittens, and scarves, other tables had pickles, jams, pies, and cookies.

We didn't buy any of Mrs. Bouchard's penuche fudge, but we all found something of interest and did our part to support the church, which used the money for some good cause. I got footed onesies Gabe would grow into this winter and a towel with a knit buttoned loop for hanging on a kitchen drawer handle.

Dad and Frieda left with the loot, and Donna, Dieter, and I took our free bags of popcorn onto the common, where the gazebo was being used as a bandstand. A group was hammering out toe-tapping tunes on fiddles, guitars, and banjos. The men wore suspenders and the women wore floor-length calico dresses. Under straw hats with red, white, and blue bands, every head, if it had hair at all, had gray or white hair.

"They're called The Old Timers," I said to Dieter. "They play around a lot."

"They're good," he said.

"Yeah."

The lyrics were old fashioned, but they were fun, and you could hear every word. Between the music and the colorful flag-themed bunting hanging from all the verandah railings, I was snapping out of it. Still, I wondered, who was more patriotic? The kids chanting or the adults clapping?

The music wasn't Donna's taste, but Dieter and I liked it and hung on to the last song. By then I think she started to enjoy it, since she sure didn't mind standing next to Dieter, who, even with the fishing hat, was recognized now and then. If it had been Donna instead of me at the beach with him, the reporters would have taken plenty of notice right from the start.

He nodded or said hi to acknowledge everybody who recognized him, even if they rudely stared and talked about him like he couldn't hear them. He really took the responsibility of his role seriously. To the glory of God. What did Donna think of that?

My mood let up almost as quickly as the rain had. There was a big family atmosphere at the Arms because so many more kids were there for the holiday, and unlike other major events, I'd get to join the crowd at La Terrasse and watch the fireworks later. That was nothing to sneeze at.

Dieter always had something interesting to point out about architecture, and one day he had said, "Considering the property nearly bumps up against the forty-fifth parallel, the Arms was built to maximize the outdoors as much as possible."

That was especially true on the Fourth of July. A party always booked the Excelsior Room and watched from its balcony. Some guests watched from their rooms, while others had cocktails and canapés and watched from the verandah, but what drew the crowds was La Terrasse.

A wide flagstone path stretched from the front door of the inn and around the west side overlooking Île de L'eau, where the fireworks were set off from the public beach below. The path ended at a broad step to a terrace surrounded by a concrete balustrade and massive flower urns. Several yards in and up another step was a covered terrace. At the third step the wall of French doors led to the enclosed dining room. La Terrasse was named for its stepped terraces into the landscape. We had dining *al fresco* in common with the North Shore Restaurant, which would be doing a bang-up business tonight, too.

The flagstones had steamed in the heat and the terraces were dry by the time Mom and Gabe and Frieda and I took a table next to one of the urns overflowing with flowers. Mom had developed tonight's menu to include patriotically colored items, and from the moment a tourist said, "It's that swimmer," Dieter was on the run, selling the specialties *du jour*—of the day.

Gabe was excited by having all the kids around, seeing Dieter, and watching Donna, who whirled sparklers for him, since Mom was leaving before the fireworks started. Gabe's ears were too young for the booming sounds. Even I had to cover mine.

"You won't miss anything," Frieda said to Mom. "You've seen enough fireworks for one night," referring to the attention Dieter got.

Mom laughed. If she had stayed just a while longer, she would have seen Dieter's grand finale. Frieda and I lingered over a bowl of strawberries and blueberries with Chantilly cream, watching the action until the regular fireworks started.

Working the outer terrace near Dieter all night, Donna's face was lit up the whole time, until a man vacated Dieter's deuce—a table for two, next to us.

"Sorry I can't stay for the fireworks," he said to his wife. "I'll see you Monday."

Most of the patrons at the Arms were very well-groomed, especially the women. This one topped the charts. She waited until her husband was gone and held up a $100 tip between two fingers, obviously over and above what he had signed for on their room tab.

She eyeballed Dieter coyly. "I'll be up late."

He took the bill. "Thank you, ma'am," he said. "This goes a long way on the foreign mission field."

The look on her face fizzled, and so did Donna's.

Chapter 23

GOING TO CHURCH WITH Dieter had been nerve-wracking the first time, and the second time had been awkward at the start, but today, probably because I'd missed a week, the look on certain people's faces tipped me off that they were watching to see if I'd show up with him again. Once was a novelty, and twice started a pattern to keep an eye on, but three times confirmed it as an official matter of record and steady grist for the gossip mill.

With the article out and guests from the Arms recognizing Dieter, the previous attention was minor compared to what followed us as we walked the aisle to the front. If I intended to keep going to church with him, or doing anything else for that matter, I'd have to get used to it.

And I did intend to go with him—no, that sounded too much like we were going together in the other way. Attending, that's what we were doing. I liked how Dieter had explained things to me about Luther's bulwark. In fact, I thought his explanation was more interesting than the sermon itself.

Timothy took seeing us in stride, but Paula had that look of curiosity herself, so I wondered how long it would be before she, and Debbie, started pestering me about attending with him. She'd already spilled the beans on us swimming, and if they found out how often we swam, I'd have to answer for it again.

I looked up the song numbers posted on the wooden roster while Dieter read the bulletin, which was two sheets of paper printed on both sides and folded like a booklet. Besides the order of the service and prayers everyone said aloud, it included announcements, such as weddings, births, baptisms, funerals of members and deaths of other people, and other events, like the thrift table, food drives, and the autumn chicken pie supper.

I didn't need to see the sermon title to know what Rev. Bouchard would be talking about again. The hymn lineup started with #342, "Rock of Ages, Cleft for Me." I knew what a cleft chin was, so I understood the rock of ages was God and the rock was cut out for me to hide in.

This was definitely familiar. Last week's sermon must have been on the rock theme, too. It looked like we'd be on rocks in the Psalms all summer.

Instead, Rev. Bouchard veered off from Psalms and went all over the place. He said, "You recall that Moses struck a rock and water came out for the Israelites to drink."

Well, I didn't, so that must have been what I had missed last week. Then he quoted, "'they drank from the spiritual rock that accompanied them, and that rock was Christ.'"

I tried to piece it together. First there was rock, then there was water out of rock, and now there was water, but it was from a spiritual rock, not a physical one.

Dieter was flipping back and forth to the verses in his Bible and scribbling notes on every empty space in the bulletin. I'd never seen anyone take notes from the sermon. If we weren't in the front row, he would have stuck out like a sore thumb. As it was, the Bouchards noticed.

Speaking of being struck, I was thinking that, later, I'd ask Dieter to help me out figure the spiritual rock when Rev. Bouchard said something that really stood out to me.

He went back and quoted Isaiah. "'You will be like a well-watered garden, like a spring whose waters never fail.'"

Never failing was also familiar. It was what the Psalms and hymns said about the rock. As it turns out, the waters never fail either.

But not just any water. Spring water. Now that was a year's worth of sermons in Neston. Anybody from Wortham County understood springs.

He skipped ahead to Jesus meeting a woman at a well. "'Jesus said to her, "Everyone who drinks this water will be thirsty again. But whoever drinks the water I give him will never thirst. Indeed, the water I give him will become in him a fount of water springing up to eternal life."'"

The Neston common had a fountain, and it was nice, but the town of Billington Springs was famous for its fountain. Fed by its main spring, it gushed like a geyser. Back in the day, the largest house had been a resort. Locals still took to swimming holes where water crashed down and pooled. Time and again, people were warned that the water looked still on the surface of those pools, but it had a strong current running underneath, pouring over one set of falls to another.

Rev. Bouchard skipped again to where Jesus told the crowds at the temple, "'Whoever believes in Me, as the Scripture has said: "Streams of living water will flow from within him."'"

Suddenly, everything jelled.

Springs bubbled up out of rocks. Besides feeding fountains, the waters formed flowing streams. They were living waters.

But these springs and fountains and streams of living water came from Jesus inside you. He was the source, the spiritual rock.

I got it.

I took a deep breath, just thinking about how beautiful it was.

Finally, it was interesting.

I mulled that over until the service ended. I expected we'd help with cleanup again, but two boys presented their bulletins for Dieter to sign.

"Like a trading card," demanded the bigger boy.

Dieter signed with flourish but kept on.

"What are you writing?" he asked. He looked concerned.

Dieter handed the bulletins back. "My life verse. Do you know what that is?"

They read what he'd written and scowled.

"We gotta go, mister," said the other boy.

After that, Dieter excused himself and we ducked out the side door. I decided to wait for a better time to tell him what I figured out, but he didn't dwell on how the boys had reacted.

"For a small town, Neston puts on a nice Fourth of July celebration," he said.

"What'd you like best?"

"The parade was right up there, but I'd have to say The Old Timers. How about you?"

"Probably the same." Although the protesters weren't the only thing that bothered me. "I like the fireworks, but the noise is so loud. It must scare all the animals." It probably hurt their ears, too.

"Temporarily. To them, the fireworks may be like thunder. Animals are smart enough to take cover until it passes."

That was a better way of looking at it.

"Too bad you won't be here for the fair," I said. "That's really nice."

"The one where parents can *f-i-n-e-d* their missing children?"

"Check."

We parted at the Arms with smiles on our faces.

"I'm really looking forward to tomorrow," he said.

Ditto, I thought.

Chapter 24

IT WAS THE FIRST time everybody at home had a full day off since the picnic at the beginning of summer, and the air had that nice lazy holiday feel. As always, we enjoyed holidays after providing the celebrations for the guests at the Arms.

I had helped Mom last night so she could relax, too. The ratatouille and chicken and clafouti were baked and the liver potted, and all that was left to do was warm them up with the baguettes, toss the salad with vinaigrette, and open the wine.

Dieter was finally coming over.

Donna, who had spent an inordinate amount of time primping, cheated Dad out of answering the door.

"Oh, you brought a gift," she gushed, as if it were for her. Except for Marcia, who was shielded in a wing chair where she was reading, we crowded Dieter.

Dad held Gabe, and Mom and Dieter exchanged *deux bisous*. He glanced up at the hall chandelier while she unwrapped the gift. The cloth ribbon fell to the floor and Donna picked it up.

"Oh, Dieter," said Mom. "This is wonderful."

It was the newly published Official World's Fair Edition *International Cookbook*.

"The Olympic trials are held near the Fair," said Dieter, "and I hope to taste some of those dishes in the international pavilions."

"You've hit the bullseye," said Dad.

"Thank you, sir. I'm glad you like it."

"Please, it's Ray," said Dad. "Come in."

As we went in, Dieter looked up at the pontil marks in the glass panes of the transom above the door to the living room, where he continued looking up at the crown molding.

"Is this all original?"

"Most of it," said Dad, "but some has been restored, like the shutters. It wasn't a difficult job but time consuming with all the louvres."

"Did you do the work yourself?"

"No," laughed Dad. "I don't have the time or the talent. John Lacroix handles the restoration work and any sort of repair and keeps up the grounds as well. We've had to replace some things, like the wainscot in the dining room. It had gotten pretty banged up over the years, but of course the replacement is a copy of the original. Care to see? I understand you're eager for a tour."

"I am, very much so. I admit I've been looking forward to it as much as visiting with everyone. How many fireplaces are there?"

"Six."

"All working?"

"Yes. When we don't use them, they're covered with Isabelle's hand-painted panels to keep out the draft. You'll see."

"Ray, would you mind if we started in the basement?"

"Not at all. How about if we grab a couple of flashlights."

"Going from the foundation to the attic follows the house in the order it was constructed," Dieter explained as they went to get them.

Donna returned to her room. I really couldn't fault her or Marcia for wanting some time off from helping. They were both working hard to save for college.

In the time it took Dad and Dieter to look over the house, Mom and I had set the table under the shady oaks, and she showed me how to arrange dried vines on the weathered kitchen porch sideboard with fruit, nuts, lemons, and linen-covered cheese on our special pewter. The wine was breathing.

"Looks like we've got a Dutch decorating theme today," said Dad as he came out with Dieter. He kissed Mom and kept his hand on the small of her back as he said, "It's always a nice surprise element to me. Artistry is just one of Isabelle's many talents."

"It's remarkable," said Dieter. He was almost as excited about the display as when he first saw the house. "The layout looks like some still lifes I just saw at the Montreal Museum of Fine Arts. One was so beautiful and lifelike, I thought it looked good enough to eat, and you've brought it to real life."

"Thank you," said Mom with a smile. "I've seen them myself, and I created this one for the outdoor setting."

Mom.

I knew it looked artistic, but I had no idea.

We said grace together and helped ourselves at will.

"Pinot Noir, Dieter?" asked Dad.

Dieter didn't bat an eye. "Thank you."

He and Marcia and Donna got half as much as Mom and Dad, and I got what amounted to two thimble-sized sips. If I didn't like it, I could have a full pour of grape juice, but I knew this one was good.

"À ta santé," toasted Dad. To your health. We raised our glasses.

"With your company and such a meal, I'm certainly going to enjoy the best of health," said Dieter.

You can't live in a food-loving family without a great deal of commentary on whatever is served, and Dieter was no slacker in the culinary appreciation department. Neither was Gabe, the little king over his board. With some mashing in their juices, the vegetables in the ratatouille were soft enough for him to eat, and he signaled his favor by slapping the tray of his highchair.

In between compliments, Dieter propelled us through the main course, telling about how he and Carl had gone to the Meyer house. Of course, the Frohlichs knew who the Nordens were in the world of real estate, and after Carl and Dieter had toured all but the first floor, which had become the offices of Wortham Realty, they insisted he have a look there as well.

"The only thing that impressed me more than how the Frohlichs worked with Uncle Carl and Aunt Frieda to retrofit the house was the scope of their business operation."

He also got a kick out of the secret compartment where Carl and Dad beat the neighbor kids at hide and seek.

"Uncle Carl said you and he used to race in Stony Creek."

"From time to time. Usually we took the path," said Dad. "We practically lived at each other's house."

"It's a grand place, but I'm equally partial to this one."

Dad smiled. "Me, too." He winked at Mom.

The oak boughs fanned the table. For us, this was the marrow of life. It was almost perfect.

We'd just gotten to the clafouti and coffee, which was another low dose tasting for me, when Dad said, "So, how are Etienne's swimming lessons going?"

"They're more practice sessions than formal lessons," said Dieter. He looked at me. "Wouldn't you say?"

Donna, who had put her hair in a ponytail and tied the gift ribbon in a looping bow, went from comedy to tragedy face.

"Yes, but they make a big difference."

"How's that," egged Marcia.

"I can swim a lot longer now, and I'm getting a little faster, but that's all, nothing fancy."

"That's all?" laughed Dieter. "Speed and endurance are my constant focus. You've come a long way, Ette."

Donna piped up. "How do you find the extra time?"

"It's not extra, just the usual morning laps," said Dieter. "We've been at it, what, almost since I got here?"

I nodded.

Donna looked like a cornered cat. Usually, everybody except Mom, Gabe, and I slept in from having worked dinner, unless they left early to work breakfast, so it wasn't surprising she didn't know.

"Doesn't your girlfriend mind?" she lashed out.

Mom put her hand on Dad's, but he left Dieter on his own.

"If I had a girlfriend, I wouldn't give her any reason to mind, but I don't have one. What gives you the impression I do?"

"The picture in your room."

So, she had come across it. Also unsurprising, but Dieter's explanation was surprising.

"Oh, Anna. I've never met her."

"Why have a picture of a girl you've never met?"

"She and her brother Drew, who's been my roommate for the past two years, are my prayer partners. She goes to school in Massachusetts, but she asked us to keep her in mind. The photo does that."

Nobody said a word. Gabe slapped his tray. He liked the clafouti.

Dieter smiled at him and continued. "We're part of a prayer group. All of us have vowed to remain pure, and we depend on each other's support. It's really helpful knowing friends of both sexes who won't give in to compromises. I'll never date, let alone have a girlfriend, until I'm interested enough in someone to consider marrying her. I'm a long way from there."

We had a good chew on that.

Finally, Dad said, "I admire your standards, Dieter."

"And your friends," said Mom. "Things are much laxer today."

"Things are, and that's why we rely so much on our mutual commitment. It keeps us more accountable than if we were on our own."

Dieter's honesty revealed to the whole family just how churchy he was. Marcia had the worst face she could get away with toward a guest at the dinner table. But poor Donna. You could just see her puppy love unraveling around the edges.

Before Dieter left, Mom showed him the picnic photos I had taken. He loved them.

"Take them," she said. "They're keepsakes for you and your parents of our time together."

"We're having more copies made for Frieda and Carl," I said, and for us as well. Like he had a prayer picture of Anna, I'd have one of him, and he'd have all of us. I hadn't realized that's what they would become. It was a far cry from what Donna had hoped for, but she'd also get the shot of Dieter she wanted.

She paid a high price of embarrassment to satisfy her curiosity, but what was really sad was that she would have preferred him to have a girlfriend than the real reason Anna was on his nightstand. Donna wasn't a runaround, but Dieter was probably the last boy she wanted to hear this from. Now she couldn't be of any interest to him, not even for the rest of the time he had left here this summer.

My curiosity was also satisfied, but I hadn't been suffering from a crush like she was. I figured all along that Anna was his girlfriend. It didn't matter to me, except it had seemed odd that he never mentioned her. Now it made perfect sense.

Chapter 25

IT WAS ANOTHER HOT sunny day, but the waiting room of the Guidance Offices was cool. The request to arrive a few minutes early for the appointment aimed at more than keeping to schedule. The thick rug, low light of the table lamps, and deep arm chairs helped calm students in trouble, but they weren't the only ones. It worked just as well for Mom and Dad and me as we silently waited for our eyes to adjust.

The only bright thing in the room was the yellow border of a crisp new *National Geographic*. I picked it up. There was an article about the World's Fair and a pull-out map of New York City. It was another reminder of Dieter's upcoming Olympic trials in New York. He planned to visit the Japan Pavilion at the Fair and find out what he could before competing in Tokyo.

The Fair exhibits were fantastic. People could go to the past or the future, where they'd stay in hotels underwater or live on the moon. If something wasn't gigantic in size, it was in idea, from the world's largest outdoor color photographs to atomic fusion. My favorite was the two hundred television sets in buildings throughout the fairgrounds. They showed lost children, so parents could f-i-n-d them and families be reunited. Dieter would get a kick out of that when I told him.

It put me in a good frame of mind for the meeting, and I was absorbed in the article when Mrs. Richardson invited us in. Her voice was as calm as her office.

"I'm so glad you were able to come in on such short notice," she said while she shook hands with Mom and Dad, and me, too. "There was a last-minute cancellation."

"We get those," said Dad.

"And also like to fill them," said Mom.

Mrs. Richardson smiled. We were off to a good start. She sat behind her desk and we faced her, but she focused on me.

"It's been a pleasure to consider your application to enter junior high school, Etienne. Your report cards indicate your academic ability, and your teachers' comments are very positive. Everyone I've conferred with, including your parents, strongly supports the request, but I haven't heard from you."

"No, ma'am," I agreed.

I could hear the wall clock tick.

"Why do you want to advance a year?"

"I went over the reasons for and against it, and I decided I really don't want to wait to learn new material. That's the main reason why, and the reasons against it don't matter that much because it's only a year's difference. Well, two years, counting skipping second grade, but that was so long ago, I don't think it counts any more. I'd have to face things I'm afraid of next year anyway."

Probably lots of kids were afraid of high school, but it was scary just admitting it.

"That's true." She paused. "Sometimes a year or two makes a difference in the ability to handle fears."

It was the polite way of asking if I was mature enough.

"I guess it might, but I'd rather face them now if it means I can learn things I don't already know. That's more important to me than anything."

"Learning is a powerful motivation." I nodded.

"Yes, ma'am."

She took her time again.

"You should know that, if I recommend your entry this fall, you would be required to meet with me once a week, and that whatever we need or want to discuss should be discussed with your parents as well. Your progress involves open communication between all of us, including your teachers."

I felt relieved. "Okay," I said enthusiastically.

"You seem to like that idea."

"Everybody will be watching out for me."

"Yes, we will, but you also will have to look out for yourself. High school might be tiring for you, especially at first. I would not want to discourage you from any activity that you enjoy, but I would caution you about involvement in extracurricular activities before you've had a chance to adjust."

"Does that mean you're saying yes?"

She sat back and folded her hands but had that sort of smile look of hers.

"Unfortunately, I may not give you that answer. I will provide my remarks to the principal, but the final decision comes from him."

But you didn't say no, either.

She turned to Mom and Dad. "You should receive a letter from Mr. Gaudet in a few days."

The way she talked at the end, it sure sounded like it was definite. She never would have said I also had to take care of myself or warned me about extracurricular activities if the answer was no.

Besides, I didn't think she'd make us wait for the principal to send a letter if she was dead set against it. She would have gotten into a discouraging explanation of how there were many factors to consider, and then Mom and Dad would have chimed in about how what was best for me was most important.

Instead, they stood up and hugged me.

"You've earned this," said Dad.

"We're so proud of you," said Mom.

Did they take it as a yes? Mrs. Richardson hadn't actually said so. All she said was if—if she recommended I enter high school this year, I'd have some rules to follow, and the principal, who hadn't even met me, made the decision.

I said "thank you" to Mrs. Richardson, but I was more honest with God about what I really thought.

This isn't the clear-cut answer I was looking for.

Is the door open or shut?

Chapter 26

MOM PACED THE KITCHEN floor with Gabe, holding him close every time the thunder boomed. Like the brief cloudburst on the Fourth of July, the storm passed quickly, but Gabe's whimpers didn't. He wouldn't let go of her, wouldn't let her put him in his highchair. Mrs. Lacroix arrived, and Mom wasn't about to have the noise of the vacuum cleaner scare him again, but she had to go over numbers with Frieda, so she said she was taking him with her to the Meyers' apartment.

"I might go to the library," I said.

Mrs. Lacroix poured herself the last of the coffee and sat with me while I finished my breakfast.

"Jack says the Amidon crew's been out on Neston Avenue for days." She took a sip. "There won't be a parcel of ground left."

The Lacroixs' son Jack had a short haul truck route that took him out to Wentwick, down to Bestbury, and back again. She said Jack said Amidon Surveying was the bellwether of construction in Neston, and it was true.

Wherever Henry Amidon's company surveyed, buildings followed. Mrs. Lacroix enjoyed passing on what Jack said about Amidon sightings across Wortham County. It gave her a conversational edge, which lasted until the sites got chain link fences with signs announcing Future Home of you-name-it.

Grocery Giant had gone in, a fluorescent behemoth that took three times longer to shop in than the A&P, but it was cheaper, so residents of the outlying towns planned trips and loaded up.

There was a lot of grumbling, but Frieda said the choice of shopping in the Historic District or the New District was an inalienable right. It only depended on what was more valuable to you, time or money. For just a few items for us at home, we still walked across the common to the A&P.

The Giant Store, as everybody called it, was part of an ugly stretch of Neston Avenue, next to the five-bay Town and Country Tires, where hills of used car, truck, and tractor tires were piled up. If you parked near that side of the Giant Store lot, you could feel the ground rumble under your feet, matching all the clanking and banging and whirring.

On its other side, a Ford dealership paved a half-acre and filled it with new and used models. The Buckminsters must have seen you couldn't have more cars without more gas. Their first filling station was near the dealership, so they got east-west traffic, and with a second on Connecticut River Road, they got the north-south traffic, including border crossers and truckers. I wondered if they had torn down the old wooden warehouse where they put the new station. I wasn't sure if it was inside the Historic District, and everything outside it was first dibs. Would that stretch of the River Road turn into another Neston Avenue?

But it wasn't all bad. The junior-senior high school was on Neston Avenue, and the Wortham County Fairgrounds had sprawled into a collection of buildings that hosted events year-round, which the farmers loved. The Fairgrounds brought so much more business to Neston Farm & Hardware that it expanded, yet nobody grumbled about how giant that got. It was the Tedeschi's of landlubber life and had as much under the sun: feed and equipment, overalls and muck boots, electrical and plumbing.

The whole New District brought in folks from the outlying villages a lot more often than they used to come into Neston, and whatever business went in next probably would bring them in, too. All I had to do to find out was go to Neston Avenue when the fence went up, but I could tell Mrs. Lacroix wanted to talk, so I said, "I wonder what it will be."

"Word's out, a bowling alley."

That wasn't so bad.

I was thinking it definitely would bring them in when she said, "Needed special approval."

"How come?"

"It's going to have a restaurant with a bar. Right next to the school, a bar could spell trouble."

That wasn't so good.

We heard Mr. Lacroix hammering.

"I best get to work," said Mrs. Lacroix.

It dawned on me that this might be the last chance to take whatever baby pictures were left of Neston Avenue. I couldn't wait. I had to take them—right away—and every other place in Neston. It didn't matter what it was.

I changed my plans.

Gone to Putnam's and a walk to the high school. Love, Ette

In less than an hour, I was the owner of an Instamatic camera. I'd still have to keep it dry, but the film popped right in and out, and all I had to do was point and shoot. It couldn't be any easier. I bought three rolls of 20-exposure and had plenty left over to get them developed. I couldn't earn a paycheck for helping at the Arms, so I got bonuses with my allowance instead, plus I had saved all my tooth fairy and birthday money. I was flush.

I walked Parker Street at top speed, which in summer could be as challenging as stepping in Stony Brook. Neston was becoming more popular in general, and with Parker Street smack in the Historic District, tourists flocked to its quaint old stores. I would have stopped in the bookstore and window-shopped the patisserie and antique shops, but I was afraid that the chain link fence might have already gone up, and I would miss what might be the last open view of the last remaining piece of pasture that used to run the whole length of old Neston Road.

I felt relieved when I got to Neston Avenue. Amidon Surveying had come and gone, but the site of the future bowling alley wasn't announced yet.

The lot had been a horse pasture between the school and Neston Farm & Hardware, and every once in a while, when we shopped there, we'd pick up a few apples from the seconds barrel and feed them to the friendly horses. They were so tame that the single wire fence with straggly posts was all that kept them in. The horses had been gone for a while, and now the wire fence was gone, too.

But the chain link fence wasn't up either. I really had gotten here in the nick of time.

I took far and near shots from east and west angles, some including the school and road, some not, before I crossed Neston Avenue at the well-marked school crossing. It was a busy crossing, being so close to the intersection of the River Road. Whoever owned the bowling alley was going to do a brisk business.

I waved to the groundskeepers chalking baseball field lines for tonight's summer league game. They waved back and eyeballed me while I took a shot of the ground where the fence had recently been, the post holes sprouting tufts of new grass. Across the pasture, I got a couple of men in dirty overalls coming out of the hardware store and the help taking down the Fourth of July sale bunting.

As fast as I could scoot across, I trespassed the lot over to the store. From that angle, I knelt on the springy ground so I could get a shot of the high school looming beyond the pasture. What with all the natural horse fertilizer over the years, the pasture had the greenest grass.

Like the empty raft, at first it seemed kind of stupid to take pictures of things that were gone or not there yet, but I decided that it all meant something. Photographs of things and places are as important as ones of people.

And they would change as much as people did, just like Gabe was changing in the photographs I took of him every Sunday. You couldn't see him growing before your eyes, but all it took was a couple of weeks to see the changes in the pictures.

Chapter 27

THE LETTER FROM MR. Gaudet was addressed to Mom and Dad. It must have been sent right away, so it arrived way sooner than I expected, but I had less patience waiting for Mom to open it than I'd had waiting to receive it.

Mr. Gaudet wrote that Mrs. Richardson's recommendation was strong, and he supported her plan to work with me, Mom and Dad, and my teachers on the transition to seventh grade. He welcomed me to the incoming class.

It was a yes!

I jumped up and down and thanked God for the very clear-cut answer, silently of course.

"Wow," said Donna.

Mom hugged me. "Congratulations, Ette."

"For what," said Marcia, coming into the kitchen.

"I'm entering seventh grade this fall."

"Oh," she said.

It sounded more like eew. She bit into a banana.

"Marcia," said Mom.

The banana bulged in her cheek. "What?"

Mom gave her a you-know-what look.

"Congratulations," she said. "You'll probably never see me."

She couldn't have been more comforted by that than I was.

"I'm glad I don't have to follow you," said Donna.

Sometimes teachers expected kids to follow in the footsteps of an older sister or brother who'd done well in their classes.

"Thanks," I said. It was a compliment.

"Thanks," said Marcia in a different tone of voice to Donna.

"I just meant—"

"I know what you meant." Marcia cut Donna off and looked me over. "I'll have to work on your clothes."

"Fine," I said. It was.

There was a rule in our house that whatever we earned would be split three ways: one third to saving for college; one third to general saving for the future; and unless we wanted to add more to savings, one third was ours to spend. When we finished college or turned twenty-one or got married, whichever came first, but preferably in that order, it was all ours.

Fashion magazines and sewing patterns were Marcia's spending favorites. She had known by her freshman year that she wanted to attend the Fashion Institute. She had made a very realistic cardboard-backed paper doll of herself and dressed her effigy with outfits that she designed or cut from magazines. She saved a lot on school clothes by sewing from scratch, even if she used expensive fabrics, which Mom and Dad appreciated, and she definitely had a fashion look all her own.

As far I was concerned, Marcia mostly wanted to save face for herself, but for once, I'd be on her better side. Besides, this way, how I looked compared to the other girls would be the least of my worries. She'd make sure I looked good.

But I was still tingling with suspense. I went up to my room and cleanly slit the sealed envelope Dieter had given me—his prayers for me, waiting to be opened after I had an answer from school. It had a single sheet of hole-punched loose-leaf paper with neatly lettered lines.

Durand, Etienne

6/14/1964 R1
Make your will clear in Etienne's decision to skip 6th grade and go to junior high school
A1

6/14/1964 R2
Appointment with guidance counselor in early July
A2

6/14/1964 R3

Prompt answer from the school
A3

I read it over a couple of times. He had begun "my file" in his prayer journal the very same day he had said, "I'll pray for you." I had been amazed when he said that. I didn't doubt for a minute that Mom and Dad prayed for me, but it was the first time I'd heard anyone put it that way. "Let us pray" was what Rev. Bouchard said for silent prayer in church. The only prayer we ever said aloud at home was grace before meals.

R was for request, and A for answer, and Dieter had left lots of extra lines to put the date of the answer and what it was. His prayer journal was down to a system, with requests so specific, he sure expected answers.

R1 wasn't a surprise to me, but R2 and R3 were, but then I could see why he would ask for those things. The longer the wait for the appointment, the more it would have been hanging over my head, a cloud over the summer.

If I had known R2 was in there, I would have been bugging Mom to find out if the appointment had been made.

As for R3, I had been on pins and needles to find out the answer, and it would have been another cloud if that had taken a long time to arrive.

I noticed that Dieter didn't request a yes answer, although that's what I'd really been hoping for. Instead, he asked for God's will to be made known to me.

I used a blue pen to fill out the answers, tucking in a note below my name.

7/10/1964 Friday
I opened this prayer journal entry for me from Dietrich Norden today.

A1 7/10/1964 Friday
I prayed last month for Mrs. Richardson, a high school guidance counselor, to shut the door if it wasn't right for me to skip sixth grade. She said the principal, Mr. Gaudet, made the final decision. They both opened the door, so I guess that means it's your will, God.

A2 7/7/1964 Tuesday

Mom and Dad and I got an appointment with Mrs. Richardson because of a last-minute cancellation. That was very early July. I don't know how long we would have had to wait if that hadn't happened.

A3 7/10/1964 Friday
We got the answer today from Mr. Gaudet, saying I was accepted into 7th grade this fall. That was very prompt.

Thank you, God, for everything.

Now I understood why Dieter waited to tell me what his requests were. I felt really special. But it felt so personal, too, not just with Dieter, but with writing to God like I was talking to him, like he was right there.

Dieter had said something else, too. "This is when it gets interesting." Now I understood that as well. This was a whole new way of praying. It was risky. If the appointment had taken long to get, and the mail had been delayed, and the door had shut, I would have felt awfully disappointed and not very interested in a prayer journal. Instead, it was all blue skies.

Even so, I knew better than to think I wouldn't run into some storms. After all, I'd be in the same home room as Janice and Tina.

I was willing to take the risk. I had a lineup of things I'd already started asking God for. I made a quick list until I could get to Woolworth's for a new three-ring binder, something sturdy that would last. I guessed everything would get even more interesting.

I went to the Arms and caught Dad in an office huddle with Frieda and Carl. All three read the letter.

"This calls for a celebration," said Dad.

"Your wish is our command," said Frieda.

"I want to go to the lake again, all together." That was a lot harder than if I had said pizza lunch at Leo's, but I didn't want it just for myself. "It could be a going away party for Dieter, too."

"Let's ring him and see what he says." Carl phoned and Dieter came down in a minute.

"It's an open door," I said.

"You had the appointment already?"

"And the letter." I handed it to him.

As he read, he grinned so much his pearly whites showed. He knew I had opened his envelope, and he knew all the answers to his prayers.

"We're going to have a picnic to celebrate, and for you as a going home party," I said.

"There's only one thing to do," said Frieda.

"What?"

"Look at the calendar."

What with big bookings, and the work schedule set through the following week, and Dieter leaving after that, there was one and only one day that was possible.

"There is another thing," I added. "Pray it doesn't rain."

"You're starting to sound like a certain someone I know," said Frieda.

"I do?"

A flicker of interest crossed Dad's face.

"I'll have to put my thinking cap on." Frieda tapped her temple. "Whoever could that be?"

Dieter put his arm around her shoulders.

"I knew it would come to me."

We just laughed, and I didn't say anything. That prayer, I really, really meant.

And I had another. I still had some talking to do.

Chapter 28

I HAD A LUMP in my throat at the thought of telling Debbie and Paula. I'd been the new kid, and a scrawny undersized one at that, the day I joined them in third grade, and the way they mother-henned me, they had made a jittery day into one of the happiest of my life. After that, summer camp together had bonded us in the way that, well, only camp can. We'd been three peas in a pod for a long time.

The meetup was at Paula's again, since it was on the way to Lakeshore Drive, but we left earlier than usual because it would be our longest trip yet.

There was also another difference. Since Debbie had been so put out with getting stuck at Theresa's, and then disappointed with the Chauncey Smith site, I washed my hands of any problems she might have with this week's destination. The main decision was how far we could make it in good time. Either way, east or west side of Lakeshore Drive, we'd pass the previous disappointments.

Last time, I'd said, "Here. You decide." I had handed them the map.

"So, what'll it be," I asked as Paula handed the map back.

"East side, as far as Chadwick Lodge," said Debbie.

"Check."

Stillwater Bay Road was public, so we wouldn't be trespassing on it, but the wooded paths surrounding the lodge were private. I wasn't about to contradict Debbie's choice, though. I definitely needed to keep my mouth zipped.

Since we had already traveled most of the ride, we were better prepared for conditions and made good time. We didn't pause for sightseeing and didn't slow our pace until we entered new territory past the Chauncey Smith Historic Site. The road started curving west. We were finally on the south shore, the remotest part of the lake. Despite the densely packed brush, a healthy doe and fawn silently crossed the road ahead of us and disappeared. They were there and gone before we braked.

We arrived at Stillwater Bay Road, which led to what Mrs. Racine called the gilded age colony. Unless the Wards and Cotes had us beat, after the Arms, Chadwick Lodge was the fanciest place in Neston. Being a residence now, it wasn't as well known as our inn, but it was famous enough for Debbie to want to see it as much the original Ward house on Point Droit.

The thick canopy overhead offered welcoming cool shade. It was a wonderland in winter, bowing under snow. A few narrow lanes splintered off toward waterside cabins.

As we approached, the canopy opened up, revealing the sky above and a glimpse of the lake and lodge ahead. We came to the end of the road, which encircled a round pavilion. Driveways extended like umbrella spokes from the pavilion to the houses. If we wanted to turn tail, now was our opportunity.

After circling the pavilion twice, Debbie brought us to a halt and said, "Looks like this is the end of the line."

"We can't stay here," said Paula.

"What are you whispering for? Why not?"

"You can see for yourself. There's no place for us to go."

"What's wrong with where we're at?"

"I'm not eating here," said Paula.

"Me neither," I said.

"We'll have to eat at Potash Park again," said Paula.

Outvoted, Debbie gave up. "Alright, but I'm not leaving until I get a good look."

We sat down in the pavilion. If there was anything to be seen, it was fruit trees, bushes, and flower beds galore. Unlike many places where the houses were tucked out of sight among firs and pines, the area closest to the water had been cleared of all but shade trees, but the houses were still concealed. Privacy walls of arborvitae were trimmed to a uniform height.

All the same, you could tell the houses were unique works of art with at least two massive stone chimneys, tons of gables, and wide sleeping porches. Like every place on the lake, they were built to face the glistening water, and Stillwater Bay, which had a breakwater, truly was calm.

Towering above the others was Chadwick Lodge, which had been the gathering lodge back in the day. The Greenbergs, the people who owned it, were family friends, and I knew they weren't using it this summer. The lodge was furnished like a camp and felt like one, which was very surprising since it was so big. Even though Chadwick Lodge was a home now, it was still the Grand Central of the colony, which was named after it. It was the jewel in the crown.

Chadwick Colony had tennis courts, a small golf course, a boathouse with a covered deck on top, and parties. Mrs. Greenberg had said the summer people still gathered on the deck once a week, rain or shine, just like they had in the good old days.

We were plenty close to get an eyeful of the lodge's upper stories, but Debbie took out her binoculars. Anyone glancing toward the road would notice us just as well. We stuck out like a color guard.

"What if somebody comes out?" Paula said nervously.

"I'll say I was looking at a bird," said Debbie.

She took her time panning before she settled on a particular window. She could've read the fine print on a diploma mounted on the wall inside. Even if the Greenbergs weren't there, they often let friends stay for weeks at a time. They also had full-time caretakers. None of them would cotton to it.

No two ways about it, that was snooping.

This time, Paula dodged on looking through the binoculars before Debbie offered. "What time is it?" she asked.

I looked at my watch.

"We'd better get going."

Nobody came out, and if anybody noticed us, we were obviously not enough of a threat to bother asking what in the world we were doing. We weren't the first ones to come out to gawk.

Paula hightailed it off of Stillwater Bay Road. She must have been a little burned up because she kept a fast lead all the way back to Potash Park. From the look on Debbie's face when she dismounted, the table by the fire pit looked a little more inviting this time.

I bit into my tame ham sandwich, which I'd chosen so I'd fit in for a change, and unfolded the map again.

On paper, circling the lake seemed reasonable, but checking the map again, I saw the circumference of the lake was too long for us to go it alone. We'd thought we might make it in six or seven segments, but that part of the planning had fallen short. None of our parents would let us be gone as long as we would need in order to reach the farthest point south and return in the time limit we were allowed to be out on our own. Going fast and stopping for less time, we had just reached that limit on the eastern side. We definitely already had on the western side, since I had misjudged the distance between Leeward Lane and Mallard's Head as the crow flies and we'd had to hustle home. I wasn't misjudging this time. I knew better now, and I had to announce the bad news.

"This is as far as we can go in one trip," I said.

"What?" said Debbie angrily.

"Are you sure?" said Paula.

"Well, we're here," I pointed. "And if we went farther, by the time you add in stopping to eat and looking around, we wouldn't be able to get back in time," I said as they hovered over the map.

"It seemed a lot shorter in the car," said Paula.

"We don't have to stop and eat. We could just bike," said Debbie.

I didn't want a race. Even if breaking bread together wasn't all it could be, exploring was part of the fun.

"I can't," said Paula. "If I don't take a lunch, Mother will be upset."

"So you don't have to tell her."

"And what? Throw away food?"

"How's she going to know?"

"I am not going to waste a perfectly good meal, especially not when I know I'll be hungry."

Atta girl.

"It looks like we'll just have to leave it at this," said Paula.

"We could, but it won't be the same as saying we went the whole way around the lake," said Debbie.

Check. That would be disappointing. But I had an idea.

"We just need to get dropped off or picked up. There's enough room in the back of our station wagon for two bikes. I'm sure Mom would take us, but we'd need another car. Or we could just come separately and meet."

"We don't have chauffeur service at my house," said Debbie.

"I would never ask Mother to do that," said Paula, "and Daddy doesn't have time."

"Okay, then what if we ask Theresa George to go with us? Her father said they had a truck big enough for our bikes. A truck could probably fit one more."

"There's just one problem," said Debbie.

"What?"

"Theresa. I thought this was going to be just the three of us."

"It was, but why can't it be the four of us now?"

"Because I don't want the four of us, I just want my friends."

"You said you wanted to go all the way around," said Paula, "and now's your chance."

"Maybe you'd rather be friends with her."

Paula was surprised. "She'd be doing us a favor, you know."

This was making my big news a lot harder to say.

"I do want to be friends with Theresa. I'm skipping sixth grade and we'll both be in seventh grade this fall."

I hadn't meant to say it like I wanted Theresa's friendship only for that reason, but Paula didn't take any of it the wrong way. She jumped up and hugged me. "Ette, that's great!"

Debbie was completely thrown for a loop, so I went on.

"I thought she was nice to us, and if she wants to be friends with me, then I want to with her. Just because I make new friends doesn't mean we won't still be best friends."

"You do so know we won't," said Debbie. "We'll never be in the same classes again—we won't even be in the same school for a whole year."

This was not the one for all, all for one I hoped it would be.

"So what? That happens to lots of friends in different grades, but it doesn't change anything between them. I'm going to miss both of you an awful lot. That's a really hard part of skipping. I thought we'd be together all through school."

"You'll be in the same home room with Peggy, probably the same classes."

"I guess so," I said—and I remembered that Debbie had started getting mad if I didn't keep my distance from Peggy on the school playground.

"I'm done riding with you," she said.

Paula's jaw dropped. "What?"

"Why are you being this way?" I said. "First you want to finish, now you don't."

"If I want to be ignored, I might as well go home. It's bad enough I'm number four there, but I won't be number four with you, too."

"You're jealous!" I said.

Paula called it differently. "You are being selfish, Debbie Fortin," she said. "You wreck our plans, and I suppose you want to throw me out with the bathwater, too."

"It's up to you. You can ride with Theresa, or you can ride with me."

"Deb-bie!" said Paula.

Debbie stood up.

"Come on, Debbie, don't go," I said.

But it was too late. Debbie got on her bike.

"We can't let her go alone," I said.

"I know," said Paula, and we scrambled to catch up to her. She was being unreasonable, but if anything happened and we weren't with her, we'd get in trouble and there might not be any more bike riding the rest of the summer.

Besides, sometimes you had to stick together because it was the right thing to do, even if it hurt.

Chapter 29

THE SUN FELT GOOD as Dieter and I sat cross-legged on our towels.

"We got your note," I said. "Mom and Dad said it was really nice. I thought so, too."

It was like a grownup had written it. Donna had left the room to go cry.

I remain overjoyed with the graciousness of your hospitality, the beauty of your taste, the warmth of your home, and the enormous enjoyment of lingering over a delicious spread. Thank you for a memorable day. Your friendship is a delight. ~Dieter

"I meant every word," Dieter said. "I had a wonderful time."

"So did I."

Even if Donna had gotten a little out line. Apparently it didn't faze him, and now that she had dealt with the mystery girl, I decided to ask Dieter another personal question that had arisen in my mind. I knew what he prayed for me, but I wondered, "What do you and your friends pray about?"

"This past year, it's mostly been about overcoming temptations. They seem to be multiplying, which is why some of us took an oath of purity, and since then, we've prayed for God to provide a hedge of protection around us."

"Like a bulwark."

"Exactly. And God is faithful to protect our minds and emotions, but we have to remain faithful to do our own part, too."

"How do you do that?"

"I keep my focus on him, mainly through the Word."

"You mean the Bible?"

He nodded. "If I focus on sin, eventually it will take over my mind and feed my emotions until it reaches the physical stage, and then I'd be on the offense."

"So it builds up a little at a time."

"Usually. Just like growing in the Lord does, too." He thought for a second. "Although growth spurts can also happen. But overcoming temptation really starts at a deeper level, in the spirit."

I couldn't picture that. "What do you mean, in the spirit?"

"It's the innermost part of our being. God created male and female in his image, so each of us has a body. It's like a house for our spirit. The body dies, but God made the spirit to live forever."

"So how do you start there?"

"By choosing to be guided by God's spirit. The Holy Spirit comes to live in you when you give your life completely to Jesus."

I was sure he had. "What did you do, to make sure you were all in?"

"I prayed a prayer that Billy Graham recommends, but I saw it as more of a guideline than a script. I put the prayer in my own words. Do you know who he is?"

"Isn't he the man with crusades on TV?"

"That's him."

"Well then, I sort of know who he is. We don't have a TV, and one time, when I went to Carl and Frieda's to watch theirs, a crusade was on. I only saw part of it."

"I watched a whole crusade series that lasted for weeks, and the message stayed with me. I became very convicted of my sins. I wanted to repent—to turn my life around."

I laughed.

He looked surprised.

"Sorry. I'm not laughing at you, I just can't see you being so bad you had to turn your life around. Especially when you aren't that old."

"You wouldn't say so if you could have seen me then. I belonged to a group of well-to-do private school boys who were very good at arrogance, and I became the leader from the start because I was the most arrogant. Some older boys ingrained it in us that we were too special and too important for the rules to apply to us like they do to other people. Turning our heads like that made it a lot easier for us to believe we could do no wrong. Outdoing each other became the name of the game. Not all the boys were like that, but for me, it was a way to fit in. Usually, if someone did manage to get caught doing something serious, their parents were willing to pay their way out. We began to believe that the bad things we'd done, things that we knew, deep down inside, were wrong, would never catch up to us."

"So how did you change?"

"I was watching the last crusade in the series, and it finally sunk in that Jesus took the fall for me. I needed bailing out myself, but it wasn't anything my parents could do for me. So at the end, when people who were ready to give their hearts to Jesus were invited to go down to the stage and pray, I knew that's what I needed to do. It took a few weeks, but I confessed that I was a sinner and I asked God's forgiveness. I placed my faith in Jesus for dying for my sin and promised to follow him forever."

"That's all?"

"The basics, but it's not a prayer to be said lightly. You have to really mean it."

"What if you want to, but you're not sure?"

"You can ask God to help you be sure. The Holy Spirit is called the Helper, and God often also uses other people who are walking with Jesus to help."

Rev. Bouchard came to mind, although I thought of him as the minister, not as walking with Jesus. I guess it's supposed to be the same thing, but he never put it that way. Dieter was the only one I knew who did.

Chapter 30

WHEN I WAS ALONE in the window seat, I thought it all over. I could see why Dieter and his friends prayed for overcoming temptation, especially him. His problem wasn't only a little fame.

I remembered how he looked away from Brenda. He asked me if he could touch me when he was showing me how to do the back flip, and he hadn't touched that woman's fingers when she held out the $100 tip to him. And he'd never led Donna on, never had anything more than regular conversations. He didn't seek attention from women and girls, but he couldn't prevent them from going after him, and that was just in Neston. He'd be in New York soon, maybe Tokyo, and attending college in another year. Only boys attended Yale, like the private school he went to, but that didn't cut any ice. Maybe prayer really was the only solution, but he did take practical steps.

I noticed that he didn't wear his cross any more, but that's because it probably would have been stolen while we went swimming. One time we came back to the table and when he reached in to his duffel for his towel, everything he'd neatly folded was tangled, and a message was in his shirt pocket. Not a business card or note, but flowery stationery with a number for him to call.

"You should probably check your duffel," he said.

I didn't think anyone cared about me, but I did anyway.

"Is your change purse there?"

"Yes."

"Is all the money in it?"

"I think so."

"If I were you, I'd leave it at home from now on. I'm sure Mr. Ted would give us credit for a day if we needed it."

It kept up. In fact, it got worse. He always looked at the messages just long enough to make sure there wasn't something actually important, tore them up, and threw them in the Beach Bun trash. But then one day his handkerchief was missing, and my duffel had been ransacked, too. There was a note for me. *Girls don't belong with grown men. Stay where you belong and leave him alone.*

Mr. Ted was always at the store when we got to the beach, so we went in and Dieter asked him if we could pay him to stow our bags.

"Tell you what," he said. "There's an old locker around back. Buy a combination lock and it's yours to use whenever you're here."

So we did.

A lot of boys probably would have gone up to the room or called the numbers, but Dieter went in the opposite direction. I already didn't like the direction Debbie and Paula were going. All that talking about boys and imagining kissing and going steady. The only thing left was to give in to temptation. I was more surprised about Paula than Debbie. She stood up to looking through the binoculars that second time, but usually, she seemed to toe the line because she was the minister's daughter and wasn't allowed to cross it, not because she didn't want to. The way her parents boxed her in wasn't helping.

Not that my friends were very different from most kids, though. Nowadays, people dated and went steady and held hands and made out all they wanted. Times were different from when Mom and Dad got together.

I wasn't interested in boys yet but I would be eventually, and thanks to Dieter, I saw a choice for when that happened. I liked the idea of staying pure, of waiting to date until I was interested enough in someone to consider marrying him.

Besides, why would I want a boy who'd been around the block a bunch of times? What kind of boys would want me if I'd been?

It wasn't just help with temptations that interested me about following Jesus, though. One thing I learned from the Psalm sermons was that Jesus was the good shepherd. Jesus looked after his sheep in lots of ways. As I understood Dieter, and I did believe him, there was just one thing that made the whole thing really work. I had to give my heart to Jesus first.

I understood that Jesus died for our sins. Every week, we had a moment of silence to think about the things we'd done wrong, and then the whole church recited the "Our Father," and as far as I knew, we were forgiven.

I wasn't a juvenile delinquent, but there had been plenty of times I hated Marcia so much I wished she were dead. I figured confessing my sin silently was enough. It was only between me and God. All the same, hating is wrong even if you don't do anything about it.

But there was something else—and it wasn't only between me and God. It had weighed me down since last Christmas.

For the gift exchange lottery at school, I had drawn Norman Levesque. Norman was one of a slew of Levesques in Wortham County. He had dirt under his nails and smelled stale. It came with the territory, since he lived in one of the tenements on Connecticut River Road.

The timber frame units had been built back in the day to house lumberjacks, river log drivers, and sawyers. If the General Store hadn't been in their midst, the buildings might have been torn down, but the penny candy and dry goods emporium anchored them, and once Neston got its historic preservation status, the apartments were there to stay. After all, it was the oldest part of the original settlement, even if it wasn't the prettiest picture. The second floor porches jutting out toward the river were held up with rotting beams. The buildings couldn't be propped up much longer, but there was no place else so cheap to live in town, and without those renters, Neston's saw mill would be over a barrel.

That should have inspired some gift giving generosity in me, but it didn't. Somebody had given Norman a PEZ dispenser for Christmas the year before, so I figured he'd be happy if he got a puzzle. I bought the cheapest, cheesiest puzzle ever. The cardboard box it came in was so flimsy the seams cracked when I wrapped it.

You should have seen his face when he first saw it. And then you should have seen his face when he unwrapped it. The puzzle was as bad as PEZ. The whole fifth grade saw it.

Worse, in the lottery, Norman had gotten one of the Frink twins, and everybody saw her smile when she unwrapped what he gave her, a long, warm scarf. It was hand-knit and it looked really soft and she wore it all winter, no matter what her sister wore.

I never felt so ashamed in my life. Ever since then, my conscience had bothered me, but I swept it under the rug. I never called it a sin, and I never confessed it during the silent time. But it was plain as day.

I went to my room and locked the door and knelt next to the bed. I'd confess my sins so I could invite Jesus into my heart. I whisper-prayed into the quilt, but God would hear.

"God, please forgive me about Marcia."

What about her?

I don't know if it was only my conscience talking, but it was just like God was right there.

"For hating her sometimes."

When?

"Well, there was that time..." I went into it, and I said it was wrong and said I was sorry and would Jesus forgive me?

Yes.

Is that all?

No, no it wasn't.

I could see where this was going. I named the other times and confessed the awful things I thought, like how glad I was whenever something went wrong for Marcia, even the time she sprained her ankle so bad she had to use crutches. The hardest was admitting my favorite word for Marcia was crummy, since it wasn't any different from Janice and Tina calling me Eddie. Eddie was just another name for crummy.

But by the time I got to Norman, I was feeling I was getting the hang of asking God's forgiveness.

"God, please forgive me for giving Norman Levesque that puzzle. It was cheap and awful."

Which really meant I was cheap and awful. I scrunched up the quilt and cried into it. "I was mean."

I didn't like thinking I was mean at all, but if you think mean things and use mean words and do mean things, you're mean.

"I don't want to. Be mean."

I didn't have anything else to say. I took a deep breath. Dieter had told me he felt cleansed after he confessed his sin. That's how he put it. Not clean. Cleansed. It's true. I felt cleansed. I felt a lot better.

How does Norman feel?

I heard Mom calling me to dinner.

"I'll have to get back to you on that, God."

What about him?

Meaning, will I get back to Norman? Confessing to God is one thing, but owning up in person, well, that was different. If I also had to get back to Norman, I'd need some help. Besides the Holy Spirit, I knew just who to ask.

But something else, way bigger, was holding me back from giving my heart to Jesus.

It was promising to follow him forever that I wasn't sure about. Jesus sure wouldn't like it if I broke my promise.

I knew the drill on that. It was better not to make a promise in the first place.

Chapter 31

THE ONE TIME I'D been around to see tempers flare in the Arms kitchen, Carl had said, "Cool your engines." That's all Debbie needed to do.

I figured a whole day was enough time, so after I got home from the beach, I called her. Cathy answered, and her palm only partially muffled the mouthpiece while I heard Debbie telling her to say she wasn't home.

I gave her another day. That should be plenty of time to cool off. The second time, she answered, and when I said, "Hi, Debbie, it's Ette," she hung up.

Finally, I called after church on Sunday. Even if she wasn't cooled down, it didn't seem possible she could stay really mad right after going to church.

She answered the phone, and I pleaded with her. "Debbie, don't hang up."

"*What* do you want?"

"I want to talk to you. I don't understand what's going on."

"I told you."

"Theresa?"

"Bingo, Einstein."

"I want us to make up."

"Then say you're sorry."

"Me! What did I do wrong?"

"Forget it."

She hung up. This was three strikes. I was out. She wasn't just still too hot to patch things up, she had no intention of cooling off.

She dumped me! Just like Tina and Janice. I didn't get it. Girlfriends and boyfriends broke up, but who ever heard of your regular friends dumping you, especially your best friend? And calling me Einstein just to make me feel bad for skipping again. If she ever heard Janice and Tina calling being called Eddie, she'd chime right in.

Well, imagining another way she'd hurt me wasn't helping anything, and holding a grudge back at her because she had one toward me made no sense. A grudge doesn't make you feel better, either. The pit of my stomach was already bunched up, and that would make it worse. But I did wonder if I'd have to avoid her, too.

I wracked my brain. Had I done something wrong?

I'd called her jealous, but she must have seen I was more surprised than mad when I said it. And she was jealous.

She didn't want to be friend number four when she was kid number four at home. It wasn't my fault her parents called their children to dinner by number. That probably wasn't such a good idea. But Paula and I never numbered her off that way. I always called them both best friends.

And she was jealous that Peggy and I would be in seventh grade. Once that happened, there wouldn't be anything she could do to keep us apart.

It seemed like she flipped as quickly as a coin, but now I could see that her reasons had been building up for a long time.

Anyway, I wasn't the one who let go. Or hung up. Or refused to make up. It hadn't been up to me or Paula to lose Debbie's friendship. I didn't understand it or like it or want it, but she made that choice. All I could do was forgive her and hope she'd change her mind.

But Debbie didn't get to tell me I couldn't be friends with somebody else. If Theresa was interested, I wanted to bike with her, and Paula sounded like she did, too.

The way Theresa looked so happy to see us, had she thought we stopped by deliberately while we were out biking? Theresa's mother had called us her friends. I wondered if that's how Theresa described us at home.

Friendly definitely described her. When we saw her in the cafeteria and on the playground, she was always nice, but what with two best friends in the same grade who lived near by, I thought it would be disloyal of me to become friends with Theresa, and because her parents and mine had restaurant businesses.

That seemed silly now. It was thinking like Debbie: you can only have one and not both. Besides, neither business lost customers because of the other, and another friend would have been really nice. But business did affect friendships, or the lack of them.

As a daughter of two owners of the Arms, it could be hard to make friends, especially with kids whose parents worked there. Mom, Dad, Frieda, and Carl held the senior positions, and other management positions were few and far between. On the other hand, many junior positions kept the Arms running, and although those jobs were just as important in making the inn special, the kids whose parents did them kept their distance from me. It wasn't the sort of place where they could pop in and see their parents at work like they did at the A&P or the Giant Store, and they treated me like I was off-limits, too.

Debbie and Paula were the exceptions. Their parents didn't work at the Arms and they weren't intimidated by it or my family or our house, which they'd been to lots of times.

Then there was Lisa Ward. When you owned the fanciest restaurant and inn in the county, most kids hated you because they figured you thought you were better than them, but she despised me because she wanted to rub it in that we were beneath the Wards, just like everybody else.

But those threats did not exist at all between Theresa and me. If anything, as daughters of restauranteurs, we were equals. Sure, she would have her loyalty and I would have mine, but we could get along. If I'd been as nice to her as she was to me, we might have been friends a long time ago.

Like they say, there's no time like the present. I wasn't counting on Debbie changing her mind by Thursday, and Paula and I needed to figure something out. I called her.

"Mother only let me bike around the lake when I promised her there'd be three of us," she said. "I can't go if it's only you and me."

"Yeah, I wouldn't be allowed either."

This is what they call between a rock and a hard place. Four was too many for Debbie, which I didn't understand, and two was too few for our parents, which I did.

"What about asking Theresa?" I said.

"I don't know. I mean, it's fine with me, but Mother will have to agree. She doesn't know the Georges like she knows the Fortins."

In other words, they didn't attend the Meetinghouse.

"Alright."

I looked up Theresa's phone number. Four Georges were listed with the same number. They had their own party line. The line picked up after a single long ring.

"Theresa George speaking."

"Hi, Theresa, it's Etienne Durand."

"Ette! Hi! Can you hold on while I pick up in my room?"

I held. She had her own phone? She sure sounded excited. I heard her phone open.

"You can hang up now, Mama."

I heard the other line click.

"I'm really glad you called," she said. "Do you want to come over?"

She was making this very easy.

"Yeah, but I was calling to see if you want to go biking on Lakeshore Drive with Paula and me this Thursday."

"What about Debbie?"

"I don't think she wants to any more."

"Really?"

"It's kind of hard to explain. Anyway, there have to be at least three of us to go biking. Paula and I thought you might want to go."

"Want to? I'd love to!"

Theresa was a lot more enthusiastic than I knew.

"The thing is," I hemmed, "we wanted to bike past your house, to where we haven't been, but we can't be gone that long."

"I'll ask Nikky to take me to pick you up at the restaurant, and we can ride out from my house."

"Are you sure?"

"Oh, yeah."

"And there will be enough room for all of us and the bikes?"

"Plenty! I'll call you back."

Chapter 32

THE WHOLE THING WAS settled in no time flat. In fact, Mom and Mrs. Bouchard preferred that we were biking from the Georges instead of asking for twice as much time to ride all the way over so we could head out from there.

"Bring a windbreaker," said Theresa. "The breeze can get cool."

I filled my duffel with my rolled-up jacket, map, and camera case with extra film. The time to drive to Theresa's still had to be taken into account, so Paula and I left her house earlier than usual and rode to the North Shore Restaurant. We were on the lookout for a pickup truck when the inboard with the wheelhouse that Dieter and I had seen several times came gliding toward the Marina—and there was Theresa, as tan as a sailor, waving from its railing!

"Ahoy," she hollered.

The crowd eating on the North Shore wharf all turned to watch as the *Odyssey*—she was close enough to see her name now— slowed to a crawl. Nikky was in the wheelhouse. Theresa let down some tube-shaped bumpers to protect the boat while docking. Gregory was waiting on the Marina pier, and as soon as Nikky cut the engine, he caught the lines Theresa threw and knotted them onto cleats. She hopped off.

"Ahoy," I said back. "This is great."

"I thought we were going in a truck," said Paula.

"Didn't I say?" Theresa laughed.

"No. I don't know if I can go in a boat."

"Oh, there's nothing to be afraid of."

"I'm not afraid. I have to ask my mother."

"Oh, of course. You can use the phone in the Marina. Do you need to call, too, Ette?"

"Maybe I should."

Theresa took us into the cool damp building.

"Let me call first," I said to Paula, "so you can tell your mom that mine said I could go."

While Dieter and I had first seen the boat from the raft on the day of the picnic, we hadn't been the only ones. Mom said everyone else had noticed the *Odyssey*, too. She was all for me having a ride in it.

Paula was readied for her call with additional assurances from Gregory that all the George men were licensed marine pilots. After all, they owned the Marina. He promised life jackets were used at all times, even on calm water days like today.

She dialed and I held my breath. I could just picture this whole thing falling apart in no time flat.

The phone rang and rang.

"There's no answer," said Paula like the sky was about to fall.

"Then hang up," said Theresa practically. "There's really nothing to worry about."

Paula hung up. "I'm going?" she giggled.

"Then let's go!" said Theresa.

The deck diners watched as we went into the bow cockpit, where she fitted us with orange vests over our windbreakers and gave us kerchiefs for our hair. Gregory handed our bikes over to Nikky, who secured them snugly in the stern cockpit and stored our bags in the wheelhouse.

As soon as Nikky picked up speed, all that bundling made sense. The air whipped around us, and was a lot cooler on the broad lake than on the shoreline.

Paula and I were amazed at how the places so familiar to us looked so different from the middle of the lake. Theresa, however, was the Mark Twain of Île de L'eau. She'd known things from the lake point of view for her whole life, and she explained the navigation buoys and markers, which I'd never paid attention to. They were like words you never noticed until after you learned what they meant.

Long before we recognized their houses on it, she pointed out Mallard's Head and said, "There's our starting point. We could bike over there to Fish Hook Point."

We followed her finger to another spot.

"It's a few miles by land," Theresa warned. "If you want."

"Let's!" said Paula. She was picking up Theresa's enthusiasm.

"Okay," I said.

If Theresa recommended it, I figured she had her reasons. It would also take us farther around the circumference of the lake. Maybe she would bike all the rest with us.

Avoiding the red buoys near the sandy beach end of Mallard's Head, Nikky slowed for the approach and steered toward a deep water boat house, where the waterfront was built up with a stone seawall. We watched Tony, who stopped mowing the lawn to help unload. We grabbed our bags and got out.

"They'll bring your bikes up," said Theresa, leading us across the flagstone porch. It was almost as impressive as the outermost terrace at the Arms.

We went into her house, where she slipped off her boat shoes next to a line of varied sizes on a sisal rug. We followed suit with our sneakers. The hall tile was cool under our muffled sockfoot steps.

From the outside, the house looked regular, but inside, the doorways and valances in recessed windows were arched. Paula and I lollygagged past a wide arch to an open area.

Theresa backtracked. "I'll show you around in a minute," she said, smiling.

Mama met us at the kitchen. "Come, come in," she said. "Have a glass of milk, to tide you over."

We eyeballed the white domed breakfast nook and the arched cast iron door of an oven built into a white brick wall. Meat with garlic was resting on the counter.

"That smells delicious," said Paula. She was full of surprises today.

"Gyro, for the pita," said Mama. "I have it ready in a minute."

"What's that?"

"A lamb sandwich," said Theresa.

She led us past the dining room, a large and formal room with a massive polished table. We crossed the hall for a peek in a study used as an office, and back to the living room. The end tables were topped with ship models, the pillows were embroidered with anchors, a ship's wheel was mounted above the fireplace, and an interesting piece of driftwood had been made into a floor lamp. All the walls were bright white and covered from floor to ceiling with framed nautical charts.

We passed closed doors, including one where a television blared *I Love Lucy* through the door.

"That's Pappouli and Yaiyai's room," said Theresa.

We came to Theresa's room. The aquatic theme continued there as well. A chart of Île de L'eau took up the better part of the wall facing the lake. All she had to do was look out the window and match everything up. Her mirror was set into a brass porthole. Her bookcase was made out of an old rowboat, and it was filled with containers of shells and sea glass.

"Did you collect these yourself?" asked Paula.

"Yes, in Greece. Papa and Mama and I went with Pappouli and Yaiyai last year. We didn't think they'd ever be able to make it back again. The day you came by was their sixtieth-fifth anniversary."

Sixty-five years—they'd been married in 1899!

"Is that why you were all here?" I was dying to find out how they managed it.

"Yes, but you only just caught us all together before the cake. Everybody went back to work after that."

I grimaced. "Oh."

"We interrupted you," said Paula.

"Not at all. What's a little more company?"

She was awfully nice. We really did crash their party.

She picked up an old photo. "This was my family in Greece."

Paula gasped. "But they're all..."

"Royalty? Yes." She pointed to the king. "Through him. But they were all driven out. Or killed. We had to leave."

"You mean you're really a princess?" I said. "It's not just a nickname?"

"Can you keep a secret?"

Of course we could.

"Yes, but my family is so far down the line we're very minor, and it really doesn't matter since we're Americans now."

Paula and I both gasped.

"Really, there's no need to be impressed. We're so unimportant we couldn't get in to see anyone in the royal family when we were there last year. They probably thought we were gold diggers. They must have people saying they're family crawling out of the woodwork."

"But still," I said.

"I don't tell just anybody about my family," she said. "I want you to know my history. I want to learn about yours, too."

Saying things that nice was better than being a princess. I wondered if I had any good family secret to share.

"So why did your family come to Neston?" I asked.

From Theresa's smile, I could see that telling their story was as important as sharing their food.

"After Pappouli and Yaiyai and Papa left Athens and went to New York, they opened a restaurant in their Greek neighborhood. Then Papa went to work on cruise ships and worked his way up in the galleys. Once, when he came home, Mama—she wasn't Mama yet—was working in the restaurant. She was from Greece, too. He wanted to settle down, and after they were married, they took a trip Upstate and came through Vermont on the way home. They loved it here, and Pappouli and Yaiyai wanted to leave the city, so they made a fresh start."

It made sense, how they had the restaurant and the marina.

Tony came to the door. "Ready?"

"Almost. Be right there." She turned back to us. "Did I tell you to bring a whistle?"

"No."

"What for?"

"Tony said we should all have one in case we need to signal SOS or scare off a bear. I have an extra I haven't used that one of you can have. Two should be enough, unless you don't mind a used one."

"I don't mind," I said. This sounded frightening and exciting at the same time. Better safe than sorry. I didn't think a used whistle could be have any more germs than Gabe's pacifier, which I thought nothing of picking up off the floor and sucking clean before I gave it back to him.

We went to the kitchen for Theresa to get her lunch. Tony and Nikky were there to make sure the time on our watches matched theirs.

"You've got an hour and fifteen minutes," said Nikky.

"One o'clock," said Theresa, tacking on another fifteen minutes.

"At the very latest, Princess," said Tony, "or we'll come looking for you, so stick to the plan."

That settled it, just as if they'd been in cahoots with Mrs. Bouchard. From the look on Paula's face, you could tell she was seeing her mother's strictness in a new light, just as I was seeing Theresa and her brothers and the whole George family.

Theresa sure could hold her own. She was the Princess with her brothers at her beck and call for everything from a boat transport to lugging. But her brothers being old enough to be her father, they bossed her like one, too. She had a father and three brother-fathers. In comparison, one Mrs. Bouchard was a cinch— if Paula handled things the right way.

The nieces and nephews were out at the pool with Maria and Lina, and they screamed, "Theresa! Theresa! Theresa!" as we set out.

She waved and tore past. "I love them all, but you know."

We understood.

"I'm so glad to get away!" she said out of earshot. "Yippee!"

She laughed and we laughed. She slowed to chat. "Watch out for that salamander. Did you see the fireworks? The sidewalk sale is starting next week."

At first, the way she went on, I figured she was starved for company her own age, but the way we chimed in, maybe we needed to let our hair down, too. With Theresa, we weren't worried about saying the wrong thing. It felt like we had started over with a clean slate. If it kept up, this ride would be the best so far.

But once we dismounted, Fish Hook Point didn't look anything like it had seemed when Theresa had showed it to us from the boat. The whistles were a must.

The shank of Fish Hook was all we had seen, and it had looked substantial enough, but the bend was an isthmus barely wider than the narrow lane on top of it. It curved so sharply that the point of the hook almost touched the shore, and water lapped up against the rocks piled on either side like a jetty. One good gust, and whoof! off you'd go, into the cove on one side or into the lake on the other side. The only protection was trees defying the rocks and waves, growing skyward true on either side like guardrails.

Thankfully, the lake was as calm as it ever got.

"This is a good place to leave our bikes," said Theresa. She put down her kickstand but nestled her bike against a tree, just in case.

"Whew," said Paula. "I was afraid you wanted to ride out there."

She took the words right out of my mouth.

"Oh, I'd never do that. I didn't mean to scare you. I want us to have a fun time, and this place is so pretty."

And here, I'd gone along with wading in Stony Brook even though I knew Debbie and Paula could get hurt. I wished I'd been as considerate.

The water in Fish Hook Cove was a much lighter blue-green. It wasn't just pretty; it was way prettier than anyplace we'd seen so far while biking, maybe than I'd ever seen on the lake. It was a *Vermont Life* kind of spot, and I had my camera.

We walked slowly, watching each footfall for stones that might throw us off balance, stopping every few feet to see the changing view or to yield to chipmunks skittering across. Chickadees flitted between the boughs.

We were far from alone.

Across the cove, a blue heron stalked in the shallows, four turkey vultures sat on a fallen log, and rows of turtles warmed on rocks. We froze. If I so much as moved a finger to take a picture, it would scare them all away.

As it was, only three seconds passed before they were all warned off anyway. The heron and vultures were so big that we heard the sound of their wings flapping as they took flight, while the turtles slid soundlessly into the water.

"Wow," I said.

"That was amazing," said Paula, and when Theresa just smiled, she added, "You probably see this all the time."

"Pretty often, but we don't take it for granted. I should warn you, if you surprise a turkey vulture, it will vomit on you. They've got good aim."

"Didn't we just surprise them?" I asked.

"Not enough."

"What?"

"If you make them really mad, like getting near their nest, they might poop on you."

"Did you—"

"Almost."

"Let's not surprise any of them," said Paula.

"Don't worry," said Theresa. "We aren't near their nests."

She didn't say they wouldn't come back.

I made up for the missed shot. By the time we got to the hook, I had used half the roll with 360-degree views of the cove. Midday reflecting photos of Île de L'eau were unusual.

We sat on the rocks and ate our lunches. Based on the smell alone, I would have traded for the gyro pita, and I never traded. Paula didn't complain, either. In fact, we didn't talk at all. Just looking around was good enough. We were no strangers to wildlife, but this place was something.

When we were done, I snapped a couple shots of Paula and Theresa.

"You should ask first," said Paula.

"Sorry." I saw her point, but if I asked everybody ahead of time, I wouldn't get good unposed shots.

"Why didn't you bring your camera before?" she asked.

"I just bought it. I wanted to get some pictures of places before they change," I said, although I didn't want to get into the postcards.

"Like what?"

"So far, only Neston Avenue. A bowling alley is going to be built there."

"Really?"

"Oh, yes," said Theresa, "with a restaurant."

"Really?" Paula ratcheted it up.

"You know about it?" I asked Theresa.

"Papa reads the legal notices in the paper, so he saw the one for a meeting to review the plans. He and Tony went. They said they'd never seen the room so full before."

"Because of the bar next to the high school, right?"

"A bar next to the high school?" echoed Paula.

Theresa nodded. "In the bowling alley. The school board had a meeting, too."

All the sunshine went out of her face. The situation became crystal clear. I wanted to share my new photography interest, but I wished I hadn't brought up the bowling alley. Apparently the Georges were far from alone in opposing it, but they had the most to lose. The North Shore Restaurant would be hit hard by another restaurant that served regular food, especially one with high school kids for customers right next door, plus heavy traffic from being on one well-traveled road and near the intersection of another.

Its location couldn't hold a candle to the North Shore's beautiful setting, but a bowling alley would be a big draw, especially in the winter. People would go even if the food was so-so. Plus, the North Shore only had a service bar, not a regular bar. That would add a whole other bunch of customers, and everybody in the restaurant business knows drinks have a high markup.

"But they're building it anyway," she added. "Papa said it was bound to happen, sooner or later. Do you like bowling?"

"I tried to play once when we went to Burlington," I said, "but the only ball light enough for me had finger holes too wide for me to hold on to it." I wouldn't have liked it anyway. The racket was as loud as Beatles fans.

"Sounds like ten-pin bowling," said Paula. "We play candlepin when we visit our family in Georgia. It's a lot easier. Which kind will they have here?"

We didn't know. We'd find out.

"If you spend enough time looking, you might get a picture of the Dragon of Neston," Theresa said to me. "It would be worth a fortune."

"It sure would," said Paula. "Do you think the dragon is real?"

"I don't know," said Theresa in a tone that indicated she was very open to the possibility.

A dragon? In Neston? That was ridiculous.

"I never heard of it," I said.

"It's like Nessie, the Loch Ness monster, only in Île de L'eau," said Paula.

"Oh." I knew about Nessie, but I had never known people thought any lake dragons were here. "I heard there's one in Lake

Memphremagog." Of course, there had to be more than one to reproduce—if they were real.

"The Memphre Monster," said Theresa. "And Champ in Lake Champlain. The stories go way back of people seeing them."

"I saw a book at the library with drawings of them," said Paula. "I don't think people would make them up."

"There are a few photographs now, too," said Theresa. She looked at me. "But they're all fuzzy."

I got the hint. Tales were one thing, but drawings upped the ante, and pictures were a whole different ballgame. I was warming up to possibility myself.

"I'd like to see the Dragon of Neston," I said. Any of the lake dragons, in fact. Scotland was out, but here I was, smack on one lake, and the other two were also in-state.

It was still an awful long shot, though.

"Won't you be scared to swim in the lake now?" said Paula.

"No. The Fish and Game Department would post warnings if it was dangerous."

All I ever saw were run-of-the-mill fish. But if I did bump into the Dragon of Neston, wouldn't it be worth it, even if I got hurt?

"Maybe nobody hardly sees them any more because they mostly got caught," said Paula.

"Maybe," I said. Maybe they all had, but I was already hoping they weren't extinct.

"But if somebody did catch one, maybe they'd put it in a big fish tank, so everybody could go see it." She paused. "But eventually it would die of loneliness because they'd never find a mate for it."

Paula was more logical than I gave her credit for.

We kept our gaze on the cove. I kept my finger on the shutter button.

We were sitting quiet and still and after a minute a heron swooped fearlessly over our heads and landed in the shallows a few yards away. We were on his turf. Suddenly the smooth surface of the cove broke and a colossal creature headed toward us.

Paula shrieked.

I shrieked.

Theresa whooped for joy.

Tony was waiting for us.

"Right on time, Princess," he said.

"We saw a sturgeon!" she said excitedly. "It *had* to be Stu!"

"It was huge," said Paula.

"Enormous," I seconded.

"I believe you," said Tony, as blasé as if we'd seen a large-mouth bass. "I'll take Papa out and see if we can catch him. He's been trying for years."

Theresa clapped her hands. "I can't wait!"

So, no aquarium for Stu—not that he was the Dragon of Neston. But I could see how people might think he was.

"Why not just leave him alone?" I said.

"Stu's had a good long life. I'd rather see him on our table than leave his carcass for catfish." He went to pack our bikes.

Or any other angler, I thought.

Theresa said Stu was famous. He was definitely real, a trophy catch probably nobody would ever beat. It would be big news.

I really, really wished I'd gotten the photograph of Stu breaking the surface, but I'd been distracted by the heron. You had to be in the right place at the right time for a shot like that—it was one in a million, or maybe once in a lifetime—and I was there, waiting, which made losing it hurt that much more.

On the other hand, once you knew what you were looking for, and the best place and time to spot it, maybe the odds weren't so high after all. Of course, there's more to it.

If you're going to photograph dragons, especially ones that spend most of their time below the surface of the water, it takes constant vigilance and a trigger finger—and based on that glimpse alone, steady nerves, too, all while you were watching out for vomiting vultures.

Tony took us back in his station wagon without Theresa, since he was going to work at the restaurant after he dropped us straight off at our doors. He'd worked on the yard all morning, and he was going to work all night.

I had vastly overestimated the Georges' free time. They all put in long days and took turns helping each other at home. A whole day like we'd had together didn't exist for them.

Sure, they had a lot to show for their efforts, but their struggle for success came by the combined efforts of every family member and had been long and more difficult than I could imagine, and it all started because they lost their royal standing and their country. Not all the grass on Theresa's side was greener.

Chapter 33

THE *NESTON NEWS* HIT the porch with a soft thump and I went out to get it. I unrolled the rubber band onto my wrist to save it with the rest of them, and as soon as I smoothed out the paper, the headline blazed at the top of the front page.

TEDESCHI'S BAIT & TACKLE
ROBBED, VANDALIZED

Police responded to Tedeschi's Bait & Tackle on Lakeshore Drive at 6:00 a.m. on July 16 following a report of a vandalized Coca-Cola machine. According to Roland Tedeschi, Jr., "It looks like they took a hammer to it and clawed out the cash box for all the change. They broke the glass, took some soda, and smashed the rest." The vending machine, located outside the entrance to the store, is a total loss. Roland Tedeschi, Sr. said theft inside the store has become a problem in recent months. "No more warnings. From now on, I'll report every one of them to the police." No suspects have been charged and the investigation is ongoing. Anyone with information is encouraged to contact the Neston Police.

Claw hammer? Theft? A shock ran through me. I had information!

Well, maybe I had information. I had a hunch, anyway.

There was a full-length picture of Old Mr. Tedeschi and Mr. Ted on either side of the machine. The dispenser glass was broken and the metal peeled back, and the coin return was gashed open. A puddle of Coke had seeped into the floorboards beyond the pile of shattered glass.

Had Old Mr. Tedeschi caught Sammy stealing? Even with a kiddie pool, I figured the Fortins still went to the beach at least once a week, like they always had, and they went into the store every time they went to the beach. If Sammy couldn't go in there any more, like Putnam's wouldn't let him, I wouldn't put it past him to make Debbie go in for him, and if that was true, it would help explain why Debbie disliked Old Mr. Tedeschi.

It also might be one more piece in the puzzle of her attitude toward Paula and me, but I doubted it would solve the puzzle. I wasn't sure I'd ever find that piece. This would be exactly the time a person needed friends. She had shared with us about why she thought Sammy stole her penknife, but I wondered, would she ever have said anything if we hadn't been there when she realized it was missing and caught him red-handed?

Dieter must have seen something when he went swimming yesterday. Even if the police were gone by then, the machine would still be there, and the mess on the porch.

I put the paper on the table with my note and left before Mom came back in the kitchen from bathing Gabe.

When I met up with Dieter, I said, "Did you see the paper?"

"No."

"Tedeschi's got robbed."

"I know. Mr. Ted was cleaning up when I got to the beach."

Without him saying or my asking, I knew Dieter had given him a hand.

I stopped. "Wait. I've got to tell you something."

I looked around.

"Let's go over there."

I ducked behind the tree line.

Dieter didn't hesitate to hide with me.

He listened intently while I gave him the scoop, and when I finished, I asked him, "Do you think I'm off base?"

"Not at all. You're thinking like a sleuth, but there's no way to be sure if you're on the right track unless you report it to the police. If they find the evidence, they can interrogate suspects."

"But if there aren't any eyewitnesses or fingerprints, and they can't find the evidence, the, um, suspect would have to confess for the crime to get solved."

"I suppose so."

The consequence hit me like a wrecking ball.

"And then he'd go to jail."

"I don't know exactly what the charges would be, but if the damages are misdemeanors, and if the suspect is a minor, he might get probation for a first offense."

If it was Sammy's first offense—or at least the first official one he got caught at besides Debbie's penknife. Still, I breathed a sigh of relief. I couldn't really see the Tedeschis throwing the book at Sammy. But if he really was in as much trouble as it looked like to me, he needed to stop. He'd gone way past feeling and thinking and was charging full speed ahead.

"I have to go back home," I said. "You can go swimming without me."

"I can go later. Unless you're booked."

"No, I can go later."

"Good. It's tough at times, but competitors have to push through a lot of obstacles to stay disciplined with training."

It was nice of him to put it that way, and not just to encourage me. He was affected, too.

Dad closed the door to the den, and I told him and Mom. He got on the phone.

In fifteen minutes, an older model Buick pulled up and quiet Mr. Pecor from church came in. All this time, I never knew he was a detective. He was very nice, and I told the same story for the third time.

"I don't want Sammy to know I told," I said.

"Your identity won't be revealed," said Detective Pecor, "although suspects try to figure out who the informants are."

"All he knows is that I know he stole Debbie's penknife, but what if he remembers I heard his father say he showed him how to use the claw hammer? I'm scared."

"Is Etienne in danger?" said Dad. "Or any of us? I wouldn't want this traced back to my family or our business."

"Claw hammers are very common objects, Mr. Durand, but evidence of use on a metal vending machine isn't. The paint can be traced. We'll follow up on this tip immediately. As for your safety,

I suggest you go about your business as usual. There is no evidence personal violence was involved in this case."

All the same, he stood up and put his hand on my shoulder and said, "You're one brave young lady."

Sammy may not have acted violently toward any person, but if my guess was right, he was getting back at Old Mr. Tedeschi just like he did to Debbie. It was the next best thing, and pretty close to it.

Who knows? Putnam's might be next. Detective Pecor couldn't guarantee there wouldn't be any violence, but all in all, his advice was the best thing to do. Nothing would get my mind off everything like a good swim.

Chapter 34

DIETER NOTICED MY TIME as the fastest so far. It wasn't from bravery.

Hosing off the porch hadn't gotten rid of the Coke stain, and I wasn't the only one who gawked at the smashed-up machine. Neston was tainted, and it was frightening.

But there was another thing. I knew what it felt like to be in Sammy's shoes. I was guilty myself. I was trying to run away from it, or swim, in this case.

Mine wasn't exactly the same as Sammy's crime, but I had my own meanness to confess to Norman Levesque. It must be weighing on Sammy something awful, but how could I expect him to confess to his sin if I wasn't willing to make things right myself?

"I can't invite Jesus into my heart," I said to Dieter.

"Why not?"

"There's this situation." I gave him the scoop on Norman.

"That shouldn't hold you back, not if you purpose to ask Norman's forgiveness. After I invited Jesus into my heart, I had to do that with some guys at school. I had more than one situation to confess."

"The boys in the pack?"

"The same. Admitting my wrongs to each one of them was the hardest thing I'd ever done, but it made a big impact on them. We're all seriously competitive, and I thought they'd see me as weak, but it was the opposite. You shouldn't put it off. And don't let it hold your heart back from Jesus."

"There are other reasons."

He nodded. When I didn't say what, he said, "I can understand that. I had to work through my own. A big one for me was, I thought

I was already a Christian just because I went to church, but Jesus said no one comes to the Father except through him. It's not a church membership, it's a personal relationship, and I knew without a doubt I didn't have one. I do now, and I will for my whole life."

He hit the nail on the head, but I said, "The part about sticking with God is exactly what bothers me. It seems like the Christians you talk about just get into trouble. Stephen got stoned, and Dietrich Bonhoeffer went to prison and then he got hanged. I thought they were supposed to be protected. The rock and bulwark and all that."

"They were, but that doesn't mean it's always easy. They knew the cost of being a follower of Jesus."

He gazed over the water.

"There are places in the world where it will cost you your family, your job, and your home. Every real believer in Jesus will experience persecution in some form or another, so you're right to give thought to the most important decision you could make."

I didn't say anything.

"Once you are his, though, you see things differently, in ways you can't see until after making that decision."

Even so, I said, "Well, I'll have think about it some more. For now, I just want to make it up to Norman. Will you go with me?"

"I think it would be more appropriate for your dad to be with you."

That would mean another explanation, but he was right. It wasn't really above board to do something so important without Mom and Dad knowing.

What with the Arms and La Terrasse fully booked, another distraction wasn't needed, but I had to get this talk out of the way first thing. I had thought of something else, too, a reason just as important for making things right as soon as possible: my conscience wouldn't be completely clear unless I did this for Mom and Dad.

Here we were in the den for Round Two. Just twenty-four hours earlier, I'd held their attention more than I could ever remember, and once again, they heard me out without interrupting, just as amazed. But this time, Dad kept swiping his nose with his handkerchief, so Mom had to wipe her tears with her apron.

"I know it's a really busy day, and I would have waited, but there's another reason why I thought it was important to talk to you right away. I don't want anyone thinking you haven't raised me the right way. I knew all along what I did was wrong. My reputation is already wrecked, at least with Norman, and I don't know who else in class. But I don't want your reputation as my parents to suffer, especially being business owners."

I came up for air, but they were still in shock. I raced to the finish line.

"So, besides helping me pick out something to make it up to Norman, I was wondering if you'd go with me," I said.

"I'd be proud to go with you, Ette," said Dad. "Just as soon as you're ready, I'll make time. Whenever you say."

"I was thinking Tuesday. That will give me time to pick something up, and you won't be so busy. But I don't know what to get for Norman. It should be something better than we're allowed to give at gift swap at school, since it's for making up, but I really don't know him very well."

"You said he lives on the river, right?"

I nodded.

"How about a fishing pole?"

I thought of the boy and his father at the boat launch. "I don't want him to think I feel sorry for him, like he has to catch fish for his dinner."

"Ette, people catch fish to eat them," said Mom gently, "whether they have to or not."

Of course they did. Mom was right, and Dad's idea was good, and I knew just where to go.

Chapter 35

DIETER AGREED IT WAS a great idea. He went to Tedeschi's with me after we swam, and I picked out a combo fishing kit. Mr. Ted promised it could be exchanged for something else if the person didn't like it. It was a win-win.

Next on my to-do list was planning to have Paula and Theresa over for lunch. I could share our family history, and we could plot our remaining bike rides. It would be a short visit, but that was just as well, since everybody was straight out with work, including me.

There had been wedding receptions, anniversary parties, Eugénie Cote's organizational meeting for some women's auxiliary club, and thanks to her and Claude's wedding, a retirement gala for one of Senator Perry's state staffers, which was the sort of thing that had always been held in Montpelier, the state capital. The Arms *No Vacancy* sign was out, and except for a few weeknights, La Terrasse was booked solid.

Day after day, Dieter and I filled boxes with folded napkins, and I returned to looking after Gabe. The Perry party had made last-minute special dietary requests with several restrictions, and Mom needed to work without interruption on their menu.

"We're going to have another picnic at the lake next week, Gabe, and if you hold still at the water's edge, you'll be able to see minnows, but they'll swim away if you wave your arms."

I wiped his hands and highchair dry.

"You'll be a minnow in a couple years, when you learn to swim, but you have to start out as a tadpole and a guppy, and then you'll be a minnow and a dolphin and a shark. That's what I was."

I kept an eye on him over my shoulder as I rinsed the dish cloth.

He kept his eyes on mine.

"Can you say min-now?"

"Dadadadada."

"Atta boy! You're getting the hang of it. Now, *monsieur*, may I take your order for lunch with Paula and Theresa on Wednesday? Nothing fancy. The chef is very busy lately."

He dada-ed back.

"Tomato soup! Of course. We've got to pick all those ripe tomatoes. I'll get on it later. What else?"

He dada-ed back.

"You sure? The whole table has to like it." I waved my hand over the kitchen table.

He waved back.

"Well then, grilled cheese it is. Classic. I'm sure they'll both like dipping grilled cheese in tomato soup. Like they say, Gabe, it's the simple things that count."

I tilted my head. "And you know the best thing?"

He leaned, following my eyes.

"You can try it, too. So it really is for the whole table."

I lifted the highchair tray over his head, and he reached out his arms.

"Ahh."

If I loved Gabe before, I adored him now. And he loved me back!

His baby love was so simple and accepting. I would do anything for him. I would love him forever.

The moment I took him in my arms, I realized that Jesus loved me the way I loved Gabe—and he wanted my love back. Even if it was just a baby love to start, Jesus would give me all his love forever. He wanted the best for me, just like I did for Gabe.

It was way more than Mom and Dad or anyone else could give. He had already given his life for me so I could go to heaven. He wanted me to be his child so he could bless me while I was on earth, too.

If I could love Gabe for the rest of my life, no matter what, why not give my heart to Jesus for the rest of my life?

Chapter 36

NOTHING GOT MY MIND off of what I had to do at Norman's house. I went out to the hut, I read to Gabe, I read the comics but none of them seemed funny. I didn't want to arrive too early, in case the Levesques were late sleepers. Every minute dragged by like hours.

Swimming would have taken just the right amount of time and probably taken the edge off my nerves, but Dieter and some waiters had gone to Burlington for the day, and I didn't want to swim alone, so that was off the table. But when Dad and I finally drove over, I was more jittery than ever.

The grass was long gone from the patch of ground in front of the weather-beaten apartment houses. An empty fifth of Old Grand-Dad stood upright next to a broken stroller.

I knew where Norman lived but not which apartment. We looked at the mailboxes and Dad knocked on the first door where a Levesque lived. A woman wearing a worn housecoat answered the door. She eyeballed Dad.

"Well, if I'd known company was coming," she croaked in a gravelly voice.

"I'm looking for Norman Levesque."

"No one here by that name, but you're welcome to a cup of coffee."

"Thanks, we have to move on."

We continued to the next apartment.

"There's a Levesque on the top floor," said Dad.

The railing was so rickety, I held Dad's hand. The paint on the stairs was worn off in the middle and dust banked like snow at the edges. We passed doors with babies screaming inside and disgusting smells seeping out. The door we were looking for was unmarked, but it was the only apartment left. Could Norman live here? It was just a space under the eaves. Dad knocked a second time.

The door opened slowly, only as far as an eye behind a chain link lock, and shut again right away.

"Go away! I ain't got it to give you."

"I'm not here to collect anything," said Dad loudly. "We're looking for Norman Levesque."

The volume of the radio broadcast increased.

We went back out into the light and checked the mailboxes in the next building. There was one more Levesque, on the far end. The rotted door was beneath a rusted fire escape.

Dad knocked. Norman answered.

"Hi, Norman," I said like it was a regular social call. It was all I could do to keep my voice from shaking.

He sure looked surprised. He came out and closed the door behind him before I could see in, but the stale smell came out with him.

Dad stepped away to give us privacy.

"Norman, that puzzle I gave you last Christmas was really cheap and I'm really sorry."

I held out the fishing combo. "Please take this. I should have given you something nice but what I did was mean and I'm really sorry about being mean, too."

He took it.

"Will you forgive me?"

He looked me straight in the eye.

"Yes. I forgive you."

I stared back at him for a second. I was probably more stunned than he was.

"Okay, well then, I just want you to know my dad didn't make me come here. I asked him to come with me, but the fishing pole was his idea. I told him I wanted to make it up to you."

"I've always wanted to go fishing with the fellas. Thank you."

I made it out to the car before the floodgates opened. I never knew being forgiven would feel so good. I was cleansed all the way, from God and from Norman. Not that I wanted to have to make things right again any time soon.

Chapter 37

PLANNING LUNCH HAD BEEN the easy part. I was still scratching my head on a secret. If there were any in our family history, nobody had told me, which is why they're called secrets, and which is why I wasn't going to bump into them left and right, but I could probably find something interesting. I went up to the attic. It was the most obvious place to look.

Besides, I liked the attic. The beams of the house showed, holding us safe and sound year after year. My pedal wagon was there, covered with an old sheet. The last time I'd ridden it, I had to be pulled out since I was really too big for it, but I cried and cried for Mom and Dad to keep it.

Same with my Dutch wooden clogs. I'd stuffed my feet into them until my toes turned red. They were with all the baby shoes, which hadn't been bronzed, but they'd gone too stiff for Gabe to wear. The way he was growing, he would fit into the clogs and the car soon. Good thing we kept them.

I sat in the heavy wooden swivel chair and opened the roll top desk, where I neatly stacked the contents from one of the old steamer trunks so I could return them to their carefully chosen order. I'd seen most of it before for the simple reason that I'd helped Mom sort the trunks. Being as it's one of those chores that hardly anybody ever gets around to doing, there hadn't been time to look closely at each item. Organizing was the goal. That done, the contents were for digging into later. We'd dug into Great-grandmother Durand's recipes, but that was only one needle in the haystack, and today was later.

I got to what I was looking for, one of Mom's scrapbooks. The oversized heavyweight pages had been filled so that the expanding binding had been let out as far as it could go and still hold the book together. She had begun it after college when she went to Atlantic City. Papa and Maman and even Uncle Robert had passed on. Isabelle Benoit needed a fresh start.

The pages took a tour from the moment she arrived. She met Frieda, and they met Ray and Carl, who were at the Army Air Forces Training Center.

There were stubs from every amusement ride they took, every movie. According to the receipt of June 26, 1942, they splurged at Dock's Oyster House just before Ray and Carl were sent to Fort Meade School for Bakers and Cooks in Maryland. After that, bus tickets and receipts from Hot Shoppes recorded Isabelle and Frieda's rare trips to Odenton to visit them.

Then the men got shipped out, and the next three years were pretty sparse, just Isabelle and Frieda, until Ray and Carl came back in one piece and married them. They bought their wedding dresses and suits off the rack from Macy's and had the hand-written receipts to prove it.

The last thing in the scrapbook was a manila envelope. Its metal clasp was still flexible, so it hadn't been opened often. It might not contain a secret I could share with Theresa and Paula, but I felt like I was unwrapping a gift, since I didn't know what was inside.

There were two *New York Times* clippings. The first one was the wedding notice for Norden-Sinclair. Frieda Norden to Edgar Sinclair. It was a high society wedding, Helen Rose gown, swanky bigwig reception, the works.

The second clipping was an obituary. Edgar Sinclair. Tragic accident, majority holder of a fortune cut off in his prime, great loss to society, grieving heiress bride.

Talk about surprised. When I came to my senses, I saw the obituary was less than a year after the wedding. Three years before Frieda met Carl.

The letter beneath the clippings was in Frieda's handwriting, and I wondered if I should read it. I never set out to snoop.

I decided the damage had already been done.

Isabelle and Ray, my dearest friends, it is time to trust you with this. It will explain a lot. You deserve to know. Carl knows everything, of course, always has. I saved the clippings, supposing if we ever had children, I would pass them on. As you are now parents, they ought to go to you.

There is another important reason. Carl and I have discussed beneficiaries and are in complete agreement that, after each other, we are naming you and your children as our heirs. Albert and Penelope's children will also receive something.

We'll talk, but we thought this the best prelude to discussion. If there's anything I've learned, you never know the day or the hour.

~Frieda

I felt a flush spread from my face to my feet. If this was supposed to be a secret, it was not hidden very well.

At first, I thought Mom must have forgotten it was in her scrapbook. But then I thought that wasn't like Mom. She put it there, knowing where she could find it again, or it would be found by others. If something was really meant to be secret, you hid it in the bottom of your underwear drawer or put it in a locked box, someplace nobody would find it without deliberately spying.

But it still wasn't anything I could tell. It wasn't even a Durand secret. I was stuck with it.

But it wasn't awful, either. Just something Frieda didn't advertise. In fact, I knew beneficiary meant you got the loot, so taking the obituary into account, it wasn't bad at all.

Which made a whole other way of looking at discovering it. The things in the trunks were for handing down. They were being kept for sharing, not hiding. It was meant to be told, sooner or later. Maybe Mom meant to show us the clippings, just like Frieda planned to tell her kids, if she'd had any.

She wrote that it would explain a lot. I put myself in Mom and Dad's shoes. What would it explain?

Frieda and Carl knew they wouldn't have children. The note was written after Marcia was born, but Frieda said Mom and Dad and their children were the heirs, plus something for Stefanie and Dieter—but not Albert and Penelope, I noticed—and that many people might stretch the loot.

But maybe not too thin. Frieda was rich. Not "taken care of," like Mom had been from what her family left her, and what she got from selling their home and business later. Very rich.

And maybe that had something to do with why she hadn't gone into real estate. Maybe she was too rich for it to look right to go to work. Men could do that, but society women, not so much. But eventually, she did, in her own way.

There was a lot to chew on. It would take some time. I tucked the manila envelope back where it had been.

Chapter 38

THERESA BROUGHT THE CUTEST little zucchini croquettes, some of that tangy tzatziki, and a paper bag full of zucchinis.

"Know anybody who wants these?" she said. "They're perfectly good."

Mom and I shook our heads. Everybody had zucchini to spare. If four George families had this much to give away, it must be coming out their ears.

I was about to suggest the Kovacs would take it for their pigs when Paula said, "We would."

Of course. Mrs. Bouchard didn't have a garden. Not only was it dirty, gardening mussed manicures something awful. Gardening gloves were the only kind not in her collection.

"Mother is too busy to grow our own," said Paula, "although she always says fresh from the garden is the most delicious. This is too much for just us, but we know some other families who would really appreciate it."

Good thing I hadn't opened my mouth too soon.

Paula uncovered the Tupperware carrying case she brought. The smell overtook the croquettes as soon as she lifted the lid.

"Is that your mother's peach pie?"

"Mmm hmm."

"Wow," I said.

"Yeah," said Theresa.

"What treats," said Mom. "So generous."

This wasn't just generous, it was the royal treatment. Mrs. Bouchard's peach pies had taken blue ribbons more often than native Nestoners wanted to keep count.

Paula must have told her mother that Mrs. George was bound to send something along. I would have done the same. And Mrs. Bouchard couldn't have her daughter dining with the daughters of restauranteurs without sending something over the top.

Or was I being judgmental, like I'd been about gardening? Mrs. Bouchard had done something really nice, and Mrs. George had, too. They both had put in a lot of effort.

Still, it seemed like a competition. Hospitality gifts weren't expected for kids getting together and having soup and sandwich lunch.

The zucchini bites were so good, Paula even tried the dip.

"Theresa, I have a favor to ask," I said.

"Sure!" she said before she even heard it.

"Paula and I have almost biked all the way around Lakeshore Drive. The ride with you to Fish Hook Point took us farther, and if you go with us the rest of the way, I think we can finish in a couple more trips. If you can go with us."

"I'll make sure I can!"

"Whew," said Paula.

"But that's not the favor."

"What is?"

"Well, the last two sections we have to cover are the farthest away, and we'd be out too long, unless we could start where we left off. Would one of your brothers be willing to take us out again?"

"They better be."

"It would mean taking us home on time, too," said Paula.

Theresa shrugged. "Tony and Nikky can go fishing while they cut us loose for a little while. They don't have to be to work until the dinner shift."

Theresa surprised me to no end.

"Does that mean we'll have to ride in the back of the truck?" asked Paula.

"Either that or the *Odyssey*."

"Oh, good!"

The new Paula surprised me to no end.

"So, how about if we plan for next Thursday," I said, "depending on where we go tomorrow. We should be able to make good distance."

"Oh, I was going to tell you, I can't go next week," said Paula. "My aunt and uncle and cousins are coming up from Georgia and staying with us. I can't plan for biking while they're here. We usually do a lot of things. I could go the week after."

"I guess we have to move that date out, then," I said. "Maybe we could pick a different day of the week."

"Sorry," said Theresa. "I'll be going on trips with each of my brothers right up until school starts. We have to take turns on vacations, and they're counting on me to go with them and babysit."

"But, then that only leaves tomorrow, and we've still got to go all the way from Stillwater Bay Road to Fish Hook Point."

"We can swing it," said Theresa.

"You think so?" Paula sounded doubtful.

So was I.

"Sure. Remember, that's only Point A to Point B. You've been used to planning that includes getting there and back."

"That's true," said Paula.

It was. "But we should still start extra early."

"All the better for fishing."

It was true, tomorrow was the one and only day to finish the entire circuit of the lake this summer. It was now or never. *Carpe diem.*

We had just enough time before lunch for me to show Theresa around, since it was her first time over. I'd never given the tour to friends, but Paula and Debbie and I had played at each other's houses long before any of us would have thought of it. We ignored our houses like we had the navigation buoys; they were just there. But our house was part of our family history, and Theresa was interested in that.

"Durands have been in this home for five generations," I said. "Two brothers who worked in the timber business built it and lived here together with their families. I feel like I know them all the way back just because of the house."

"What are these?" said Theresa, looking at a row of long-handled covered pans in the hallway.

"Warmer pans. When the weather was cold, the pan was filled with hot ashes from the fireplace and run over the bed linens to warm them before people got in. We tried doing it once. You have to be careful not to scorch anything. The fireplaces don't warm up the house like the heater does, but I like when we use them."

"You do?" said Paula. "All that carrying wood in and cleaning ashes out."

"We don't use them very often."

I took them up to the window seat. "This is one of my favorite spots. I like to imagine all the other kids who must have sat here. Or waded in Stony Brook. Which reminds me, next time we can get together when it's hot out, let's go to the stick hut out back. We can wade in the brook."

"Sounds like fun," said Theresa.

"Not to me," said Paula. "I'm not going in the brook again."

"There's a way to skip to the birch so you won't get hurt at all," I said. "It's just like hopscotch."

She didn't believe me, and Theresa looked like she couldn't believe all the fuss over a little brook.

"I didn't get hurt, did I?" I said.

"No," said Paula.

"That's because I know where to hop. I'm sorry I didn't show you before. It would've been a lot more fun."

"I will if you will," said Theresa.

"Well, okay," said Paula. "But I'm not going in until both of you make it without falling in."

"Sounds fair," said Theresa.

It was another mean thing I'd get to make up for, but it would be fun.

We went down the library, which had old, old books I'd never read, but I'd spent plenty of time looking at the two sets of oil portraits.

"These are my great-great grandparents. The portraits were done by an itinerant painter, somebody who travels."

"Look at that." Theresa was in awe.

We stared at the paintings like we were at a museum.

"But Great-great grandfather Durand painted that sign himself." The battered old *Durand Printing* sign hung on another wall. "He opened the shop. Printing was a really good job then."

"What about your great-great grandmother?" said Theresa.

"What do you mean?"

"What did she do?"

"I don't know. The same thing other women did, I guess, raise kids, keep house. There was a lot of work to do, and everything was harder then."

We moved to the paintings of my great-grandparents. "These were done by an itinerant painter, too."

They were as mesmerized by the brushstroke details as I always was.

I showed them an oval framed flower bouquet.

"My great grandmother made this out of hair."

"We've got those. I think they're spooky," said Paula. "Is it her own hair?"

"Maybe. It could be anybody's. Who knows?" Starched bonnets covered most of the women's hair. Too bad she hadn't labeled, like we did with our photos.

"Anyway, this is my great-grandfather. He eventually took over the shop. They printed all sorts of things. You can still find things that say Durand Printing on them."

"Where's the shop?" said Theresa.

"It was on Parker Street, where the bookstore is now."

"I didn't know that."

"It was a long time ago."

"Why did it close?"

"A different kind of printing machine got invented. After his father sold the shop, Grandad went to write for the *Wortham Weekly*. He'd printed it enough times that he learned what to write."

But as they say, their legacy lived on. Our largest dictionary sat on an antique easel. Both came from Durand Printing. I used the dictionary all the time, and I always thought my interest in words had been handed down to me.

On the shelf next to the portraits, the photos continued the story.

"This is him and Grandmom. He was the first Durand to work in an office, although he had to travel all over the county to get a week's worth of stories. Dad says he worked fifty hours a week fifty weeks a year, and he and Grandmom were married fifty years."

"That's so sweet," said Paula.

"Did you know them?" said Theresa.

"No, they died after Donna was born."

"That's too bad."

"First Grandmom, and Grandad died hours later."

"Aw," breathed Paula.

"And these photos are Mom's side of the family, the Benoits. Her ancestors ran Chez Benoit in Sainte Anne de Bellevue. It's an inn, close to Montreal. That's her parents Papa and Maman, and this one is of Mom with her brother Robert."

They stared.

"Chez Benoit is still there, only Mom sold it because..."

Theresa and Paula looked from the photos to me.

Finally, the secret came to me.

It was time to tell. Not that it was the kind of secret that I wished I had to tell.

"They all died. From diabetes. Well, complications from diabetes. I never met them either. Mom always says they were wonderful, warm people. Everybody liked them. They might still be alive if they'd taken care of their health. But it's hard when food is your living, and you're always tasting. They were great cooks and bakers."

Theresa put a hand to her mouth.

"You should have said so," said Paula. "All those times you wouldn't have any dessert, I thought you were being finicky."

"Sometimes I am."

They laughed.

"But your mother is slender," said Theresa. "Doesn't diabetes run in the family?"

"No, they didn't have the type that gets passed on. Anybody can get the kind they had if they're not careful. Mom studied nutrition, so we're very careful all the time, even Carl and Frieda are."

"Oh, no," said Paula.

"What?"

"The peach pie."

"It's okay. I can't wait to have a piece. Mom, too. A little bit is okay. We just can't go overboard day in and day out." I don't know how the Bouchards did, and the Georges were just as much at risk.

"Anyway," I sniffled it all away, "this is Mom and Dad and Frieda and Carl's double wedding picture."

I knew Paula was checking out the suits and hats.

"Mom and Frieda were the first women in their families to go to college and have careers."

"Finally, women doing something besides having babies and keeping house," said Theresa.

My hackles rose. Her grandmother was the first to have a career when she opened the restaurant in New York City, and George success and nice houses included all the women, all mothers and housekeepers.

"Yeah," said Paula.

From her tone of voice, you'd never know she had high hopes for a big engagement ring and long wedding train.

"Managing a home is just like running a business," I said defensively. "Mom had us and runs the house, and she works at the Arms, too. Your mothers work."

Even if they didn't, running the roost is nothing to sneeze at.

"Oh, Mother works, she just doesn't get paid," said Paula. "The church gets a two-for-one."

Theresa shook her head. "I'm getting a college degree."

"In what?"

"Aquatic biology. I want a career."

"What kind of work do you do with that?" asked Paula.

"Work outdoors on the water, in it actually, the ocean, rivers, lakes, any body of water. Study plants and fish. But first I'm going to become a marine pilot, like my brothers."

"Whew," said Paula.

No kidding.

"Don't you want to work at the North Shore?" I asked.

"Of course. At the Marina, not the Restaurant. For a while."

"Oh."

"What do you want to do when you grow up?" Paula asked me.

I thought everybody knew. "Work at the Arms. I mean, run it. I'll own it one day, or at least be one of the owners. As soon as I turn fourteen, I'll go to work and start learning the whole business. That way, I'll figure out what parts I like doing best, but I'll have to learn all of it anyhow."

"That's a career," said Theresa.

Well, at least she didn't think you had to go to college to have a career. I was saving for it already, but I'd get so much training I wasn't sure I would need to go, and since Gabe was born, if I even wanted to go.

"What do you want to do?" she asked Paula.

I wanted to know, too. Here, we'd been friends so long, and I had no idea. As it turned out, neither did Paula.

"Anything except marry a minister," she said. "Weddings are the only thing I really like about church."

If her lack of interest in a minister husband and in church itself were indications of her lack of interest in Jesus, she and I were headed in opposite directions. Of course, ministers and church aren't exactly the same thing as Jesus, but you'd think they were so related that she and I would be headed the same way. I doubted it. And I had no idea where Theresa stood.

It was enough of a damper for me not to bring up wanting to give my heart to Jesus. I'd just barely realized how that would be the best thing ever—yet I felt I shouldn't talk about it. Dieter was the only one I could trust with that, and he'd be gone in a week.

You should be able to talk to your girlfriends about what's most important to you, but I was afraid it might drive a wedge between us. Marcia and Donna had gone their own ways a long time ago, and Tina, Janice, and Debbie had dropped like flies. I didn't want to lose Paula's friendship, too, or Theresa's, even though she and I were not as alike I as thought.

Or not in the ways I imagined. I thought the restaurants were what we had in common. It was the water. Fine. We shared a love of the water, and we shared a love of good food, if not the business end. At least we could have those in common, at least until she flew the nest for college.

And we had tomorrow.

Chapter 39

MAKING SURE I DIDN'T forget anything mattered, so I made a list: map, camera in its case with extra film, whistle around my neck, penknife in a pocket, change purse in the other pocket, canteen filled with water, watch on my wrist, windbreaker tied around my waist; plus a chicken drumstick in foil, peanuts in a bag, and a banana, each wrapped in their own handkerchief. It all fit in my duffel, which I tied down in my bike basket. I had plenty of room in case I found some interesting rocks or small driftwood. I liked Theresa's style. Now I had a complete list that I could just check off instead of finding out later there was something I wished I'd taken, although I didn't know when I'd need the list again. This was the end of the road.

As soon as Paula and I arrived at the North Shore parking lot, a couple of boys pushing carts loaded with bussing bins of ice came around from the rear service area of the restaurant. They waited nearby until Nikky drove in a minute later.

The Georges hadn't been kidding about the truck having enough room for us and our bikes. It was a farm truck. Theresa was sitting on the wooden lid of a galvanized watering trough placed under the rear window panel of the truck bed.

She dropped the tailgate. "Good thing we're starting early," she said.

"Why's that?" said Paula. "It's so hot out."

"Oh. Yeah."

We were sweating already. I glanced up. No clouds, but no sunshine, either. The haze was the color of old paper.

"Don't worry, the ride on the ice chest will feel cold." She eyeballed me. "You'll want to sit on your windbreaker."

Good. Paula got hers out of her bike basket, and I took out my camera.

"Okay, boys," said Nikky. They heaved up the bins and dumped the ice into the so-called ice chest. It took up the entire width of the truck, enough room for all four families to stock up, but I guessed it would be holding their catch for Friday's fish fry at the restaurant.

Once they were done, Theresa said, "Careful with the bikes, Nikky. Their baskets are full."

"Yes, ma'am." He saluted her. He lifted each bike like it was a feather and roped them, like hers, against the slats.

At first, I had thought the George brothers bossed Theresa, but I'd seen enough to know it was mutual. She could match them any day of the week. It had to be more than just being the spoiled baby, even if she was a princess. What with all that babysitting she did, she had leverage, but it probably had mostly to do with her strong personality. I could learn a thing or two. Paula already had.

"Need anything before we leave?" said Nikky. "Last chance."

He didn't need to remind me there was no turning back.

We shook our heads and climbed up. He closed the tailgate and tested it to make sure the lock caught. "Alright, get yourselves situated."

Paula the new adventurer sat next to me on the ice chest. Theresa settled on one of the rectangular straw bales. She pounded the metal side wall three times, and we were off.

"Whee!" Paula and I squealed.

That turned to "whoa!" when the road veered west at the bottom of the lake and we hit a patch of washboard. We grabbed the slats.

"Nikky!" Theresa hollered. "Heave to."

"Couldn't help it," he hollered back, but he slowed way down, so I figured that's what heave to meant.

Theresa laughed. "It's like sailing. You'll get the hang of it."

"I thought sailing was smooth," said Paula.

"Sometimes," said Theresa.

Not for Roald Amundsen, the explorer who led the first expedition to reach the South Pole. His journeys were anything but smooth. I looked *Amundsen* up when I saw it painted on the stern of a rowboat, and I realized the name was a joke. But the story of the Norwegian explorer was very interesting, and it so happened the shoe fit us. We were traveling to our own south pole.

Although Nikky heaved to over the swells, even at a snail's pace, we felt every bump. I wished I'd sat on a straw bale instead, but it was too late. I knew I'd be sore in the morning. Keeping cool was the best medicine in the meantime.

"Here's the plan," said Theresa. "Nikky will drop us off, and then he's going to the house to pick up Tony. They'll drive to Fish Hook Point, and we'll meet up there. If we're not on time, they'll head out to check on us."

I reminded myself again, all we had left was the leg between Stillwater Bay Road and Fish Hook Point, but it was at least twice as long a haul than we'd done, and even though everyone expected us back late, we still had to make good time if we were going to explore Île de L'eau State Park and pick a spot for lunch on its beach before the final stretch.

Nikky did a U turn at the entrance to Stillwater Bay Road and unpacked us. He drove off and Theresa took the lead at a brisk pace. She knew this neck of the woods the best.

A couple of minutes later, a loud white Olds full of boys passed us. A hairy arm waved out the driver's window. Then the car stopped right in the middle of the road.

"Uh oh," said Theresa.

We went on high alert—but what good would slowing down do? Or speeding past them?

Suddenly, a boy's rump appeared out of the backseat window. The boys hooted and hollered. The driver gunned the engine and took off fast, spinning the wheels and sending dirt swirling. I turned my head and a sharp pebble hit my temple, but Theresa and Paula got a hefty dose of dust.

We came to a dead halt.

"Ow," said Paula.

"Don't rub," said Theresa.

"What else can I do?" said Paula.

"Just close your eyes. Keep them closed."

"What was that all about?"

"We've been mooned," said Theresa.

"That was awful."

"It's supposed to be. Wait until I tell Tony."

If we'd been right next to the water, Theresa and Paula could have dunked their faces, but closing their eyes would help them tear up. I opened my canteen and held my fingers over the opening.

"I'm going to drip some water into your eyes. Tilt your head so it runs off, but then open your eyes until I'm done and shut them again after that." It wasn't an eye wash kit like we had at home, but it would do.

I repeated the process for Theresa, and afterward they picked some grit out of their inner eyelids.

"Better?"

"Good enough to keep going," said Theresa.

"Yeah, me too," said Paula. "Wait! You've got blood on your face."

I felt my temple. Sure enough, there was blood.

"A pebble hit me."

I doused my hand and face and dabbed the spot with a handkerchief. "How's it look?"

"It's clotting," said Theresa. "You just got a nick. We'll disinfect it later."

We set out again. We rode a long stretch through woods where private lanes led toward the most secluded summer houses on the water. Usually, it was cooler in the woods, especially where breezes came off the water, but the humidity was steamy under the tree cover, and the hazy openings were just as hot as standing in the parking lot; worse, since we were making time faster than we ever had before. My shirt stuck to my back. This definitely wasn't as much fun as the other rides had been. Well, the last one, anyway.

Come to think of it, I was the one who always seemed to have the most fun, but even I never did completely. I'd had my share of disappointments, but my reasons for them were different.

If we hadn't biked the lake in the first place, would I have found out how much less it seemed I had left in common with my friends, or felt I had to hide things to fit in, or lose a best friend? Compared to all that, what were nice views, a few good pictures, the ride on the *Odyssey*?

On the other hand, I was making a new friend. And the whole point was to bike entirely around the lake. Paula and I were finishing what we started.

Finally, the sign for Île de L'eau State Park came into view. We dismounted and took a few good glugs from our canteens.

The park ranger came out of the log hut. He was just as neat as a pin in a pressed short sleeved uniform, badge over the heart, *R. Porter* nametag over the other pocket, official patch on one sleeve.

"Morning, ladies," he said, touching his Smokey Bear hat.

"Good morning."

"I see you've got an injury there," he said to me.

"Yes, sir, but I'm okay. It doesn't hurt."

"I have a first aid kit if your party needs it. Name of your reservation?"

"We don't have one," said Theresa. "We're just here for the day."

"Actually, not even that long, sir," I said. "Just a look around and lunch."

"Are you expecting an adult to join you?"

"No, sir."

"As unaccompanied minors, you're not allowed in the Park."

"Why not?" said Theresa.

"It's a safety risk."

"We've been biking around the lake all summer," said Paula. "We've been to Potash Park and the boat launch on—"

"I can't make an exception to the rule. If I do it for you, others will want me to break rules for them as well. They're for your own good."

Theresa put her hands on her hips, but R. Porter was not about to budge.

"I'm sorry to disappoint you, but if anyone saw you unaccompanied, I could lose my job. You're welcome to eat your lunch right over there," he said, indicating a picnic table a few yards away in a stand of pines. "First, let's get that cut cleaned."

We went into the hut. It was nice and cool. Paula and Theresa browsed the pamphlets on the wooden shelves while Mr. Porter cleaned the cut with iodine.

"How'd you get this?"

We gave him the scoop.

"Do you know those boys?" he asked.

We shook our heads.

"They're summer people," said Theresa. "I've seen them around the lake for the past two weeks."

"It was a white Oldsmobile with New Jersey plates," I said, and Paula and Theresa agreed. The license plate game was now worth more to all of us than whiling away hours on the road.

He shook his head but said, "It's a good thing you noted that information. I'll report the incident."

He dabbed petroleum jelly over the cut and covered it with a Band-Aid, and since he had eye rinse cups, he also had Theresa and Paula flush their eyes with a solution.

"Where are you headed?"

After hearing that scoop, he seemed less skeptical of us being out on our own. "You can fill your canteens at the outdoor spigot," he said. "The water's good."

"Thanks, Mr. Porter."

The picnic table was far enough away to be out of hearing distance, but close enough that he could keep an eye on us. We walked our bikes over.

"Didn't you know we couldn't get in?" said Paula. She hardly ever got mad, but she was peeved.

"Of course not," said Theresa. "We wouldn't be in this mess if I did. But you didn't think of it either."

"We're all to blame. We should have known better," I said. My temper was short, too. "So should everybody else."

I guess our families were just too busy to think it through for us, especially since we'd been to the other places, but we hadn't learned our lessons either.

Paula sighed. Her whole body deflated. Yet another disappointment.

"We'll just have to keep going," said Theresa. "Unless you've got a better idea."

I couldn't think of anything. I was as disappointed as Paula that we would miss exploring the park, but I said, "There are other nice places where the water comes near to the road. Anyway, you and I will finish circling the lake today, Paula."

"That's true," she said. She perked up.

We unpacked our lunches.

"Those boys are sitting ducks," said Theresa. "The police will catch them alright."

The problem, as I saw it, was that we had been the sitting ducks. What if they meant to hurt us? What if they came back? Our whistles wouldn't be any help if nobody else heard them.

If we or a single one of our parents had foreseen the slightest danger like this, we'd never have pedaled any farther than Stony Brook Road. We probably never would again. For the first time, I felt the danger we were in.

Paula put down her sandwich. "I'll have to tell Mother," she wailed. "And it will be in the paper."

"No it won't," said Theresa. "Mooning happens all the time."

"It does? I've never seen it before."

"Me neither."

"There's always a first time. It's just a prank."

"But the dirt could have damaged your eyesight, and I'm going to have to explain how I got this cut," I said. "That's not a prank."

"That's right!" said Paula. "It *should* be in the paper. Mother will just have to understand it could happen to anyone. She's probably been...mooned. It's really disgusting, and, and, just plain stupid."

Atta girl.

Now that we spat that out, we ate in silence. Theresa had another gyro sandwich. I really had to look up that recipe.

"Where are you going on vacation?" I asked her.

"Cape Cod. We rented a bigger beach house this year, so I'll have more privacy when I'm not helping look after the kids, but I'll have to travel back and forth three times so my brothers can cover for each other a week at a time at work. It will be fun anyway. The house is right on the water."

Their whole lives revolved around the water, living and working and vacationing on it.

"It all sounds fun to me," said Paula. "I like traveling."

"I do, too, but not that much back and forth. Are you going away?"

"No, not with Mother's family flying up here. It's really their vacation, since they like to get out of the Georgia heat during the summer. We usually go down there right after Easter during the school spring break."

"Do you fly there?" Theresa looked very interested.

"Yes. Mother hates flying, but it's the fastest way to get there and back."

"Wow. I've never flown."

"Me neither," I said. "Weren't you scared?" All this time, and I'd never asked her.

"I was at first, but after a couple of times, I got used to it. It's fun."

Like they say, you learn something new every day.

"Do you like Georgia?" I asked. All this time, I never asked about that, either.

"Lots. It's pretty, and it's so warm there then, the flowers are already bloomed. Mother really misses it. She hates the cold."

"Where are you going?" Theresa asked me.

"We usually go somewhere during Easter break, too," I said. Unlike the Georges, we couldn't take turns vacationing during summer. "We were supposed to go to Atlantic City this past spring, but Gabe and I had colds."

It was where Mom and Dad and Frieda and Carl met. I'd been looking forward to my first trip to the ocean, but we had to cancel. At the last minute, Marcia finagled a stay with the Wendells, Frieda and Carl's friends in New York City, and Donna went to Washington, D.C. with Kimmie Hart's family.

"Maybe you'll go next year," said Theresa.

"Maybe." I was about to say it would be our last vacation together before Marcia left for college, but we were all surprised when the truck appeared.

Mr. Porter came out of the park ranger hut. Maybe we'd get into the park after all if Theresa's brothers would go with us. Tony came around from the tailgate while Nikky got out of the cab. We waited while they shook hands and spoke with the ranger first, and then all three came over.

"How come you're checking on us so soon?" said Theresa. "Is everything okay?"

"Never better," said Nikky.

"We caught Stu," said Tony.

Paula gasped.

I gulped.

Theresa jumped up. "Where is he? Can we see him?"

"Right here," said Tony.

196

We walked around to the back of the truck.Mr. Porter whistled. Theresa clapped a hand over her mouth. Paula and I stepped back. Nikky and Tony laughed out loud.

You couldn't help but see. Stu was so big, the tailgate was open and he didn't even fit. His body was nestled in straw and ice. His tail was tied to a piece of plywood so it wouldn't flop around, and the wood was roped so he wouldn't slide out.

"Don't touch anything," said Nikky. "We've got to get him to the Marina as soon as possible. You can help uncover him then."

"Why do you have to go there?" asked Paula.

"The Marina has a certified scale," said Tony.

"I've got the number for Fish and Wildlife," said Mr. Porter. "You're welcome to call from here."

"Thanks. I'll do that."

"What about our bike ride?" said Paula.

"We have to finish," I said.

"Can you girls hustle to wrap it up?" asked Tony.

"I can," said Theresa.

"I promised you," she said to us.

Paula and I looked at each other. It was either that or give up forever.

"It's our final lap," I said to Paula.

"We can make it," she said, grinning.

"Mind if I make a few other calls?" Tony asked Mr. Porter.

"Not at all."

"All right, you girls get going. We'll catch up with you."

We took off faster than ever. We hadn't even told them about getting mooned, but Mr. Porter probably would. We'd have to keep an eye out, but I guessed if those boys meant to hurt us on purpose, they would have already. It really was just a nasty prank.

In a minute, I wasn't thinking of anything. My legs were burning, but by the time we flew by the backup plan scenic spots, all three of us had turned into machines, pumping automatically. I hardly got a glance, let alone a photo.

Eventually the truck lumbered by, and we raced the rest of the way to Fish Hook Cove, site of the newly deceased. We took the corner hard and dismounted, panting for air.

I felt what it must be like to be in Dieter's shoes, pushing for my best time, and then, after all that effort, celebrating the tie for gold with Paula—the moment of victory as short as it would take for medals to be placed around our necks.

"We made it!" I said.

"We made it!" she said back.

We hugged hard.

Theresa took our victory picture.

Chapter 40

THE ACHIEVEMENT WOULD LAST, but once the glory was gone, the thrill was put aside for the Georges' excitement over the capture of a different kind of record-breaking trophy. We only stayed long enough for Nikky and Tony to rig up our bikes onto the outside of the slats, where there was no danger of them falling on Stu.

Theresa stepped carefully and sat on the ice chest, Tony sat on the tailgate protecting him, Nikky took the wheel, and Paula and I sat next to him. This time, the drive was as slow as a funeral procession. Nikky heaved to at the smallest bump. We arrived at the Marina parking lot looking like the Clampetts rolling into Beverly Hills.

The place was packed. Two men with *Neston News PRESS* tags on their hats had set up shop. The photographer was adjusting his tripod, which was pointed at the scale, and the reporter was talking to Gregory and two men from Fish and Wildlife. The younger one wore khaki, but the warden, Lt. Allaire, was dressed as sharp as Mr. Porter—and his holster kept people from crowding them.

Apparently, that and Tony's calls were all it had taken for Wortham County's ham radio operators to spread the news. Anglers fishing from boats and Tedeschi's pier and the Sherburne River bridge flocked in anticipation of seeing The Big One. The new police cruiser was near the bridge, its lights flashing silently while an officer kept traffic moving.

Beachgoers and diners joined in to see what the commotion was. Except for Pappouli and Yaiyai, the whole George family had arrived, and they were the only ones allowed near the truck. The whole slew of kids stood dutifully by Maria, Doris, and Lina.

Paula and I stood behind Mama and Papa. The photographer started snapping before Theresa was out of the truck. There was Stu, packed in straw and ice, and her sitting behind him on the trough. That peek alone was enough for tongues to start wagging.

"Will you look at the size of that thing!"

"It's a monster."

It took all three George brothers and the man in khaki to slide Stu onto a gurney.

"Get a good grip."

"Easy, easy."

"You got him?"

Theresa was on cloud nine. She helped lift Stu's head, and as soon as he was half transferred, Tony said, "Can you get his tail?" and she got out and held it up even with the gurney since Stu was too long to fit. There she was, holding him while volunteers ran a bucket line from the water to wash him off.

With each rinse, the crowd went wild, whooping and talking. Most said they'd never seen anything like it, but one man said he'd seen him spawning up the Sherburne. "Look for him every year," he said. "Seen him a few times."

"He really does look prehistoric," Paula said to me.

"I guess so," I said, agreeing more than not. I didn't know how you could know what something prehistoric looked like, but all the same, Stu did.

Like everyone else, I'd never seen anything like him. We were fascinated. His upper body was battleship gray, white lines like basting seams ran along both sides, his underside was white, and his chin had four whiskers like a catfish. If only his tail had been sticking up out of the water, you would have thought it was a shark. But he didn't have any teeth, and with his upturned mouth almost like a smile, when his open eyes looked at me, I felt sorry for him, even if he had lived a long life. Stu wasn't a regular fish. He was a giant among fish and men. He was famous, and he was dead.

He was laid out. It turned out the man in khaki was a state biologist, and he and Lt. Allaire did the measuring and weighing and recording. Stu was officially 105.6 inches long—twice as long as I was tall. He weighed 352 pounds.

The crowd reacted every which way. I saw money passing hands.

Along with the photographer, I got pictures of Tony and Nikky, the official catchers, carefully holding Stu for the vertical measurement because he was too heavy to hang, Theresa and her brothers kneeled behind him on the horizontal—and he still stretched beyond them—but I was the only one who got family members posing with Stu. The Georges sure were glad.

"How old is he?" asked the *Neston News* reporter.

"First of all, we don't know if it's a male," said the state biologist. "It's more likely a female. Sturgeon never stop growing, and females are known to live longer, which would explain its size, but we'd have to do an examination to confirm its sex. As for its age, at this point, I'd estimate it's at least sixty, seventy-five years old, possibly much older, but that's only an informed guess at this point."

There was a lot of handshaking and congratulating, and a good chunk of crowd dispersed.

"What's your plan?" said the biologist. "We'd like to study it if we could. We'd take fresh samples today, and then freeze it for further work."

Tony rubbed his chin. He looked at Papa.

"It's up to you boys," said Papa.

They talked it over. Stu was probably Sue, but she was still Stu to the Georges.

"We have to let them study Stu," said Theresa, and before her brothers could answer, she asked the biologist, "We'd get him back, wouldn't we?"

"That's your call."

They decided to let Stu be taken to the laboratory, where he'd be for several weeks, if not months. They made the biologist promise that Stu's show side would remain intact in order to be preserved for the taxidermist. He said the specimen would get the best treatment.

The only thing Stu wouldn't get was eaten.

The eventual plan was to lay him to rest, like a prize marlin, on Mama and Poppa's living room wall. Maybe someday, when business was slow, they'd encase him and show him off at the Restaurant. They had enough publicity for now.

Chapter 41

THE HAZE BUILT UP into a storm overnight. Although I was completely tuckered out, the thunder woke me. Rain battered the window, and in the flashes of lightning I could see the trees thrashing. I was glad the storm had held off. The weather was about the only thing that hadn't kept us from the finish line, although it tried hard.

The last leg of our journey turned out nothing like we planned. We never could have thought of it, let alone planned for it. It also turned out to be a lot more interesting. For that matter, had any part turned out the way I thought it would?

I had to hand it to Paula for sticking with it and making it to the end. We had made it together, even after it seemed the rug was pulled out from underneath us.

For that, I had to hand it to Theresa. I don't know what we would have done without her.

I had to hand it to myself, too. I had endured as many losses as gains along the journey. I hadn't calculated that there would be so much bad with the good.

They say it's the journey, not the destination. Tell that to Amundsen. Tell that to martyrs. As far as I was concerned, the destination really matters. It's what makes the journey worth taking.

And I would be on a new journey soon. Destination: high school. If it was going to be anything like this summer, it was a brook full of slippery stones. But I guess all of life would be. It wasn't enough that I could see that. I needed somebody I could count on to guide me, hold my hand if I slid anyway, and pick me up when I fell.

The only one I could think of who would always be there for me for my whole life was Jesus. In fact, I was starting to think I couldn't make it without Jesus. The risks of a hard journey were far outweighed by the eternal benefits. What was the point of life's rocky journey without arriving in his arms?

The *Neston News* was spread flat on the breakfast table when I finally went downstairs. The jumbo headline and Stu's photograph took up the entire front page above the fold. I peered at the photographs below the fold and discovered I was among the people in the crowd scene photo. Even though I knew the story, I read every last word as if it were all new, and I handled the pages carefully; this paper was going into one of the steamer trunks in the attic.

There was also a brief article in the local section about an uptick in the number of reports of mooning incidents, as well as drag racing on Neston Avenue. "Anonymous sources" had reported a white Oldsmobile with out-of-state license plates. Those boys were definitely sitting ducks now.

Detective Pecor came to the house again in the afternoon. He told us we could expect to see another news piece featuring yours truly run in the next day's paper. He said the gist of the story was that police had solved the vandalism and theft at Tedeschi's in no time flat, thanks to "a quick-thinking citizen" who brought valuable evidence as soon as the crime was reported. He thanked me. He said crimes were solved faster when evidence was brought quickly, before cases go cold.

The case of the claw hammer had never begun to cool. As soon as Detective Pecor had heard my story, he had returned to the police station. The police had gotten a search warrant and gone to the Fortins' house. The metal-damaged tool, with traces of vending machine paint on it, had been found under Mr. Fortin's work bench in the garage. The stolen coins, coated with Coca-Cola, were in a coffee can. Sammy had confessed immediately.

Detective Pecor assured us that Sammy believed his friends had turned him in. They had not taken part, but they had been interrogated, and they'd said Sammy had told them what he planned to do. It had all gone according to plan—except getting caught.

The claw hammer was the hook that caught him. And Sammy wasn't done with that claw hammer. He had learned how to pry up floor boards, and when Dieter and I went to Île de L'eau on Saturday morning, that's exactly what we saw Sammy doing to the porch at Tedeschi's Bait & Tackle. The vending machine had been hauled away.

The Tedeschis never pressed charges, which would have become public, so Sammy was never revealed as the perpetrator, but all anyone had to do was put two and two together.

It wasn't likely to help mend fences with Debbie.

Or raise Mr. Fortin's reputation as a teacher.

At church, Paula and I were still giddy over our accomplishment. We were also giddy because of our secret as "anonymous sources." Mrs. Bouchard never guessed that Paula had gotten mooned.

Paula was especially excited. It was Dieter's last day at church before returning home, and he was going to have Sunday supper with the Bouchards. She was storing him up like a battery charging.

I had never said anything to her about Sammy, but she noticed, like I did, that the Fortins weren't in church for two weeks in a row. They'd been seen, though. They hadn't gone away on vacation yet.

I mentioned it to Dieter after we went swimming Monday morning. Dieter said it was a natural reaction, like Adam and Eve, who hid from God after they sinned.

"But that's exactly when we need to turn to God," he said.

"Maybe Rev. Bouchard will go visit them."

"I imagine so, but they still need our prayers. Would you pray with me?"

"Here?"

"I think it would be better to pray somewhere that's private and quiet."

"I know a good place."

"You booked after lunch?"

"No. That would be a good time."

Chapter 42

WE MET AT THE service entrance and I took us the back way behind the Arms and cut across to Stony Brook and the stick hut.

He broke into a grin when came to the clearing. "Did you build this?"

"The first time, Paula and Debbie and I did, but it was so flimsy, it fell down. Mr. Lacroix set up the frame the second time, and we started over. We've been building since then. Well, I'm the only one who works on it any more."

He gave it a good once-over. The whole time, he had that architecture appreciation smile.

"Welcome to the hut," I said, and we went in.

His smile turned to laughter. "Now, that's not your regular picnic set."

"No, I guess not. Mr. Lacroix made that, too, out of scrap wood." He'd pieced together odds and ends and sanded, stained, and varnished them to make a rustic table and benches. "But it looks like it belongs here."

Dieter looked around at the what-not hanging from branch pegs and tucked into nooks: bird nests we found that had fallen on the ground, wasp nests that Mr. Lacroix had knocked off the house and barn before they got out of hand, baskets for collecting berries or whatever, a Plaster of Paris mold of our handprints we made at camp, a wooden box with paper and pencil inside, bits of rope and string, some dangling lavender for keeping bugs away.

"Thank you for bringing me here. It's a great place to pray. You know, the temple was God's house of prayer, but you've got a hut of prayer."

"You're welcome. I figured if I wasn't going to play make-believe here any more, at least not until Gabe is old enough, we might as well use it to pray real-believe."

"Nicely put." He raised his elbows to the table and clasped his fingers together. "In that case, shall we?"

I did the same. "Will you go first, and pray like you do with your friends?" Even though he had told me what they prayed about, I wondered exactly how they prayed.

He nodded. "You've already told me about some situations, but I just want you to know that everything we bring before the Lord is only between us. I won't share it with my prayer group unless you want me to. You're welcome to join the group."

"Okay. I'll think about it."

"Lord God, our father in heaven," Dieter prayed, "what a privilege to meet with you. We bow our hearts as well as our heads to you."

We closed our eyes and sat that way, like before we stepped into the lake, settling down until we heard the crows cawing to one another, settling down until we heard the soft crackle of squirrels scurrying over dry leaves, settling down until we heard an unknown bird's wings flitting off of a branch.

"Lord, thank you for this special place and the beauty of your creation." He paused. "We turn to you today as the almighty God of the universe, able to help in time of need."

I was with him in every word. He paused again.

"We come to you on behalf of the Fortins. Only you know all the reasons why they have stopped attending church, but we do know that the family is hurting."

He stopped. We prayed silently for a long time.

"God," I finally said out loud, "Sammy's in trouble, and not just for breaking the Coke machine and stealing the money. He's been sniffing glue with his friends and maybe stealing and maybe getting girls into trouble."

"Mmm," I heard Dieter say sympathetically. He waited another minute and said, "Lord, we ask you to intervene for Sammy's own sake and for the sake of his friends and companions. Deliver them from evil."

After another silent time, I said, "And Sammy's being mean to Debbie."

"Lord, we ask you to bring wholeness and peace to the Fortin family."

"Especially when they're on vacation," I added.

I swallowed. "And now—now Debbie doesn't want to be my friend and I don't understand why she doesn't want me to be friends with Theresa at the same time. So I'm hurting, too."

Dieter didn't wait. "Lord, we ask you to minister to Debbie and restore her to Etienne. We ask you to heal Etienne's hurting heart. We ask you to watch over her friendships."

I held my handkerchief over my eyes.

In the long silence that followed, the deep impression I'd had a week earlier about Jesus loving me the way I loved Gabe resurfaced. Praying about Sammy and Debbie and the whole family made me see the comparison in a new way. Nothing Gabe did could ever take away how much I loved him. I loved Gabe so much I could never give up on him.

Never?

No, God. I'm sure. Even if Gabe committed a crime like Sammy did, I would love him. Even if he turned out so bad, he went to jail, I would still love him. There would never be three strikes out between us.

Why not?

I'd forgive him.

Do you think Jesus would give up on you?

No. He'd forgive me.

Do you think Jesus loves you more than you love Gabe?

Yes.

Are you ready to trust Jesus forever?

When I didn't say anything else, Dieter said, "Thank you for hearing our prayers, Lord. If there is anything needing to be confessed to you, please bring it to mind, so that our prayers will not be hindered. We look forward to your answers. We pray in Jesus' name."

"Amen."

Chapter 43

THERE WAS NO LEAVING Gabe and me behind in the car this time. The clear and sunny day was the answer to prayer I wanted, and Dieter and I met as usual. Everybody else would catch up with us before lunch. We went to put our bags in the locker for the last time.

"Do you want the lock?" asked Dieter.

"Sure, I'll use it for gym class."

"I'd like to say goodbye before it gets too busy later."

We went in the store.

"Thanks for the use of the locker, Mr. Ted," said Dieter. "It was a big help."

"Thank you," he said emphatically. "You've been good for business, young man, and you've given me an idea. I'm thinking, instead of replacing the Coke machine outdoors, we'll install a few lockers under the overhang, see if we can rent them out by the day, first come first served. As soon as the insurance money comes in, we're getting a refrigerated case. Folks will have to come in the store to buy soda. I'm thinking we'll make a lot of other sales. I wouldn't have chosen for things to happen the way they did, but it looks like they'll work out in the end."

"They're both good ideas. I hope to be a regular customer."

"So, you're coming back to Neston?"

"The Lord willing." Dieter lifted his hands. "Being here has been a blessing."

Old Mr. Tedeschi listened and squinted.

We stood at the water's edge for our usual moment of silence, eyes and ears open, praying. Many days we had done energetic laps, but this time was like the first time I'd joined him. We waded out slowly and swam gently to the far raft. Usually, we swam back and forth together and Dieter did more lap circuits by himself, but this time, I sat on the far raft and removed my cap.

He sat next to me. "You okay?"

I nodded. "I just wanted to talk to you."

"Alright."

We looked out to Île de L'eau Island.

"You remember how you said I would know when I was ready to ask Jesus into my heart?"

"I remember."

"I'm ready."

He turned to me. "I believe you."

"And you said it's good to pray with another Christian?"

"It is."

"Well, so, I want to pray with you. Now."

"There is nothing I could want more than to pray with you, Etienne. Do you want me to guide you?"

"No. I sort of memorized that pamphlet you gave me, but if I miss something, you could help."

"Alright."

I bowed my head and heart. I didn't need to look to know Dieter did, too.

"Hi, Jesus, this is Etienne. I'm ready to give my heart to you for the rest of my life. I got all caught up on confessing ahead of time, so I don't have anything else to say in that area right now, except I know I sure am a sinner. Thank you for dying for my sins. I don't want to sin any more, and I know you'll help me. I believe you rose from the dead and you're alive now, looking for people to follow you, and that's what I want to do. I know you love me very much, and I'm looking forward to being together forever and ever, so Jesus, please come into my heart now because I love you, too."

I waited for a few seconds before opening my eyes.

"Amen."

"Amen and amen!" said Dieter. His face was lit up. "Ette, the angels are celebrating with God in heaven this very moment, and so am I."

"I added some. You said you put it in your own words when you prayed, so I did, too."

"Your prayer's far more beautiful than mine was. May I pray a blessing from the Bible on you?"

"Can you do that?"

"Yes. You can now, too."

"Are you sure?"

"Positive."

"Well then, I'd like that."

"'May the LORD bless you and keep you; may the LORD cause His face to shine upon you and be gracious to you; may the LORD lift up His countenance toward you and give you peace.'"

No matter what happens or what anybody else does or says, I'm sticking with God, my family, the Arms, and Neston, and I'll stand by any friends who stand with me, especially Dieter.

Only Jesus could change my heart, but Dieter had a lot to do with changing my mind. He would never take credit for it, but without all his explanations, I don't know how I ever would have learned so much.

But it was more than that. It was the way he lived his life. He really did do everything for the glory of God.

No doubt about it, my world turned upside down. All it had taken was a few weeks.

Well, actually, it was the opposite.

My life was turned right side up.

THE BEGINNING

ACKNOWLEDGMENTS

Thanks to my parents, of blessed memory, for delightful picnics at the far end of the beach.

Thanks to the Vermont librarians who provided World's Fair information and other material valuable to *Neston* and future books in The Neston Novels Series.

Special thanks to Kathy Meninger for your constructive critical review. *Neston* is the better for your comments and questions.

All blessing, glory, praise, honor, and thanks to the Messiah. I received Jesus Christ as my savior as an adult, but through his bountiful mercies toward me, I believed on him with the heartfelt trust of a child.

NEXT IN THE SERIES

The books in The Neston Novels Series are told in sequence. Each novel builds on the previous one so that the series forms a long story.

#2 in The Neston Novels Series:
The Dragon of Neston

When Ette Durand enters junior high school in the fall of 1964, the perils of fitting in and doing well pale in comparison to discovering the emerging counterculture, race riots across the United States, and combat looming in Vietnam. War isn't just on the other side of the world. The Dragon of Neston—that ancient foe called the devil—is alive and well and on the prowl in the least expected places. The battles start at the bus stop, inflict injuries in the gym, and take captives in the classroom. Dieter Norden warned her that her new faith would be tested, and Ette wants to take him up on his promise to help her, but between his Olympic swimming trials and the pressures he faces before graduation, how can he find the time? Ette needs to find a way to slay the dragon, and for that she must take up the shield of faith and rely on the Helper who will never leave her nor forsake her.

ABOUT THE AUTHOR

Tess Adone holds an M.A. in English. Her background includes teaching expository writing and assisting executives. Her first novel is *Respect and Respectability: Susan Price at Mansfield Park*, a standalone Jane Austen sequel. Currently, she is writing The Neston Novels Series, a continuous story told in sequence, beginning with *Neston*. The series is set in her home state of Vermont.

Learn more at www.tessadone.com

www.ingramcontent.com/pod-product-compliance
Lightning Source LLC
Chambersburg PA
CBHW020319260626
47156CB00004B/1293